Born in Birmingham, United Kingdom, E J Had   ....ee siblings brought up by working-class parents. At seventeen, she started a journey that took her to countries far and wide and through adventures one would never expect. She didn't return to the UK until twenty-nine years later.

It was during the first year of her return to the UK that she started to note down events of her life. Whenever she told people about her life and events, they would all listen in astonishment. Some fifteen years later, E J Hadley put pen to paper and started writing her life story. She is a well-travelled and well-spoken lady who has more than just an ordinary tale to tell.

This book is dedicated to my two daughters, who gave me the support and strength to make it happen.

I would like to thank them for their understanding and help, during the long and sometimes difficult process. Without their help and support, I would surely have given up.

They have always been and always will be 'my life'. Love you more than words can express.

I would also like to thank my sister-in-law, Lucinda, for her contribution. She filled in a lot of the missing pieces of the jigsaw, without which the book would have been less intriguing.

E J Hadley

COFFEE, SEX & CHARDONNAY

To Jax, my best friend &
confidant.

You know the story already,
and I hope you enjoy the
final thing.

lots of love &
always best wishes in all you
do. xx

E J Hadley

AUSTIN MACAULEY PUBLISHERS™

LONDON * CAMBRIDGE * NEW YORK * SHARJAH

A CIP catalogue record for this title is available from the British Library.

ISBN 9781398400511 (Paperback)
ISBN 9781398400528 (ePub e-book)

www.austinmacauley.com

First Published 2022
Austin Macauley Publishers Ltd®
1 Canada Square
Canary Wharf
London
E14 5AA

Prologue

Jan Smuts Airport – AUGUST 1998

I was jolted awake by the sound of Sarah's excited voice.

"Mummy, wake up. Come and see the view from the window. There are hundreds of cars and there are lots of people everywhere! What's happening?"

"It's alright, Sarah, it's just the morning traffic in downtown Johannesburg. People who commute to the big city every day for work. Is Annie awake?"

"Yes, Mummy, I'm awake." Annie was standing by the door still looking very sleepy-eyed.

"Come here you two." They both bounded across the room and jumped up onto the huge bed.

"What does 'commute' mean Mummy?"

"Well Sarah, it means that people travel from their homes to work at the same time every morning and it causes traffic jams. Unfortunately, here in South Africa there are no buses for people to use, well at least not like the public transport system in England. If there were buses here, then people could just get on and off the bus and wouldn't have the hassle of sitting in traffic trying to find parking. So that's what 'commuting' means, and that's why it looks so busy on the roads. Now who wants breakfast in bed, or would you prefer to go down to the restaurant?"

"You shouldn't eat in bed, Mummy; remember you always say no food in bed."

"Quite right, Sarah. The restaurant it is then. Do you want to go for a morning swim before or after breakfast?"

"Mummy, what's wrong with you today? You told us never ever eat, and then go swimming straight afterwards with a full tummy!"

My dear babies. Heaven knows when they would be able to swim outdoors again once we arrived in the UK. Sudden pangs of guilt started creeping in. *Am*

I really sure I want to do this? Just thinking about the weather in the UK makes me get goose bumps, for all the wrong reasons. You couldn't plan anything in the UK because of the awful weather. Then the other side of reality of 'staying' popped into my thoughts. No contest.

"Alrighty, let's go for a swim and maybe a jacuzzi too. Come on, let's get our swim suits out of the cases."

"Yay, a jacuzzi too, Mummy? This is the best day ever! Well, almost the best day. The wave pool at Sun City was the best day ever, wasn't it, Annie?"

"Ya, Mummy, the wave pool and the slide tubes with waves in them and the Palace of the Lost City with all the elephants, and lions in the rocks. Can we go there again one day?"

Oh, dear Lord, another pang right where it hurts. "I'm sure we'll go there again one day, but for now, let's see what the pool here is like."

After our swim and jacuzzi, I decided we'd have breakfast at the poolside café. It was pretty busy for a city centre hotel, not that I'd ever stayed in a city hotel before. Rex always stayed at five-star luxury hotels, with or without me and the girls. Mostly without. After years of his going away overseas on business trips for 2–3 weeks at a time, I started to smell a rat, and boy was I right. I'd had my suspicions for a while and on one of his trips to the US, I had asked why the girls and I couldn't go with him. He'd just laughed at me and said how boring it would be in Des Moines, as he was just going to tie up a deal with a huge agricultural company to export equipment out to them. While he was in the shower that particular time, I looked quickly in his suitcase and found a zipped toiletry bag right at the bottom of the case. When I opened it, there was a manila envelope with wads and wads of cash and books of traveller's cheques. I mean hundreds of thousands of pounds worth of cheques. That's when the 'light bulb' went on.

By the time we'd finished our leisurely breakfast, the pool bar began to fill with office workers coming for lunch. "Come on, girlies, we'd better go back to our room and get ready for our long flight to see Nanny."

With an hour to go before the taxi arrived to take us to Jan Smuts Airport, I called my best friend Penny.

"Hi, Penny, it's Margot. How are you?"

"Margot! I was wondering what had happened to you, long time no hear. How's life?" There was a pause.

"I've left Rex."

"Oh my God, Margot, when did this happen?"

"I only decided two days ago, Penny. I just couldn't take it anymore. I'm not 'me' anymore. Somewhere along the way, I've lost my identity. I love Rex with all my heart but you know what, Penny, I love me more and I have to get away from the 'life' I don't have."

"Where are you going? To the house in Cape Town, I hope, and how did you manage to leave without him knowing?"

"Slow down, Penny, I'll explain everything. I'm not going to the house in Camps Bay. I've decided to go home to the UK. I don't know anyone in the Cape and besides, I think the girls will love the UK. Plus, if I stay in South Africa and he finds me, he won't leave me alone. It wasn't too difficult to organise as you know Rex goes to the office at the crack of dawn, so two days ago, I got ready as usual, as if I was going to work and waited for him to leave. As soon as he'd left, I asked Sophie to pack the girls' cases, and then went into Bryanston Travel and booked the tickets one way to the UK departing tonight."

"Hold on, Margot, how are you going to get out of the house for your flight? It's a night flight, isn't it?"

"I stayed at the Sandton Hotel last night, so he doesn't know where I am or what I'm doing. Maybe he thinks I'm just with you or one of the girls. I take it he hasn't called you?"

"No of course he hasn't. I'd have rung you. Surely, he'll see that you've taken all your clothes and the girls' things too, he's not stupid?"

"That's why I stayed in a hotel, just in case he thought I was going back to the UK. He would have gone straight to the airport last night and boom, I'm not there."

"Hmm, Margot, I hope you know what you're doing. He's a control freak, and believe me you haven't heard the last of him."

"Look Penny, don't worry, I'll be fine. This time tomorrow the girls and I will be safely out of his reach. I've got your address and number, so I'll be in touch when I'm settled. Look after yourself."

"You too, Margot, give my love to the girls."

As the taxi pulled into the drop-off zone at Jan Smuts, I realised that this was the last time I would stand on African soil. My heart sank and it took me a few moments to compose myself. I retrieved two trollies while the taxi driver offloaded the cases onto the pavement. With three cases per trolley, Sarah pushing one and Annie holding tightly to my trolley, we made our way to the departure lounge. Twenty minutes later, we were standing in the South African Airways check-in queue. The girls were sat on the suitcases singing the South African national anthem, '*Nkose sikelel Africa*' and everyone in the queue started singing along with them. I was overwhelmed with the enormity of what I was doing, and my love for this country which had been my home for the past 16 years.

"Okay girls, quiet now, we have to show the lady our passports." I wiped my eyes and retrieved the passports from my bag and passed them across the desk into the waiting hands of the South African Airways flight attendant.

"What adorable children Mrs Charrington." The attendant smiled as she opened the passport to the relevant page then looked up at me and nodded.

I realised she wasn't nodding at me when I felt a strong hand gripping my shoulder, and a deep voice saying, "Mrs Charrington, I have a warrant for your arrest." The queue of people around me fell silent.

I spun around to see a plain-clothed gentleman, accompanied by two uniformed officers, standing in front of me. He moved his grip from my shoulder and took my arm pulling me away from the check-in desk.

"Take your hands off me!" I insisted in a raised voice.

Sarah started screaming hysterically and wrapped her arms around my legs. Annie was still perched on top of the cases and started crying as one of the officers started to wheel the trolley away from the check-in desk, through the stunned crowds of onlookers, while the other officer grabbed Sarah's hand and pulled her away from me.

"Mummy, Mummy, what's happening?" screamed Sarah.

"Where are you taking my children? Let them go, take your hands off my children – do you hear me?" I tried to grab the trolley but the officer had too tight a grip on my arm.

"Please calm down, Madam, and follow us."

Once in the confines of a small office beyond the check in desks, the officer began to explain.

"We received a call from your husband. Apparently, you're leaving the country with his two children, both minors, without his consent, and that Ma'am, is against the law here in South Africa."

I was at a total loss for words, bewildered as to how Rex had found out that I was leaving. Apart from the travel agent, no one else knew. Had he been following me, or even worse having me followed by some private investigator?

"So, what happens now? I have a flight to catch," I said matter-of-factly.

"Your husband hasn't agreed to it Ma'am, so you can't board that plane." The officer was so arrogant.

"He's not my damn husband. We're divorced and have been for four years. I was granted custody of the children and as their legal guardian, I am acting in their best interests, and you have to believe me when I say that."

"Divorced or not Ma'am, the children can't leave the country without the father's consent."

"But that's ridiculous. He doesn't have anything to do with them. He never wanted children in the first place and I refuse to be dominated by him anymore. You have to let us go. Please. You could say we weren't here, tell him anything, but just let us go."

The officer fell silent for several minutes and glared at me. The girls had stopped crying and were sitting with the officers playing 'eye spy', totally oblivious to what was going on.

"How much is it worth for me to let you board that plane Ma'am?"

I stood up and flung my arms into the air in disbelief. "My God! are you blackmailing me?"

"Sit down. Now. This warrant states 'expressly' that I have to bring you back, with the children, and under no circumstances should I let you board that aircraft. Yet I could turn a blind eye, as you so blatantly suggest, but everything in life has a price don't you agree, Ma'am?"

I felt the bile surge in my throat and the sudden urge to slap him, so intense, that I had to restrain myself. "That sounds just like Rex, 'expressly', how dare he, what right does he think he has?"

I was just about to say something I would have regretted later when the officer said, "Twenty thousand Rand should do it. Such a small price to pay for your freedom, don't you, think Ma'am?"

"Good evening, ladies and gentlemen, this is your captain speaking. I would like to welcome you aboard this South African Airways flight to London Heathrow. Please make sure your seat belts are fastened for take-off. Crew, prepare for take-off." The aircraft sped along the tarmac until it reached the required speed before floating up into the sky, making my stomach churn over. There was no turning back now.

"Mummy, look at the tiny swimming pools down there, it's awesome."

"Ladies and gentlemen, flight time to London Heathrow is approximately thirteen hours and we will be cruising at an altitude of thirty thousand feet. In-flight attendants will be coming around shortly with refreshments before dinner is served, so just relax and enjoy your flight. Please keep your seat belts on until the seat belt sign is switched off. Thank you."

"Can I get you a drink Ma'am?" the young airhostess asked.

"Yes, thank you, I'll have a glass of wine please. Do you have any Chardonnay?"

"Yes Ma'am." The airhostess passed the small bottle of wine and a packet of salted peanuts. "Dinner will be served shortly, Ma'am, but if you need anything in the meantime please just ask."

"And what are your names?" she asked, turning her attention to the girls.

"I'm Sarah and this is my sister, Annie."

"What beautiful names, and I believe you can sing too," said the young attendant as she winked and smiled at me. "What can I get you to drink, my sweeties? Coke, Sprite?"

"Orange juice, please, and some more Pringles," said Annie.

"No more Pringles Annie darling, dinner is coming soon." I smiled at the young hostess and sat back and took a large sip of wine as I looked out of the small window and watched my beautiful Africa slowly disappear as the plane soared high above the clouds.

"And what can I get for you, Sarah?"

"Do you have rooibos?"

"Yes, we sure do, and would you like some crayons and a colouring book?"

"Oh yes please, do you have felt tips?" replied Annie with delight.

"I'll see what I can conjure up."

With the girls settled and busy with their colouring books, my mind started to stray.

Chapter 1
March 1987 – The Job Offer

Since arriving in South Africa back in 1982, I had worked at several companies, all on the outskirts of Johannesburg. I never really fancied working in the centre of Johannesburg; too busy, and don't even mention the commute time and parking. That is, until I received a call from my friend Vanessa who worked for Kelly Girl Employment Agency.

"Hi Margot, how are you. Are you okay to talk?"

"Hi Vanessa. I'm good thanks, how are you?"

"I'm very well, thank you. I've just had a job spec come in that sounds just up your street. I know you don't want to work downtown, but the salary that this company is offering is just, well, I'm so excited. You must come in and let's talk. Can you come in at ten in the morning?"

I arrived at Kelly Girls' offices ten minutes early at 09h50. The traffic was horrendous and not knowing downtown too well, it took me a while to find parking.

"Good morning, I'm Margot. I have an appointment to see Vanessa."

"Good morning. I'm Trish. Follow me." Trish showed me to a small office and I took a seat near the window and made myself comfortable. "Can I get you a tea, coffee or cold drink, Margot? Vanessa is just finishing off an interview."

"Yes please, coffee, black no sugar."

"This job sounds perfect for you Margot. The gentleman, Mr Charrington, is an entrepreneur, British, and quite young to be a Managing Director. He's looking for a personal assistant with very particular credentials. The lucky candidate must have a minimum of 80+ wpm shorthand, together with audio typing, as he is out of the office quite a lot and you will receive tapes in the post.

You must also be proficient in taking minutes at meetings, of which there are many, and be proficient on all computer packages, especially graphs, as he does a lot of presentations. He also likes to be driven to his appointments. You fit the criteria perfectly Margot. He's had two new assistants in the past two months, the last one apparently just walked out." Vanessa raised her eyebrows.

"Oh Vanessa, that doesn't sound good, does it? He sounds scary as hell."

"I'm sure you will get on just fine. The last girl was Afrikaans, so maybe there was a slight language barrier. You'll soon find out as I've arranged an interview for 11 am, today. You have all the qualifications he's looking for."

"What salary package is he offering Vanessa?"

Vanessa smiled and wiggled her head. "Let's just say it's very competitive. You can discuss that with him. I know that annual leave is 25 days per annum, and there is a pension fund scheme. What salary are you on now Margot?"

"R8000 per month with a bonus in December."

"Oh yes, you also get an annual bonus. A whole months' salary. Mr. Charrington indicated that he was willing to go up to R12,000 for the right candidate, so I suggest you ask for R12000. Do you have any questions?"

"Yes, what type of company is it?"

"It's a large Lighting company. The offices are very plush with a huge showroom over two floors. You have your own office which is adjoining his."

Upon arrival I was greeted by Martha who showed me upstairs to a small area outside an office with 'Managing Director' written on a brass plaque on the door.

"Mr Charrington will be with you shortly, he's just in the board room with a client."

Ten minutes later, I heard footsteps to my right and started to feel really nervous. The footsteps got closer and I turned to see who was approaching. A man in his late thirties wearing a deep blue suit, definitely 'designer', with a dazzling white shirt and red silk tie, stopped when he reached my chair. It wasn't his looks or the way he was dressed that made me look twice; it was his uncanny ability to command respect without saying one word, the way he owned the room. He knew exactly where he fitted in the universe. I noticed everyone at their desks promptly started to look busy, all eyes on their computers and not at me or him. I felt my cheeks flush slightly, and had that freefall sensation in my stomach.

14

"Hello Margot, come in, please take a seat."

"Hello, nice to meet you," I said, as I held out my hand to shake his. As our hands touched, our eyes met, and the innate charisma he exuded was overwhelming. My heart started palpitating and I couldn't take my gaze away from his.

"If you let go of my hand Margot, I'll get you a coffee. You seem a little flustered?"

"Yes, sorry. I'm not used to so much traffic, and well, it took ages to find parking." I smiled. "Thank you. Coffee would be good, black, no sugar."

"What a coincidence, that's how I take mine."

I let go of his hand and sat down. He went over to a small kitchen area where there was a pot of coffee already brewed and he poured two cups. I watched him as he moved slowly towards me. It was like slow motion, like in a movie with my eyes scanning every inch of him.

He placed the cup in front of me and said something, but I was in a daze. I shook my head.

"I'm sorry, what did you say, I was miles away then."

He raised his eyebrows and looked at me quizzically. "I said when are you available to start Margot, do you have to give notice?"

Wow. And that's his opening question. Does this mean he's offering me the job?

"No, I don't have to give notice, I can start straight away, on Monday. Will there be a handover period?"

"No, unfortunately not. My last secretary up and walked out without giving notice, but judging from your CV, I'm sure you'll manage just fine."

"Well, yes, thank you." I sipped my coffee while I tried to think of something to say but nothing came. *I bet she couldn't handle that 'power'. She was probably terrified just like I am right now.* My palms were sweating and I couldn't stop looking at him. Those intense blue eyes looking at me, waiting for me to say something. There they go again, those eyebrows going up and down; well, actually just the one eyebrow, the right one, almost winking at me. He took another sip of coffee and was about to say something when I blurted out, "So having read my CV, Mr Charrin—"

"Please call me Rex."

"Having read my CV, Rex, is there anything else you would like to know?"

"No, Margot. The job's yours if you want it."

"Can I get you a refill, Rex?"

Looking slightly dumbfounded, he said, "Yes, another coffee would be lovely. Thank you."

"Do you have any biscuits, Rex, my tummy is rumbling?"

"No, I'm afraid not, I don't tend to snack in between meals. Do you have any questions?"

"No, not at all. I'm happy to start on Monday. I can see from your overflowing 'in tray' that we're going to be very busy for a few days clearing your desk."

There was an awkward silence. I was sipping my coffee when he looked at me, raising his right eyebrow. "What salary are you hoping for Margot?"

I swallowed rather loudly, and replaced my cup before spurting out "Oh right, yes, that would be helpful. I was thinking R12,000."

My insides were quivering. What the hell was going on with me. I am normally so confident and in control, yet here, right now, sitting opposite this man, I felt so inadequate. My emotions were all over the place, and not on the job in hand at all.

"Right Margot, R12000 it is. I'll ask Personnel to have your contract typed up for you to sign on Monday. Have a great weekend."

"Thank you, Rex. You too."

It was just after 18h00 when Debs and the girls arrived home. The girls went to their room to put their swim suits on while Debs and I started to prepare dinner.

"I went for an interview today. Debs."

"What! You never said. What brought this on, I thought you liked your job in Spartan."

"There's something I didn't tell you Debs. When Grant and I got back from the Carnival in Rio, Heinz fired me because we got back four days later than planned. I tried to explain to him why, but he just said it was the end of the line."

"I think we need a glass of wine; this sounds interesting."

We took our glasses out to the pool side.

"Well, do enlighten me. Margot."

"Heinz said that every time I booked leave, I always left it to the last minute and it made the other staff members cross. I was on the verge of tears and went to my desk to retrieve a present I had bought for him. When I gave it to him, I

16

could see that he was sorry for having to fire me, and he said he would speak with the other members of staff, and try and sort something out.

"I told him that I understood completely, and explained that Grant's job, as a Pilot for South African Airways, occasionally means that he has to do long haul flights. I continued to explain that when he does, he takes the opportunity to take leave if there's a long stopover of more than seven days. So when Rio came up unexpectedly, as he was covering for someone who was off sick, he didn't have time to give me notice, hence, I couldn't give him the required notice either. I told him that the situation would probably happen again, so it would best if we parted company. 'A change is as good as a rest, so they say,' I told him. Anyway, he wished me well and then passed me an envelope. He said he'd paid me until the end of the month, but I should leave straight away."

"When did this happen Margot?"

"On Wednesday. I didn't say anything because I wasn't sure what I was going to do. I was toying with the idea of maybe moving to the Cape, or Durban, and then Vanessa called me, out of the blue, with this 'too good to refuse' job offer."

"So how did the interview go?"

"I start on Monday."

"Where is the job and what sort of company is it?"

"It's a large lighting company and Rex, the Managing Director, who is a young British entrepreneur needed someone to start straight away. His last P.A. walked out."

"Rex! on first name terms already Margot. Did you get his life story too?"

"Not yet, but it won't take long. All I know is that he is handsome with dazzling blue eyes, dark blonde hair and very well spoken. Not married, in his late thirties and wears designer clothes. What more do you need to know?"

"So why did his last P.A. walk out?"

"He didn't say, but judging by the extreme power he exudes, I imagine she couldn't handle the intensity of him."

Chapter 2

First Day at New Job

Bright-eyed and bushy-tailed, I arrived at my new job feeling very nervous, which is only to be expected when you start a new job. But these nerves were not because of the job.

I was shown to my office by Martha who kindly showed me where the toilets and kitchen were, and introduced me to some of the office staff.

"Mr Charrington is running a little late but he should be here within the hour."

"Okay, thanks Martha."

Once Martha had gone, I went through to Rex's office and saw that the piles of mail on Rex's desk hadn't been touched. I put on a pot of coffee and got started with the mail. I removed all the unopened post from his in-tray, which was overflowing onto his desk, and piled it onto my desk. Once opened, I date-stamped each letter, discarding any junk mail, dealt with what mail I could, and put the rest back into his in-tray.

By ten thirty he still hadn't arrived, so I put on another fresh pot of coffee. His office was very masculine. There were two brown leather Chesterfield sofas, two side chairs and a rosewood coffee table. Rows of dark wooden filing cabinets filled one wall and beautifully framed landscape pictures adorned the other walls.

I was busy filing when I heard footsteps on the wooden floor. He came into the office with his briefcase in one hand and a large bunch of flowers in the other. He looked amazing. His suit was pale blue which complemented his eyes. He wore a light blue shirt and contrasting bluey-grey tie.

"Good morning, Margot. I see you've been busy finding your way around. Coffee smells good; black, no sugar, thanks. Can you find a vase for these? I do like fresh flowers in the office. Pour yourself a coffee and bring your notebook through."

His voice was soft yet authoritative, and sincere. I could have listened to him all day long. He went through the files on his desk and one by one, writing a small note on each and handed them to me. He dictated several letters corresponding to each envelope. Two hours later his desk was clear, and mine was full, and my fingers ached from all the dictation.

At around 15h45, Rex buzzed through and asked me to come in and pull a couple of files ready for a meeting. While bending down retrieving the files, I noticed in the reflection in one of the pictures on the wall, that he was looking at my 'behind'. Just to make sure I'd seen correctly, I went to the next filing cabinet and bent down. Yes, he was definitely having a good look, and he had a slight smile on his face.

I turned around to look at him and said, "I didn't see any appointments in your diary for this afternoon, otherwise I would have had the files ready for you."

He was slightly taken aback but quickly recovered. "It was a last-minute thing, a good friend of mine wants to see me. In fact, I need you to come with me to take minutes and if you wouldn't mind driving so I can do some last-minute calculations. If you bring the car around to the front door, I'll be down in five minutes." He put the files into his case, handed me the keys and said, "It's the Bentley. Bay five."

"Bentley?!"

"Yes. Silver Bentley. Okay, see you out front."

Did he know I drove an old VW Beetle? Was he mad? What am I going to do? You're going to get in the Bentley, drive it to the front of the showroom and show him that you are not afraid. That's right, walk – come on, move your legs. Hello, legs, why aren't you moving?

Eventually, I managed to move forward and once in the confines of my own office, I let out a great sigh of relief.

Now calm yourself, I told myself. *It's just a car. Oh sorry, it's not the car, it's the man. Silly me.*

I picked up my bag and notebook and headed for the basement. Thank God the Bentley was reverse parked in its bay. I clicked the remote and slid into the huge driver's seat. With my hands shaking uncontrollably, I inserted the key into the ignition and turned the key.

My heart was pounding so hard I could hear it ringing in my ears. I released the handbrake and rolled slowly forward out of the bay. The steering was as light as a feather and, with no effort at all, I manoeuvred the huge vehicle through the small car park, up the ramp and through the automatic gates.

As I pulled up in front of the building, I saw him walking towards the car. He opened the back door and jumped in.

"Okay, Margot, go straight up onto Market Street and take a left at the robots."

I was sweating but tried not to show that I was nervous. The short journey through downtown Johannesburg, in this huge vehicle, was not what I had envisaged on my first day at a new job, but hey-ho, headfirst, in at the deep end, as usual.

I was dreading parking the Bentley. Rex pointed to a large building on the left, which had several flights of steps outside, and as I came to a halt at the kerbside, a man in uniform came towards the car.

"Good afternoon, Sir," he said politely as he touched his cap. Then he turned to me. "Hello Madam, please allow me to park the car for you."

My sigh of relief was audible.

"Oh, thank you so much," I garbled as I got out of the car. My knees were shaking slightly as we made our way up several flights of stairs, through large revolving doors and into a huge reception area.

In the centre of the expansive reception area was a very impressive water fountain, which cascaded down a flight of marble stairs into a huge pool, and was full of tropical fish. We approached the lift and once inside, Rex pressed the button for the 24th floor.

The lift was on the outside of the building and made of glass. As the elevator ascended, I tried to take in the magnificent vista of Johannesburg, but my stomach churned. I turned my back to the glass and closed my eyes.

"Are you all right Margot?"

"I don't like heights; don't worry, I'll be fine."

Rex took my arm and stood close to me.

The elevator 'pinged' at the 24th floor, and as the doors opened, it was like stepping into another world. To say what I saw was opulent would be an understatement.

A young man in his early thirties, six feet at least, dressed top to toe in designer clothing, stood in front of us. His hair was the colour of coal and his eyes were jet-black. "Rex, old boy, fab-u-lous to see you. How are you? You look great, darling." They shook hands.

"Hi, John, I'm good, thanks. This is my new PA, Margot."

John turned to me, held out his hand and said, "Oh my, sweetie darling, aren't you delightful? And such an improvement on the last one, Rex." He turned and winked.

"How are things with you, John? Still playing golf four times a week?" enquired Rex.

"You bet, it's the only bit of peace and quiet I get these days. Please come through. Can I get you a coffee or something a little stronger?" he asked.

"Just coffee, thanks, for both of us," Rex said, looking over at me.

"Great, yes, coffee's good." Though I would have loved something stronger to calm my nerves, but then, of course, I had to chauffeur Rex back to the office.

There was a lot of small talk and it became apparent that they had been friends for a long time. They rattled on for quite some time before they got down to business.

John asked Rex, "Do you fancy a round of golf next week?"

"I'd love to. Just give Margot a call to arrange a date. Now what can I do for you this time?"

"Well, darling, you know those Italian chandeliers I bought from you last year for my private suite? Well, do they come in a bigger size? I would love to have a huge one hanging in reception above the waterfall so that it twinkles like diamonds on the water."

Rex laughed and said, "Bigger? Christ, John, what size were you thinking of?"

"Well, sweetie, I went to a casino in Monte Carlo and I took a picture of the most magnificent chandelier I have ever seen – look, this is it." He showed Rex a picture.

"That must be bigger than my office! How the hell are you going to get it installed?"

"Don't you worry about that, sweetie, can you get me one or not?"

"Yes, of course! If they have one in Monte Carlo, then they must be available somewhere. Leave it with me and I'll get back to you. Hopefully, I'll have some news by the time we play golf next week. Good doing business with you again, see you next week."

There hadn't really been much to write down and I had to wonder whether it had really been necessary for me to be present, or whether it was simply for show.

When we exited the building, the car was already parked up in front of the building. "I'll drive back, Margot, come and sit in the front."

I'd never been so relieved in my entire life. Peak traffic time in downtown Johannesburg in a Bentley! We made slow progress down Market Street and the atmosphere was a little tense to say the least.

Eventually, he said, "How long have you been married Margot?"

A little surprised at the question, I replied, "Since October last year."

"What does he do for a living?" he asked.

"He's a pilot."

"Lucky you. Plenty of free flights, I guess?"

"Yes, indeed. We went to the carnival in Brazil earlier this month and I've been back to the UK to visit my family – and Grant and I went to Mauritius too."

"Do you plan on starting a family straight away, Margot?"

Oh my God, I thought, *what sort of question is that? Surely, he should have asked that at the interview.*

"It hasn't been discussed and, anyway, I can't have children. Well, I don't think I can."

"Oh, I'm sorry to hear that. What happened, if you don't mind me asking?"

"Nothing 'happened' as such, it's just that I was married previously for fifteen years and we never used contraception. Jorgen had a child from another relationship, so I guess it must be me that has something wrong. Anyway, Grant and I don't live or sleep together actually – he's gay."

"What? So why did you get married?"

"It's a long story and I don't want to bore you."

"It's hardly boring, pray tell me."

"Well, where to begin. When I divorced Jorgen, I was terribly depressed. I hadn't seen my family for almost five years. I was invited to a party by my neighbour and I met Grant. In fact, all of the people at the party worked for South African Airways. We got on so well. We danced and talked and I really liked him. Anyway, during the evening, and after a few too many drinks, Grant asked me why I looked so sad. I explained that I was recently divorced and feeling homesick, and that I couldn't afford the air fare to go and visit them. Then he said something really odd like; *'why don't you marry me, and you can have as many free flights as you like!'*

I saw Rex turn to look at me. "Really!!"

"Really. I didn't take too much notice and just laughed and assumed he was drunk. The next morning when I woke up, most of the party goers were out by the pool drinking coffee, so I went out to join them. I saw Grant and he called me over to sit with him. He asked me if I had given any thought to his suggestion. 'What, to marry you and get free flights?' I said to him. He looked hurt and said he was serious, and went on to explain that South African Airways were firing anyone who was gay, and as he was, to say the least, very 'camp', he was sure that he would lose his job. If, on the other hand, he was married, how could he possibly be gay. He said it would be doing him a favour too. No strings attached, just friends."

"When did you actually get married Margot?"

"The following Wednesday, at the Registry office in Kempton Park."

It went very quiet in the car.

"Well Margot, that story is far from boring, as you put it. How often do you see him?"

"Once a week maybe, depends on his flight schedules really. I go to his house sometimes as he has lots of parties. Occasionally, we go out to dinner. He's just a lovely guy."

"So, what are your plans for the weekend, anything interesting?"

"A little retail therapy in the city, relaxing by the pool, meet up with girlfriends, that sort of thing." The small talk continued and eventually we arrived back in the office car park at around 17h15. My car stood all alone as everyone else had left.

"Would you like a glass of wine before you go home, Margot?"

"Thanks, that would be lovely. It'll give the traffic a chance to thin out a little."

When we reached his office, he took a bottle of Baksberg Chardonnay from the small fridge and casually poured two glasses. He raised his eyebrow and smiled. "Cheers, Margot."

Chapter 3

'Lady Problems'

By the time I got home, it was well after seven thirty and Debbie was sitting outside sipping a glass of wine. The girls were upstairs, playing.

"What's up, Debs? Not like you to drink on a school night," I chirped.

"Just one of those days where nothing went right," she replied. "How was your day, how's Mr Charrin… whatever his name is?"

"Oh my God, Debbie, it was unbelievable. I had to accompany him – well, actually I drove him in his Bentley – to a meeting on the other side of Johannesburg. Just hang on while I get a glass of wine."

I went to the kitchen and poured a large glass of Chardonnay, then went back outside to join Debbie.

"He makes me so nervous and I don't like it; he's just a man, what the hell's wrong with me?"

Debbie just looked at me and smiled. "Nervous! You? Well, I'll be damned."

"And what do you mean by that?" I retaliated.

"You, nervous of a man? You're normally so confident and in control, I thought you'd have known his life story by lunch time," Debbie said, laughing.

"Well, I must confess he's taken the wind out of my sails, but hey, it's early days. He asked me how long I'd been married and was I going to have children any time soon and I told him about the arrangement between Grant and I. Anyway, what's up with you to get you on the wine already?" I asked.

"I have an 'educational' arranged for this weekend as you know, in the Timbavati Game Reserve. P.A.'s from six of our top companies that use our fleet service and six managers, are all booked and ready to roll on Friday morning, to go to the reserve to check out all the conference facilities, etcetera. It's our way of keeping their business. Problem is, one of the ladies has come down with some bug and can't make it and I have a spare place." She looked at me and said nothing. Just a look.

"No way, there's no way. I can't take off for a long weekend. He wouldn't buy it. No, absolutely not," I said.

"How do you know if you haven't even tried? What have you got to lose? It's not like you to turn down a challenge, especially out in the wild, which you love. If anyone can muster up an excuse to get time off, it's you Margot."

Debbie went and fetched the bottle of Chardonnay and topped our glasses up. We sat quietly for a few moments in the warm evening air watching the sun setting in the cloudless sky over Johannesburg, with only the sound of mosquitoes buzzing around and the ice clinking in our glasses. I closed my eyes and could almost smell the bushveld in my nostrils, hear the animals snorting and roaring, getting ready for their night's hunt.

"Okay, I'll ask him if I can take the time off," I blurted out.

"Wow, that took you a while," Debbie said, laughing. "And what master plan of an excuse have you conjured up in that head of yours?"

"I'll tell him I have a 'lady problem'."

I arrived at the office early the next morning and put the coffee on. Rex arrived twenty minutes later. I took my notebook through to his office and sat down. He looked ravishing and smelt wonderful.

"I have something to ask you, Mr Ch—Rex."

"Right, sounds serious," he said, raising one eyebrow.

I opened my mouth to speak, but my voice had departed for a split second. I took a sip of coffee and said, "My throat's a bit dry."

He raised the eyebrow again, but this time looked straight at me.

Oh, my holy fuck, what is this man doing to me? I thought. *He's just a man, for god's sake. Get it over with.*

"It's just a bit personal, that's all, I'm a little embarrassed." My palms became slightly sweaty. "Well, it's quite simple really. I have 'a lady problem'. I need to go into hospital for a small operation to remove cysts from my ovaries. I've received a letter advising that there's been a cancellation and they're offering me the appointment. It's for this Friday. I can rebook if it's inconvenient but it's been pending for a while." I could hardly speak; my heart was beating so fast.

"Okay that's no problem, you can't leave things like that so you'd better get it done sooner rather than later. How long do you need?" he said calmly.

25

"Just Friday and Monday should be sufficient. Apparently, it's quite sore afterwards."

"Okay Margot, now that's sorted, is everything on track for the monthly regional managers' meeting?"

"Yes, Sir. All flights and accommodation are booked, everyone will be here, no apologies as yet."

"Sir!" now he raised both eyebrows.

"Oh, did I really say that out loud? I meant Rex." I blushed and Rex smiled and moved on quickly.

"Great. Now let's go through my diary."

Chapter 4

The Timbavati Game Reserve

The Timbavati Game Reserve was approximately 300 kilometres from Johannesburg, on the western border of Kruger Park. Debbie had arranged for two mini-vans to pick everyone up at 08h00 on Friday morning, meeting outside Debbie's work place. The drive time to the Reserve was a good six hours, mostly on dirt roads. With only one stop for refreshments and a toilet break, everyone was pretty hungry and dusty by the time we reached Tanda Tula Camp at around 15h00.

Two rangers were waiting for us with champagne and orange juice as we disembarked from the vans. When we all had a glass in our hands, one of the rangers led us to the main lodge which overlooked a watering hole. There were springbok, kudu and zebra drinking at the watering hole, while a couple of hippos wallowed like children in the muddy side-banks. There were several large stilted dwellings scattered around the far side of the watering hole.

"Can I have your attention please ladies and gentlemen. My name is Kobus, and I'm your head ranger during your stay. Before dinner this evening, we will be going out into the bush for our first game drive. Please check in at reception and get the keys to your rooms and freshen up, and I'll meet you back here at 16h00 sharp. Oh, and make sure you bring warm clothing and a blanket from your room. It gets pretty chilly once the sun's gone down."

Taking our drinks with us, we headed to the reception area and checked into our rooms.

The rooms were beautifully decorated, with the main attraction being a huge four-poster bed, surrounded by mosquito nets. There was an en-suite bathroom with a bath and shower, a cosy seating area, a balcony overlooking the watering hole, a small fully stocked mini-fridge, and a plate of snacks and a basket of fruit.

After freshening up, and raiding the mini bar for another bottle of Prosecco, we made our way back to the main lodge to meet Kobus.

We were bundled into a large jeep, with open sides and a canopy overhead to keep the sun off. On the floor between the two rows of seats were two large cool boxes. One with wine and beer and the other full of bottled water.

"Just a few rules before we start off." He pointed to a black ranger. "This is Mbeki. He's our number one tracker, and he will hopefully lead us to at least one of the big five. Under no circumstances are you to get out of the vehicle unless Mbeki says it is safe to do so. Also, if we come across any large game, please do not shout out or you'll frighten them away. Okay, are you all ready?"

The smells of nature are amazing and the first thing that hit my nostrils was a very strong smell of buttered popcorn, like when you walk into a cinema and the smell hits your nostrils. This scent is similar to leopard pee which they spray to mark their territory. Together with the smell of carrion, lemon grass, the potato bush and scented pod acacia, all blended together, they give a very distinctive bush smell.

We saw many impalas, a small deer, with a very distinct black marking on their hind quarters, which looks like the letter 'M' as in McDonald's, and are aptly called 'fast food' because they are very 'fast' and are 'food' for most predators in the bush.

The second thing that hit me was the 'sounds' of the bushveld. There is nothing quite like the sound of an African thunderstorm. It's sudden, dramatic, powerful, deafeningly loud and, gone before you know it. The rain starts abruptly, every day, at around 16h00. It can be a stifling 30 degrees, with clear blue skies one minute and then black clouds start to accumulate. Minutes later the heavens open up and the rain is so torrential you can't see a hand in front of you. If you happen to be on a motorway, it's advisable to stop, either on the verges or even better under the motorway bridges. As the rain hits the baked earth, the smells become more pungent, and all you can hear is the rain pelting down onto leaves and the earth. The rain lasts for maybe twenty minutes and then, like magic, it stops. Today didn't disappoint.

We were all huddled in the jeeps, sheltering under the canopies. After the thunderous, lashing rain, which had been so loud, a noticeable 'quiet' fell upon us.

The 'soundtrack' that followed, and the most predominant sound of the bushveld, is definitely the sound emitted by male crickets, commonly referred to as chirping. Interestingly, crickets chirp at different rates depending on their species and the temperature of their environment. What a way to gauge the temperature if there is no thermometer at hand!

Cicada beetles, another distinctive sound of the bush choir, which can only be appreciated when you've actually tried to hold conversations around a campfire in the middle of the bushveld. Without a doubt, the cicada produces the loudest insect sound in the world and those living in Africa describe the sound as very irritating, particularly at 04h00 in the morning! However, if you have been away for any amount of time, upon your return to Africa, you'll find it's a sound that you've missed the most.

"Would anyone like to spend the night out in the bush, under the stars?" Kobus asked. "A show of hands if you do."

"Okay! That's everyone. We'll make our way to the night camp. It's not as plush as the stilt houses but you'll all be safe. The camp is already set up, so let's enjoy the next couple of hours and see what we can find out here."

I, for one, will remember it till the day I die. Just after midnight, we set out in search of the big five. It didn't take long before Kobus killed the engine. "Can you hear that?" Everyone sat still. The sound of roaring lions could be heard in the distance, and my skin prickled. We all sat, excitedly, listening. Kobus restarted the engine and drove slowly towards the roaring sound. Eventually Mbeki raised his hand and Kobus cut the engine again.

"Over there, underneath the huge baobab tree." Mbeki pointed to the left of the jeep. There were a pack of lions tearing into a wildebeest. With the spotlight on them, we were able to see blood around their mouths as they ripped the animal apart. It sent chills right through me. I could hear hyenas bickering among themselves as they circled the feeding lions, waiting for the scraps. Having already eaten the nutrient rich organs, such as the liver and heart, the lions discarded what was left for the jaw musculature of hyenas, as their jaws are far stronger than the lions and, with their robust thick teeth, they can crush bones that the lions leave behind.

At the crack of dawn, the rangers had coffee on the go accompanied by 'Oumas' rusks', a giant crunchy biscuit for dunking. The sun was already giving off some heat and as we sat by the campfire, slowly waking up, we watched the bush come alive and listened to the dawn chorus, the signature tune of the African bushveld. Springbok and impalas moved cautiously through the thick terrain of thorny bushes, munching on the dewy grasses. In the distance came the sound of a hippo concerto with loud grunting, like a pig but very loud and a puffing and wheezing sound. A very distinctive sound which they use between themselves to communicate, using a huffing and blowing motion in the water, making vibrations, sending soundwaves.

The rangers doused the campfire and all camping gear was packed back on board the jeep, and with everyone reassembled in the jeep, we set off on the two-and-a-half-hour drive back to camp. Who knew what we would see along the way!

The rest of the day was spent by the poolside relaxing, and watching animals at the watering hole.

Our evening was spent quietly under the African skies within the safety of the boma. Tables were arranged in a circle around the huge campfire and we were served wild boar and venison, and locally grown vegetables such as gem squash, a small round vegetable from the marrow family. Delicious with a knob of butter and sprinkle of salt.

On our early morning game drive on our final day, we had breakfast overlooking one of the many watering holes. A sight to behold. Zebras, giraffes and elephants graced the water's edge along with the innumerable impalas and other members of the deer family.

"Okay folks, unfortunately we have to get back to camp and get ready to depart; it's a long drive back to the city," said Debbie.

Once back at camp, we all went to freshen up and half an hour later, everyone congregated at reception, bags packed ready for the drive back to Johannesburg.

Leaving a trail of dust behind it, Debs and I watched as the first minibus drove away. "Okay guys, let's roll." She put the key into the ignition. Silence. She tried again to get the engine started – silence.

"Oh no!" Debs screamed. "The blasted thing won't start. Anyone good with engines?"

There was no one who knew a jack from a wheel spanner amongst us.

"Maybe the battery's flat?" I suggested.

One of the rangers brought his jeep around and attached the jump leads, but after several attempts, the bus still made no sound. It was dead.

"What happens if one of the jeeps breaks down guys? You must have a mechanic on site!" Deb asked.

"We have to call a mechanic to come in from the nearest town, which takes several hours, sometimes we can't get one until the next day."

"Well, can someone please make the call? We need to get these people back to Johannesburg, today!" Debs said, sounding slightly panic stricken.

It was past 20h00 when a mechanic arrived in camp. The sun was already setting and the air had become chilly. The fire in the boma had been lit and food was being prepared for everyone in camp. Debbie went to talk to the head ranger and it transpired that even if the mechanic managed to fix the bus within an hour, it would be too late to leave. "We're stuck here until the morning, the Kruger Park gates are locked at dusk, no other way out until dawn."

"That's assuming he can fix the damn bus," said Debbie.

"Is that good news or the bad news?" I asked, half laughing.

"Well, it's bad news for those who need to be at work tomorrow and good news for those who don't, I guess. I'm going to call the office to let them know."

"It's a little late Debs, will there be anyone there?"

"Of course, we're open twenty-four seven Margot. You go to the boma and get us a bottle of wine; I'll be back in a jiffy."

"I'm not sure Rex will be impressed either, but I don't have his cell number."

"Well Margot there's not a lot we can do about it. Let's enjoy it."

I headed for the boma and ordered a bottle of Chardonnay. It was buzzing, literally. Several new people had arrived and everyone was sat around the camp fire, listening to the cicada symphony in mosquito minor, accompanied by the bellowing of hippos. Fabulous.

The mechanic had been unable to fix the bus in the dark but managed to get it up and running by midday the following day. We rolled out of camp shortly after twelve thirty. I tried calling Rex but there was no reception, so I decided to leave it until we got nearer to Johannesburg.

By the time we got into Johannesburg it was past 17h00, and the office was closed and I didn't have a home number for Rex.

Chapter 5

Top of the Carlton

I arrived at the office bright and early on Wednesday morning. Rex already at his desk.

I popped my head around his door. "Good morning, Rex. Coffee?"

"Margot, come and sit down please." As I sat down, I saw the envelope on his desk with my name written on it. '*Oh no, he's going to fire me. That's the second time in less than a week.*'

He looked straight at me and said, very quietly, "Margot, I don't think you and I are going to see eye to eye." Before I could reply, he handed me the envelope. "Here's a cheque. I've paid you until the end of the month, you may go."

I couldn't believe it.

"Excuse me! Don't you even want to know what happened? At least let me explain."

"No, Margot, you can go."

"But what about the Regional monthly sales meeting on Friday? Who's going to take the minutes? The least I can do is stay until Friday and help you, I insist."

He looked up in surprise and didn't speak for a few seconds, then raised his eyebrow. "Anyone else would have taken the money and run, Margot," he said, half laughing.

"I'm not 'anyone', Rex, and I think it's only fair that I stay and help you."

"Thank you, Margot, that's very decent of you. How far are you with the travel and accommodation for the managers?" he asked.

"It's all done. What can I do to help with this load of work on your desk?"

He looked over the top of his glasses, and I saw the sparkle in his blue eyes.

"You could start by making us a coffee and we'll go through these files. Bring your notebook, and thanks again."

"Pleasure's all mine," I said, and I felt my face flush.

The next couple of days were hectic, and finally Friday came around. I arrived early at the office to set up the boardroom, making urns of coffee, jugs of water and dishes full of mints and biscuits for the sales managers. With the boardroom ready, an overhead projector, flip chart and whiteboard up on the podium, I turned to see the first of the managers arriving.

I headed for the ladies' room to powder my nose and to reassure myself that I looked good. I was pleased with what I saw in the mirror and as I got to my office, Rex called out, "Margot, come to my office."

Goosebumps ran down my spine as I went through, sat down and looked straight into his eyes.

I'm going to marry this man. Oh my God, did I really just say that to myself? My cheeks flushed and I averted my eyes from his.

"Could you make me a coffee before I go through to the boardroom, please?" he asked. "And can you get John on the line for me quickly? Thanks. That's all."

Once I'd put John through, I made my way to the boardroom. When Rex entered the room, everyone stopped talking. There it was again, that power, the ownership.

He stood up on the podium and the meeting began. Oh boy, what a man. My heart was pounding so loudly, I thought the person next to me could surely hear it.

Just before the meeting adjourned for lunch, I had a sudden impulsive naughty thought. What did I have to lose? This was my last day anyway, right? I jotted something down in my notebook and, tearing out a page, quickly folded it up and passed it down the line of managers, asking that it be handed to Rex.

He was mid-sentence when the note was passed up. He took it and opened it. He coughed casually, put the note in his pocket and continued where he had left off, not batting an eyelid.

The meeting adjourned at 12h45 and I headed to my office to start typing back the minutes while they were fresh in my mind, and while I could still read my scribbled shorthand. Rex was in his office with the manager from Cape Town, Mr Gerhardt Van Der Merwe, when he phoned through and asked me to book a table for two at the Top of the Carlton for 13h15.

Fifteen minutes later, Gerhardt came out of the office and went to the toilet. About five minutes after that, Rex came out of his office with his jacket slung over his shoulder and said, "Did you book the table?"

"Yes, it's booked."

Rex stood looking at me.

"Is there something you need Rex?"

"Yes, you! I'm taking you to lunch as it's your last day. Are you ready?"

"Oh!" was all I could come up with. I was so shocked. I began to feel the heat in my cheeks as I retrieved my handbag from under my desk.

The Carlton was literally a few hundred yards from the office so we walked across the busy street and into the hotel foyer. The lift took us to the top floor where we stepped out into one of the grandest restaurants in Johannesburg. The waiter took our reservation details and seated us in a cosy little nook by the window, so we could enjoy the panoramic views of the city. I was very nervous as we sat opposite one another, neither of us speaking. I looked at the menu and although my appetite had departed, I decided to have the Kingklip, a beautiful chunky white fish not dissimilar to cod.

"I'll have the Kingklip too, and can we have a bottle of Baksberg Chardonnay." The waiter returned with the wine and when he'd finished pouring, Rex asked; "Margot, maybe you can explain exactly what you meant in your note earlier?"

I blushed. *That's it,* I told myself, *no more blushing, he is just a man, you need to 'man up', if that's the right word. Show him you are an independent woman and that you are not afraid of him.*

"I can't stop thinking about you. You make my pulse skyrocket, and I have this urge to kiss you, I want to feel you holding me close. I'm sorry, I know it's wrong but that's how I feel." I raised my glass and he raised his. "Cheers," I said.

"Cheers, Margot."

After lunch, Rex suggested going back to the office for a coffee or another drink. We were sitting on the large Chesterfield settee sipping wine, when Rex leant forward to put his glass down and in so doing moved closer towards me, his face coming nearer to mine for a kiss. Now, bearing in mind I had been waiting all week for this and had sent him an 'invite', if you like, I don't know what exactly happened to my train of thought, but in a split second, I smacked his face and stood up and backed away.

We looked at each other and not wanting to get into an altercation of any kind, I ran out of the office, grabbed my bag and ran to the car park, jumped into my car and headed for the exit. I should never have driven, but somehow, I had sobered up very quickly.

My head was all over the place. I couldn't stop crying, but I managed to drive through the curtain of tears. I reached the barrier at the car park exit and saw Rex coming down the steps of the showroom towards me, so I put my foot down and zoomed up Main Street.

I arrived home safely. Debbie was upstairs drying her hair. The girls were at their grandma's house for the weekend.

"Debs, I need to talk to you, you won't believe what's happened."

"Okay, I'll be with you in a second," she replied.

I poured a large wine and waited for Debs to come down.

"What happened?" she asked when she returned. "Have you been crying?"

"Yes. But I don't know why really. I'm not sure if I'm mad with myself or mad at him."

"Why would you be mad at him, what did he do? You're not making any sense, tell me from the beginning."

I took a sip of wine. "He took me to lunch at the Top of the Carlton, because it was my last day, I think. But he didn't talk as though it was my last day – he never mentioned it. He asked me about my life and what brought me to SA, my marriage to Jorgen etc. and Grant, that sort of thing. We had lots to drink and didn't go back to the office until well after closing time, so it was just the two of us in the office. He opened another bottle of wine and we sat on his couch. He tried to kiss me and I don't know what came over me, but I saw something in his eyes, something familiar, and I panicked. I slapped him and ran out of the office to the car park. He followed me out of the building but I drove off, leaving him standing there with his hands on his hips, looking bewildered. I can't get him out of my head. I was angry that he thought he could take advantage of me, even though I wanted him to kiss me and I sent him a note inviting it, but I wanted it to be me that made the first move."

"Hold on, what note?"

"Damn it, I can't believe I did it. I thought as I am fired anyway, I had nothing to lose, so I sent him a note while he was in the middle of the meeting saying, "I would love to kiss you all over.""

Debbie just stared at me. "Oh my God! So, what are you going to do? Do you have a job or not?"

"I don't know, Debbie, I'm scared, I mean really scared. I'm in love with this man."

"Don't be daft Margot, you've only known him five minutes."

"I can't explain it, Debs, I feel elated when I see him; when he looks at me, I get butterflies and it's as if I'm floating." *Butterflies! More like common sense leaving my body!* said the little voice in my head.

I thought about Rex the whole weekend. I went over our conversation many times in my head, and he'd definitely never mentioned my leaving. By Sunday afternoon, I had made up my mind. I would go into the office early on Monday and be at my desk when he came in and face the consequences, good or bad. What could be the worst thing that could happen?

My alarm went off at six on Monday morning but I'd been awake for ages waiting for it to bleep, mulling over in my head how the whole scenario would pan out.

When he comes into the office, I'll be typing up the minutes from the board meeting and coffee will be ready, and I'll simply say, "Good morning, Rex, how was your weekend?" and I'll smile at him, I thought to myself.

My palms were sweating and I became extremely nervous when I heard his footsteps. My heart skipped a dozen beats and my breathing became loud and raspy. He came into the office, looked at me and smiled.

"Good morning, Margot, lovely day. Please come through and take dictation. Oh, and let's have coffee."

Had he been mulling it over the whole weekend too?

I went through and poured coffee for us both, then sat down opposite him with my notebook at the ready. Our eyes met briefly as he said, "I have to go to Cape Town on Thursday. If you could get me a flight after nine, please, returning on Friday, to get me back to Johannesburg at around three thirty, and book me into the Victoria & Albert Waterfront Hotel. Thanks Margot."

Just do it, just go over to him and kiss him.

"Also, will you ask Robin to book my car in for a service on Thursday and to pick me up from the airport on Friday. How are the minutes from Fridays' meeting coming along?"

"All finished," I said and handed him a copy of the minutes.

"That's all for now, thank you. Please, can you get Gerhardt on the line?"

I closed his door, went back to my desk and put his call through. I sat down and sighed a great sigh of relief. How I got through that I'll never know but one thing was for sure, I wasn't intimated by him anymore.

Chapter 6

You've Got Some Balls

On Thursday, with Rex out of the office, I put my master plan into action. I booked an early appointment at the beauty parlour in the city and killing two birds with one stone, I made my weekly visit to the supreme court in Johannesburg to have various documents signed and stamped and booked hearing dates for clients, for my DIY divorce business which I ran from home. Between appointments, I did a little retail therapy buying a new suit and accessories. I went and had my nails done and had an hour of pampering with a deep cleanse facial.

On Friday morning, I went to get my hair done with Chris. I told him about my plan and how I was going to attempt to lure this man into my web. He looked surprised and said there was no doubt I would get my man.

"How does that look, Margot, is it blonde enough for you, my darling?" asked Chris.

"Wow, it's fabulous. Perfect, I love it. Thanks Chris. I wasn't sure of the style but you were right, it does look better short and I haven't had it this short for a long time."

"You look much younger and oh so sassy, how will he be able to resist you, you minx?"

"Wish me luck. It might not go as I want it to and how embarrassing would that be." We both laughed.

I had a bite of lunch before returning to the office. I called Robin and asked him to bring the Bentley around to the front in about ten minutes as I was going to pick Mr. Charrington up from the airport.

"Oh, Madam, I thought I was going to fetch the boss." he replied.

"No, that won't be necessary, thank you. We have to go to a meeting out by the airport so I'll pick him up and take him there. Thanks again, but just bring the car around, please."

"Yes, Madam," said Robin.

I turned off my computer, made sure everything else was turned off, locked both offices before I made my way downstairs out of the building and into the Bentley.

"My God, are you really doing this, Margot?" I asked myself out loud. *Yes, I am,* said the little voice in my head. *Go get your man.*

I drove home with a sense of euphoria. It felt wonderful. Once home, I jumped into the shower and smothered my body in sensual body creams. I opened a pair of new seamed nylons and gently pulled them up to meet lace suspenders. I wriggled my backside into my teddy undergarment and admired my reflection in the mirror.

"That should do it," I said to myself.

I slipped on my new white silk blouse and dark-blue pencil skirt and jacket. I put on my heels, my pearl earrings and necklace.

No looking back now, this is it girl.

As I drove to the airport, Chris Rea's 'On the Beach' came on the radio, so I turned it up and imagined Rex and I on the beach together on holiday, somewhere romantic like Mauritius.

After parking the Bentley, I made my way to the arrivals hall and waited at the barrier. It was too late to turn back now. Make or break, this was it.

Oh my God, what have I done? There's no going back now.

Just then the arrivals doors opened and the passengers started streaming through. I caught sight of him, head held high, looking for Robin. He looked past me and then, doing a quick turn of his head, looked back, straight at me, in disbelief. I waved to him and he nodded back.

As he strode towards me, I smiled and said, quite calmly, "Hi, how was Cape Town?"

"Windy. To what do I owe the pleasure Margot?"

"Well, I thought after a busy week, we should enjoy life a little. I thought we could go and have a drink somewhere."

"Did you now? Do you have somewhere in mind?" He smiled.

"Yes, my place. I have beer, wine, champagne, or tea and coffee if you prefer." I smiled back.

"Lead the way. You have the keys, let's go."

To say I was slightly nervous would be an understatement, but I tried not to let it show. We made our way to the car park and he got into the passenger seat. I'd made sure that I'd parked in a place where I could easily manoeuvre out of the confined space and once on the highway, I felt a little less nervy. I could sense he was looking at me.

"Apart from the wind," I asked, "how was Cape Town?"

"It's such a beautiful place but I don't think I could put up with that wind full-time. Have you ever been there?" he replied.

"No, but I would love to go, I've heard the view from Table Mountain is breath-taking. I've been to the Corcovado, you know, the statue of Christ the Redeemer on Mount Corcovado, in Brazil? Did you know it's ninety-eight feet high, and the outstretched arm span, is ninety-two feet?"

"No Margot, I didn't know that."

"It took nine years to construct and the outer two layers are made of triangular tiles of soap stone." I babbled on.

"They started building in April 1922 and it opened to the public on 11th October 1931. It's right at the top of Mount Corcovado and to reach the statue you have to go on a cog train. It's the same train that they used to transport the materials to construct the magnificent structure. I'm sorry, I'm babbling. Anyway, my point is that I would like to see if Table Mountain is as high. The Statue of Christ was so high I couldn't go to the edge and look over. It was frighteningly high."

"When did you go to Brazil Margot?" he asked.

"February this year. Grant wanted to go to the Carnival and phoned me one morning, out of the blue, asking if I could get a week's leave. I told him it was unlikely, as it was very short notice but my boss said that under the circumstances, I could take a week off. It was an experience I can tell you. We didn't have tickets to get into the Carnival and there were high walls all around. We managed to get up on to the top of the wall, with a little help from a couple of guys who gave us a shoulder lift up. When we looked down over the other side, there was a moat! Well, there was no way I was going to jump into the moat, so we had to somehow get back down. When we turned around, we saw two policeman and crowds of people standing watching us, all clapping and shouting. It was hilarious."

"So, you like taking risks, Margot?"

"Yes, I suppose I do."

We were almost home, and I took a deep breath as I tried to park the huge vehicle in the garage.

"Okay, here we are."

He followed me up the drive to the front door and through to the kitchen.

"What would you like to drink, Rex?"

"Champagne, of course," he replied.

"Are you hungry?" I asked.

"Not at the moment, maybe later."

I went through to the lounge with the champers and glasses and sat on the sofa next to him. He popped the cork and poured us a drink.

"You're a strange woman, Margot. You've got balls, I'll give you that."

I instantly felt my cheeks redden. "Well, here's to having balls then," I said, and raised my glass. *Fuck, did I really just say that?*

We had a couple of glasses of champagne and out of the blue, he asked, "Why did you slap me and run away the last time we were alone together?"

"I had a flashback; I saw something in your eyes that reminded me of something that happened years ago and I panicked. I didn't feel safe."

He raised his eyebrows and looked straight into my eyes.

"Do you feel safe now?" he asked.

"Yes, I feel safe because I'm in control. I initiated this meeting and we're in my house. Now, if you'll excuse me a moment."

I left him sitting drinking his Champagne and went upstairs. I discarded my suit and blouse. I slipped into my black thigh-length boots and elbow-length black silk gloves. I applied my lipstick and teased my hair a little. With seamed stockings and my black leatherette body stocking and whip, I made my way downstairs. My heart was pounding. As I got to the bottom of the stairs, I could see he was standing with his back to me looking out at the view of the city. He was slowly sipping his drink. I walked quietly towards him and when I was only a few feet away from him, said, "Rex, don't turn around, just put your drink down."

He placed his glass on the side table. I held the whip in one hand and gently smacked the palm of my other hand.

"Keep facing the wall. Take your jacket off and put it on the sofa!"

He silently took it off and laid it on the sofa.

"Now the shirt and tie."

He never said a word but did as I asked.

"Now the trousers, shoes and socks."

As he laid the items on the sofa, I could see that he was aroused. His white boxers were bulging, and he laid his hand on his appendage.

"Put your hands out in front of you on the wall and open your legs wide."

I moved close enough so that he could feel my breath on his bare skin. I gently stroked the whip up and down his back, creating goose bumps. I slid the whip slowly down over his buttocks and onto the back of his thighs, before sharply spanking him on his left buttock. His body stiffened, jolting with the shock, but he didn't turn around or move his hands from the wall, which meant only one thing, he was enjoying it!

I whipped his right buttock and again he flinched. I instantly became aroused. I discarded the whip and moved in close enough to feel the heat from his body, as the anticipation built. As I gently kissed the back of his neck, I pulled his hair, jolting his head backwards. With the other hand, I stroked down his stomach towards his bulge, running my fingers through his pubic hair and gently stroked around the appendage. His balls were rock hard and I knew he was ready.

"Turn around and face me, Rex!"

Like an obedient dog, he turned around. He still had his arms in the air and had a wild look on his face. He looked me up and down, taking in every inch of me. I kissed his face, then, moving slowly down his neck, I kissed his chest, gently biting his nipples, kissing all the way down to his belly button. I could feel his heart beating as he breathed heavily. My mouth moved closer to his swollen appendage, and through his boxers, I gently nibbled at his bulge and carefully began to slip his boxers down.

I teased my tongue on the bare flesh of his penis and slowly began to suck. He gasped out loud and I felt his hands grip my head firmly as he eased his throbbing penis further into my mouth. In an instant, he was out of control. He pushed me onto the sofa, pulled my thong aside, with my back arched, as he held onto my buttocks, thrusting himself into me.

Seconds later he spun me around, picked me up, and carried me upstairs to the main bedroom. He flung me onto the bed. His eyes were wild, like a man possessed.

"Spank me Rex, hard, go on spank me, for fuck's sake, go on. I'm coming! I'm coming, spank me harder, oh my God."

Within seconds of my orgasm, he let out a noise not dissimilar to that of a lion's mating call and exploded inside me. We lay in one another's arms until our breathing returned to normal.

It was dark when I woke up, and Rex was lying next to me, snoring. I just lay there and watched him sleep. He was so beautiful. His blonde eyelashes were twitching as he slept. Every breath he took, a gentle purring sound came from his throat. I adored him and I knew I was in love. I couldn't get back to sleep, so I went downstairs to the guest bedroom and eventually fell into a deep sleep.

"Margot, Margot, where are you, hello?" I heard him calling from upstairs.
The sun was just rising, and I could hear the birds singing.
"I'm down here in the basement."
He came into the room and pulled the duvet off the bed and swept me up in his arms and carried me up the two flights of stairs and threw me onto the bed.
"Don't do that again. I want you here next to me, are we clear?" he said.
"Woah, yes Sir. I couldn't sleep, you were snoring so loud. Sorry, I've kind of got used to sleeping alone; it's been a long time since I spent the whole night with anyone."
We made love again and again.
We were having a shower together when Rex said;
"I need you to do me a favour, Margot. I should have gone home last night. Janet will be wondering where I am."
Am I dreaming? I must still be asleep.
"Sorry, what did you say? Who's Janet?" I asked.
"My wife." He could see the shock on my face and he stepped back slightly. "You knew I was married, right?"
"Do I look as if I knew, you bastard? Why didn't you say so before? Do you have kids?" I shouted. "Fucking married with kids, you ass—"
"No, we don't have children – calm down."
"Oh, here we go, don't tell me, 'My wife doesn't understand me and all that crap'; you men are all the same. Get the fuck out, go on, get out!"
"Hey, wait a minute, you came on to me, remember? Not that I'm complaining. I'm attracted to you but I have to tell you Margot, I'm happily married, and it's purely physical, that's all." He looked scared.

"Okay, physical, you say? Purely physical? How's this for physical." I raised my hand to slap him but he grabbed my hand and pulled me down onto the bathroom carpet. He flipped me over his knee and began spanking me.

"How's that? Do you want more? Yes, I thought so."

The next thing I knew we were fucking furiously again.

God, if you can hear me, please help me!

While Rex showered again, I made the call, explaining to Janet that Rex had been delayed in Cape Town, and would be home later that day. She thanked me for the call and hung up.

Chapter 7
The Wardrobe

Debbie and the girls came home on Sunday afternoon and while the girls played in the pool, I told Debs what had happened.

"No way, you're kidding, he's married? What are you going to do Margot?"

"What can I do? I'm in love with him Debs, I have been since the day I clapped eyes on him. I'll just have to wait and see how things work out, I'm past the point of no return and so is he. I'm going to marry this man, Debbie, you just watch me."

"And how do you think his wife will react to that?" Debbie said sarcastically.

"I'll cross that enormous bridge when I get to it."

Monday couldn't come quick enough for me. I couldn't wait to see him. I got to the office early, put the coffee on and checked his diary which was unusually clear for the day.

"Good morning, Margot."

He strolled past my desk, briefcase in one hand and a large bunch of flowers in the other, and went through to his office. My phone rang.

"Come to my office for some dic…"

Did he say dick or dictation? He definitely said dick.

As I went through to his office, he was hanging his jacket up. "Lock the door, Margot."

My legs started to shake a little as he beckoned me over towards the sofa. He sat on the arm of the Chesterfield and put his hands around my waist, pulling me in for a kiss. He slowly unbuttoned my blouse, unclipped my bra and started kissing my nipples when his phone rang.

"Leave it," he said, sounding annoyed at the intrusion but it just kept ringing. "Dammit," he said under his breath.

He strode towards his desk to take the call. Feeling a little embarrassed but also aroused, I went over and climbed onto his desk. I lifted my skirt and slowly took my panties off, then carefully placed my flowing skirt over his head while he took the call.

"Yes, of course, Sir, I'll have to call you back. I'm just in a meeting." He replaced the receiver and pulled me down onto the desk. "For Christ's sake, Margot, that was the boss, the big boss. What are you doing to me?"

"The same thing you're doing to me; making me crazy!" I grabbed his head and pulled him in as he went down to lady town.

It was total ecstasy, out of control unabashed raw sex.

The rest of the morning dragged on and he didn't come out of his office or buzz me until at around twelve forty-five. He buzzed through and said, "Margot, go to the corner of Market and Smith Street, by the supermarket. Get a bottle of champagne, crusty bread and some ham, then wait outside for me."

Without further ado, I went to the bathroom to freshen up and off I went, already excited in anticipation of what was to come.

I saw the Bentley coming down Market Street and those damn butterflies turned into dragonflies in my stomach. That hot sensation was there again. I was so aroused.

I jumped in and 'belted' up. "Where are we going, Rex?"

"To your house if that's okay?" He gave me a raised-eyebrow look and smiled.

As he sped along the freeway towards the townhouse, I just couldn't wait. I undid my seatbelt and leant over towards him and fumbled with his zipper. He was already rock hard. I took his penis in my mouth and started sucking gently.

"For Christ's sake, Margot, do you want me to have an accident?"

"It's not good to talk with my mouth full, just concentrate on driving." My sex drive was off the scale and out of control.

"There's a guy alongside us in his lorry enjoying the action, but don't let that stop you," he said and accelerated past the lorry.

We stayed at my townhouse all afternoon. We made love several times, taking a dip in the pool between sessions and devoured the sandwiches and drank the champagne.

"We should really go back to the office, don't want wagging tongues. If anyone asks, which they won't, rather they dare not, we've been to a seminar, okay?" By the time we got back into town through the heavy traffic, the office was closed.

When we pulled into the car park, my VW Beetle was the only car in there.

"Great, let's have a glass of Chardonnay while the peak traffic subsides."

"Okay, I just need the toilet."

When I got back to my office, there was a large bouquet of red roses on my desk.

"Oh, Rex, thank you so much, you really do think of everything. They're beautiful."

He gave me a look which sent a cold chill through me. "Close the door behind you Margot." I was speechless.

I looked for a card amongst the roses but couldn't find one.

My buzzer rang. "Margot, come in here."

I opened his door and popped my head in. "Who are the flowers from Margot?"

Now call me old-fashioned, but why is it that it's okay for a man to have an affair but perish the thought if the woman has more than one lover or admirer?

"From an admirer! But I have no idea who. Is that all, Rex, or do you have some more dictation for me?" I asked.

"That's all." He was such a cool cat; why couldn't he just say he was angry, jealous, whatever, not just be so damn blasé?

"Goodnight, Rex, have a good evening... with your wife! See you tomorrow." I got my bag and left the office.

When I got home, there was a note from Debbie saying that she was staying over at her boyfriend's house. I didn't feel like being alone so I rang Penny.

"Hi Penny, what are you doing tonight?" I asked her.

"Hi Margot, how are you? I haven't got anything planned, why?" she replied.

"Do you fancy coming over for dinner and a few drinks? I can drop you into work in the morning if you want to stay over."

"Yes, I'd love to."

"Great, I'm on my way."

I took some chicken out of the freezer and put it in the microwave to defrost, then put a couple of bottles of wine in the fridge before I went to pick Penny up. Penny was a dear friend who I had met in one of the many communes I'd lived in. She was younger than me, rather old-fashioned in her ways but very clever, with a demanding job at a law firm.

We drank a bottle of wine while I prepared dinner and I told her all about Rex and the 'flowers' episode.

"He sounds really scary, Margot. Are you sure you can handle him?"

"He used to scare the living daylights out of me but I made my mind up that he was just a man. My life of being beaten senseless by Jorgen made me stronger. All the time I spent hiding and cowering in some dark place, trying to escape the beatings taught me one thing; never again will I allow a man to run my life or lay a hand on me. Never."

Eventually, Penny said, "I'm tired, I have a busy day ahead. I'm going to make a cup of tea and go to bed. Do you want one?"

"No thanks, I'll have water. You can sleep in Debbie's room, she won't mind."

The following morning at around 06h00, Penny came into my room to use the shower in my en-suite bathroom. She was in the shower when I heard a car coming up the driveway and looked out of the window to see Rex getting out of the Bentley. I banged on the bathroom door and said, "Penny? Rex is here."

"Oh my God, Margot, what the hell do we do now?" she said.

Before I could think of a reply, Penny jumped out of the shower and with a towel wrapped around her, flew past me, got into my wardrobe and closed the door.

"Penny, what the…"

I could hear Rex coming up the stairs so it was too late to do anything about Penny. I went into the bathroom and locked the door, then got into the shower. He knocked.

"Margot, open the door," he said.

"I'll be out in a minute," I replied.

"Open the door I said." He insisted.

It went quiet for a few seconds and then, BANG, the next thing I knew the door came off its hinges and Rex stood there, stark bollock naked, with a huge erection.

"Just making sure there's nobody else here."

I looked at him in disbelief.

"Nobody else here? How dare you! This is my house and you have no right barging in like this. You're the one 'two-timing', not me."

He ignored me and jumped into the shower with me.

Now I don't know what was going through Penny's mind but I knew she was going to be in the wardrobe for quite some time. I tried to get Rex down to the lounge or even down in the basement but he was adamant that we were quite happy where we were. We made love in the shower, on the floor and eventually on the bed. We were just in the middle of our manic lovemaking session when there was a 'thud'. "What was that noise?"

"What noise?"

"Sounded like someone banging about in the wardrobe."

He got off the bed and went over to the wardrobe and opened the door. He shut the door much faster than he'd opened it and said, "There's a naked woman in the fucking wardrobe, what the hell's going on Margot?"

"It's okay, Rex, calm down, it's Penny," I said.

"Who the fuck is Penny?"

"Never mind, it's a long story. Get your clothes and go into the other bathroom and get dressed."

I opened the wardrobe door and Penny was lying amongst my shoes, gasping for air. Now I wanted to laugh, really. I did, but I knew that Penny was distraught. She was flushed and her eyes weren't focussing properly, sort of hazy. I managed to get her out of the cupboard and sat her down on the bed.

"Penny, are you okay? Penny."

"I fainted. It was so hot in there I couldn't breathe."

"I'll get you some water. Just sit there and relax, I'll be two minutes." I left her sitting on the bed and went downstairs to fetch water. When I got back, she was lying on the bed.

"Here you go, drink some water. Come on, sit up." She drank the water and looked a little better. "What the hell made you get in the wardrobe you daft bugger?" I asked her.

"I'm scared of Rex, I panicked. It seemed like a good idea at the time."

The pair of us couldn't stop laughing. My sides ached and I laughed so much I cried. We were both rolling around on the bed laughing, stark bollock naked, when we heard, "Excuse me for interrupting."

Oh God, I'd forgotten about Rex.

The laughter stopped and we both sat up and looked at Rex, who had a pitiful look on his face, with raised eyebrows and his hands in the air. Shrugging his shoulders, he turned on his heels and walked out of the room. We heard the front door bang and the engine of the Bentley start up.

"Whoops. I don't know how I'm going to talk myself out of this one, Penny, any suggestions?"

"It won't matter what you tell him, he saw what he saw! Let's have a coffee, shall we?" Penny was still laughing.

We slipped our robes on and went to make coffee. "I'm going to be late for work Margot. At least your boss can't tell you off. Well, maybe not tell you off but you know what I mean. What do you think he will say when you go in?"

"I have no idea, and quite frankly, my dear, I don't give a damn."

That did it; we were now incapable of even talking. We laughed so much my whole body ached.

I dropped Penny to work at about 09h30, and when I arrived at the office, Rex's car wasn't in the parking lot.

The time went very slowly and I tried to keep myself busy. I tried to come up with a sensible reason, as to why Penny had been in the wardrobe, but of course I came up with nothing. It was so ridiculous that even as I went through it in my mind, I couldn't help but laugh to myself. I'd just tell him the truth, there was nothing else I could do, even though the truth was going to sound bonkers. What was the truth anyway; '*Penny is so scared of you that she hid in the wardrobe!*' Yep, bonkers.

I went through to his office and busied myself with filing. I was going through the papers on his desk when I found a small card – "To the love of my life, I miss you. All my love, Jorgen. Please call me."

I ran down to reception. "Martha, good morning. Did you see who delivered the flowers yesterday?"

"Yes Madam. A very tall blonde man with big dimples. Very handsome." She smiled.

"Good morning, ladies."

Just the sound of his voice appeared to put the fear of God into everyone. It was truly amazing to see.

"Good morning, Sir." Martha stood like a statue, glued to the spot.

I gave him a look. "Good morning." He walked past me and went upstairs to his office. I followed shortly afterwards.

My buzzer rang. "Come to my office, Margot."

I stood in the doorway. "You should have stayed for coffee earlier Rex, there was no need to run off. How very rude of you. You didn't even say hello to Penny."

50

"Oh sorry, what was I supposed to say? 'Hello Penny, how are you and, what the hell are you doing in the wardrobe!' Quite clearly, I was interrupting something. Would you like to explain?" he asked.

"No, not really. Nothing to explain. Would you like to explain what you were doing at my place at six in the morning?" I replied.

"So now I need an explanation to come and visit you?" he asked.

"Yes, at six in the morning you do. Our relationship is purely physical according to you, and whatever else goes on in my life is really none of your business," I said quite firmly.

"I think I may love you, Margot," he said.

"Wow. You 'think' you 'may' love me. Be careful not to give anything away."

"I love you, I'm in love with you, Margot," he said.

"Well, that's good, because I'm in love with you too, and have been since the first day I met you. So. what do we do now?" I asked.

"I assume Penny's not at the house now, so get your backside home and let's finish what we started this morning. I'll be there shortly." he said.

"Who's getting the champagne and sandwiches today?" I asked.

"We'll go get something to eat afterwards, a late lunch. Now give me a kiss and get out of here."

As I watched from my bedroom window, I could see his car making its way up the steep drive to the complex. My insides were fluttering and I couldn't wait for what was to come. I don't know why I bothered to dress up because he always just ripped my clothes off anyway. Once again, we made wild love – it just got better and better.

"I love you so much, Margot," he whispered in my ear.

"I love you more." I replied.

We lay for a while, snuggled up, just looking at each other.

"Would you like to go away for a weekend Margot. Towards the end of next month?"

"Oh yes Rex, I'd love to."

"I need to have you for more than just a few hours Margot. I thought it would be nice to go to the Drakensburg Mountains. No interruptions or strange people in the wardrobes," he said, laughing.

"So Rex, you do have a sense of humour. That's the first time I've seen you really laugh. How far is it to the Drakensburg?" I replied.

"Just over three hours. We could go straight after lunchtime on Friday, and come back on Sunday afternoon."

"That sounds wonderful Rex." I gave him a huge kiss. "What hotel is it?"

"Self-catering, they have lovely rustic bungalows, really secluded in the middle of nowhere. We'll arrange everything a little nearer the time. I just need to make the booking."

"Sounds very romantic Rex. I can't wait to have you all to myself either." I said, and leant over and kissed him again.

Chapter 8
The Drakensburg Fiasco

Our weekend away finally came around. I cleared all filing and made sure Rex's diary was up-to-date.

"Margot, come to my office," came the dulcet tone at around twelve thirty.

"Yes, Sir, can I help you?" I said as I popped my head into his office.

"Yes, you can come and bend over my desk and show me that lovely backside of yours. I can't wait until later."

On the way to the hypermarket, he asked, "What do you fancy to eat? There's a braai at the cabin so we can BBQ one night and cook indoors on the other if you like."

"I fancy Peking duck. We can BBQ tonight, because the duck will need to be hung in a draught overnight before roasting. That's what makes the skin so crispy. We can get ready-made pancakes and all the accompaniments. BBQ-wise, always rump steak and maybe chicken or ribs and salad. What do you fancy?"

"That sounds very exotic and complicated Margot, but if that's what you want then it's fine with me."

With the shopping done and packed in the boot, we headed off for our first weekend away. The drive to Kwa Zulu Natal, formerly known as Durban, was very scenic, with its fields of crops of sweetcorn and sunflowers. The hedgerows were laden with cosmos and we stopped at a designated picnic area close to an ostrich farm where we purchased a huge ostrich egg.

"That will make scrambled eggs for breakfast for a week." I laughed.

Upon arrival at the Drakensburg National Park, the roads went from tarred to dirt, and the last few kilometres of the journey were very bumpy. "All these bumpy roads are making me feel sick, Rex. How much further is there to go on this awful road?" I asked.

"Not too far, another twenty minutes or so. If you're going to throw up, just tell me and I'll stop the car."

We got to the cabin at around five, and it was extremely hot and humid. As I stepped out of the car, time stood still. All my worries seemed to melt away in this tranquil setting, like being carried away on the gentlest of breezes, a balm for my troubled soul. The cabin was picturesque. Made of logs and brick with a white chimney breast. There were stacks of logs outside and as we entered the cabin, I saw the huge log fireplace. The large open plan space was perfectly set out for ultimate pleasure. The kitchen had a breakfast bar next to a large window, where you could sit and take in the majestic views of the mountain peaks. I went through to the bedroom while Rex unloaded the car. A huge four-poster bed, surrounded by pure white mosquito nets, was strategically placed to take in the full vista through the large windows. There were African tribal masks on the walls and all the furniture was made from wooden logs, dressed with cushions of brightly coloured African-print fabrics.

"Margot, wake up. It's seven o'clock."

"What? Oh, I must have dozed off."

"I went to unload the car and when I came back, you were fast asleep; are you okay?"

"Yes, I'm fine, I get car-sick sometimes, especially on the bumpy dirt roads. Sorry."

"Nothing to be sorry for, silly. I've lit the barbecue and prepared the veggies and meat. Come and sit outside. Do you want a drink?"

"Just water, thanks," I said.

We sat quietly, listening to the hum of mosquitoes and watching the birds flitting around as we watched the sun go down behind the mountains. Not a sound of civilisation around. No cars, no kids, no planes. Just nature.

While Rex was cooking the meat, I went to prepare the duck for the next day. I found a suitable place to hang the duck in a draught, with a bowl underneath to catch any blood.

We sat a little longer by the fire and I had a glass of wine.

"It's so hot here, I don't know how I'm going to sleep. Did we bring any mosquito repellent?"

"Yep. I've lit them already and closed the windows and doors."

"Great, rather melt than be eaten alive." I laughed.

After we'd eaten, we sat quietly listening to the night critters, as we watched the embers of the fire die down. We went to bed at around eleven o'clock and fell asleep almost immediately. We were awakened in the early hours by the sound of the car alarm blaring out into the quiet night.

Rex went out to investigate.

"Was it monkeys or something jumping on the car?" I said when he came back.

"There are no monkeys around here. We'd have seen them by now."

"Well, whatever it was, let's hope they don't come back."

No such luck; all through the night the alarm was triggered, but we couldn't see any culprits. We even sat and watched, but the alarm still kept going off for no apparent reason.

"It's an omen. We shouldn't be here together," Rex said.

"Don't be stupid. What, you think Janet's put a spell on us?" I laughed.

He was deadly serious. "It's not funny, Margot. I'm freaked out."

It was already daylight. We sat outside in the early morning sun, which had just appeared over the mountaintops. The tranquillity was beautiful, with the sounds of the rippling river, the bees humming as they collected nectar from the hedgerows and the weaverbirds chirping away as they flew to and fro over the water, beneath the hanging branches of the weeping willow tree, where their nests hung precariously from the ends of the branches. It was truly amazing to watch a weaverbird build its nest.

"I don't see any monkeys, do you, Rex? Hmm, maybe it was Janet in the bushes," I said mockingly.

"That's not funny," he said angrily.

"Actually, it's very funny. You and your 'omen' theory. I'm sure there's a logical explanation for the alarm going off. Let's not spoil the day. Shall we go for a walk and then come back and have breakfast?" I suggested.

"I just need another coffee to get my bowels moving. Don't want to be halfway up the mountain and need the toilet."

Lovely, I thought. *Could have kept that to himself. Anyway.*

"Yes, okay, I'll go and get the coffee," I said.

I couldn't help thinking how regimented he was, always in control. I went to the kitchen to make the coffee when I noticed that the duck had been yanked down from its drying place in the window, half-eaten, and the remains left on the floor. There were spots of blood on the work surface and tiny footprints all around, which looked incredibly like monkey footprints.

I took the coffee outside and said, "Rex, do you really believe in omens? Seriously now, do you?" I asked.

"Janet's a very spiritual woman, Margot, really, don't mock it."

"Well, maybe you should go and have a look in the kitchen, because the 'spirits' have definitely been at work."

He raised those incredible white blonde eyebrows and stood up. I followed him into the kitchen.

"Bit of monkey business going on then, Rex, do you think Janet sent them?"

That was the wrong thing to say. He was obviously feeling very guilty about being with me and was trying to defend Janet.

"Pick the fucking duck up and clean this mess up," he shouted at me.

"Clean it up yourself," I replied.

He bent down and picked up the half carcass and plunged it into my hand, then walked away.

As he walked towards the door, I threw the duck full throttle at his head and hit him, bang on target. It made a sort of squishy thud on impact and left a patch of blood in his hair, making his head jolt forward. He turned around very slowly and I saw 'that look', the one I had so often seen in Jorgen's face.

Panic set in, my stomach knotted, and before he had time to even speak, I ran out of the cabin.

I kept running towards a treed area and managed to lose him in the dense forest and hid behind a huge baobab tree. My heart was thudding so loudly I was sure if he got close enough, he would be able to hear it beating. Sweat was dripping down my face and my palms were wet. My palms weren't the only things; I had actually wet myself from the fear.

Oh my God, I thought, *I can't live through another abusive relationship, please God, make this stop.*

I was in floods of tears and gasping for breath. I heard a twig snapping underfoot and stopped breathing and crying so that I could hear clearly. As I looked up, he was standing looking straight at me.

"Don't you dare hit me, don't you bloody well dare," I shouted, putting my arms over my face to protect myself.

"Oh my God, Margot."

He could see that I was terrified and he came slowly towards me with his arms held open wide and pulled me close and held me. I fell into his open arms and broke down in tears.

We sat there for a while, hugging one another.

"I've never seen that look on a woman's face before, and I never want to see it again. I'm so sorry if I scared you. I was angry, but I would never, ever hit you. Obviously, someone else has hit you though. Come on, let's go back to the cabin and get you cleaned up. We need to talk."

I told Rex my life story thus far. At times, he had tears in his eyes as I relived some abusive and very traumatic episodes from my past.

"Do you fancy going for a walk into the forest Margot, and maybe head towards that mountain over there. I'll pack a couple of sandwiches and bottles of water. I think the exercise and fresh air will do us both the world of good."

We went up as far as I could manage, and found shade under a large Yellow Wood tree to take a breather and have something to eat. We made love on the mountainside overlooking the open plains of the Drakensburg.

"I never want this to stop, Rex, I love you so much. I can't stand it when you go home to 'her', I feel so empty. How much longer do I have to share you?"

"Margot, not now, please. It's stressful for me too, I'm so torn. I wish I had an answer but I don't. I'm just letting things go over my head and hope that eventually it will sort itself out."

"Okay, fair enough. Let's go back down to the cabin, we've been out for hours and I'm getting hungry."

On Sunday morning after breakfast, and a morning walk, we packed the car ready to drive back to Johannesburg.

Two hours into the journey the skies started to cloud over. It didn't take long before the sky turned a blackish grey, and the first droplets of rain fell on the windscreen. Five minutes later the rain was so dense, it looked like a waterfall and we had to stop until the rain eased off, as we couldn't see a foot in front of us.

We made good use of our time in the car, and by the time the rain had started to ease a little, the car windows were all steamed up, from the heat of our bodies.

It was a little after 18h00 when we pulled up at the townhouse. Rex carried my bag up to the townhouse and said "I have to get home."

My heart sank. I felt broken. Was this how I was going to feel every time he went home, back to his wife? My eyes welled up, but I quickly got myself under control.

"What about a coffee before you go Rex. You've been driving for hours?" I asked. "Good idea Margot, I could do with a coffee to wake me up."

We were out in the garden sipping our coffee when the doorbell rang. He looked at me. "Are you expecting someone?"

"No, of course not."

I went to get up and Rex stood up and headed for the door. "I'll get it."

I followed him and as he opened the door, I heard a woman's voice. "Hello, Rex. I thought I'd save you the trouble of packing."

I heard a slap, and his head jolted backwards. As I got closer to the door, I saw a pile of clothes in a heap on the wet floor. I caught a glimpse of a curvaceous blonde woman who shouted; "Oh, now I see what the attraction is Rex, you always did prefer slim women." Janet ran away crying so loud I thought the neighbours might come out to see what was going on.

"Oh my God, all my clothes. Help me pick them up, Margot, before they're ruined."

"What? You can't be serious, Rex. Is that all you can think of to say at this very moment. Your wife is hysterical, and you're worried about your clothes?" I was dumbfounded. "Now I suppose you just assume that you can come and live here? Five minutes ago, you were going home to Janet! Only now that she's actually thrown you out, you want to come and move in with me! Wrong. Go and sort your life out and when you've made a decision, have the guts to let us know. The educated, high-flying managing director, with scores of people reporting to you on a daily basis but you can't handle your own life. Off you go. See you in the morning."

"Margot, what are you doing? Help me pick my things up off the floor."

"No Rex, I'm just your little bit on the side, not your servant, pick them up yourself. Goodnight."

I shut the door and the tears streamed down my cheeks. I sank to the floor and cried for what seemed like hours.

The next morning, my eyes were swollen and puffy from crying so much. I sliced two pieces of cucumber to put on my eyes and lay down for five minutes, in the hope that I would look less like I had just done two rounds with Mike

Tyson. I jumped into a cold shower to try and kickstart my system. It worked to a certain degree and I began to feel a little better. I arrived at the office just in time to see Rex parking the Bentley.

"Good morning. Did you sleep well?" he said sarcastically.

"Yes, I did, thank you. I feel very refreshed after a good night's sleep, especially with no alarm to wake me up." I replied, just as flippantly. We walked in silence up to the office.

"Let's have a coffee. I have something to tell you Margot."

I made the drinks and sat down opposite him.

"Where did you stay last night, Rex?"

"That's what I need to talk to you about."

"You went back to Janet, didn't you?"

"Where else was I supposed to go?"

"A hotel, it's not like you didn't have a change of clothes."

"Look, Margot, I stayed in the spare room; she didn't want to be near me. I know I have to make a decision but I can't hurt her like that. I love her."

Chapter 9
Birthday Celebration

Debbie was at home for a couple of nights, thank goodness. She'd been staying over at her boyfriend's place quite a lot recently, and we had a lot to catch up on. While the girls played out in the pool, I opened a bottle of wine and started to prepare dinner. Debs popped her head into the kitchen and said, "Margot, do you have any tampons? I've just come on."

"Yes of course, they're in my bathroom cupboard, help yourself."

"Debbie, I haven't had a period since April. I need to go to the Doctor, and before you state the obvious, I can't be pregnant. I've never told anyone this but when I was seventeen, I got myself into trouble and had an abortion. It was pretty horrible to say the least. My partner at the time was very understanding and he paid for the abortion. I never got over the pain and the guilt, and I never saw him again. Two months later, I still hadn't had a period and my mum was really worried and she insisted that we went back to see the doctor. When the doctor said 'you're pregnant again!' I started crying. "But that's impossible. I can't be. I haven't seen him. I finished with him after the abortion. I haven't had sex Mum; you have to believe me." She was livid, called me a stupid girl. She evidently didn't believe me. Anyway, I had to go back to the clinic and have another abortion, which took me almost a year to pay for. They must have damaged my ovaries or something and that's why I never conceived with Jorgen. We tried, really, we did, I never used contraception and we were together for fifteen years."

"Didn't Rex ask if you were using contraception?"

"Of course, he did, but I told him I couldn't have kids. Look, stop worrying, I'll make an appointment tomorrow. It's probably cysts on my ovaries again. That's so funny, I can't use that excuse again, can I?" We both started laughing.

As we sat out by the pool eating our dinner, I told Debs about our weekend away, and about the alarm going off all night and that Rex said it was an *omen*.

"You're kidding, right? More like his guilty conscience. I still can't believe he didn't tell you from the start that he was married."

"Well, that's not all that happened. When we got back here on Sunday evening, we were having a coffee before he went home when the doorbell rang. He got quite uptight and asked me if I was expecting anyone. As if it was any of his business anyway, and he jumped up and went to the door. Guess who was standing there?"

"Jorgen?"

"No, but obviously that's what Rex was thinking, but he got such a shock when he saw Janet, his wife, standing there crying and ranting something to him. She had thrown all his clothes on the doorstep, and before turning to leave, she slapped his face and stormed off crying."

"No! Oh my God, Margot, what did he do?"

"Well, I thought he'd go running after her, don't forget I was 'just purely physical entertainment' to him, but you'll never guess in a million years what he said. *'Look at all my lovely clothes on the floor, Margot, come and help me pick them up. They're soaking wet and muddy.'* Anyway, I gave him another slap just for good measure and told him to do it himself as I wasn't his skivvy and to get out."

"Wow, Margot. What happened at the office today? Did he come to work?"

"Oh yes, he came in alright. The nerve of the man. He said he couldn't hurt Janet, and he needed time to sort himself out and make a decision, so I made it easy for him and told him I wasn't up for playing this game anymore and that we were done with the purely physical nonsense. Work only from now on."

"And! What did he say?"

"Well, I was shocked to say the least because he said, *'Margot I need time to think. Everything is going so quickly. I think I'm falling in love with you.'* I mean what the hell. *'You think you're falling in love.'* Great. Well, when you've decided whether or not you love me, please let me know, but as of now we're over."

"But Margot, he said he loves you, that's good news, isn't it?"

"No Debs, not until he's made his mind up, *'I think,'* doesn't do it for me. I'm in turmoil here."

I got to the office the following morning and whilst I was going through his diary, I saw he had drawn lines through Friday to Sunday and written 'Seminar in Durban.' I remembered that I'd felt sick on the journey, and I became a little worried. I headed for reception and bumped into Martha.

"Hi Martha, I'm just popping over the road to get a sandwich, I won't be long."

"Okay Margot."

I popped into the pharmacy and bought two pregnancy testing kits.

When I returned, I went straight to the toilet an did a test, then sat with a cup of coffee, waiting for the longest five minutes of my life.

"Debs, have you got a minute, I need to talk to you?"

"Hi Margot, what's he done now?"

"Nothing. Well actually, I mean, he has done something. I've just done a pregnancy test and it's positive."

"Oh my God Margot, are you alright, how do you feel?"

"Honestly, I'm so excited I can't believe it. I never thought I would feel like this, but I'm so happy!"

"But you just finished it with Rex! Are you going to tell him?"

"Of course, I am. This changes everything Debbie. Well for me it changes everything. I'm going to call him right now, wish me luck."

"You're going to need it, Margot. I'll be home tonight and you can tell me what happens. Bye for now."

"Good morning, Teledex Lighting, how may I help you?" said the voice on the other end of the phone.

"Oh, good morning, Joanne, it's Margot. Can I speak to Mr Charrington?" "I'm sorry Margot he's in a meeting and said not to be disturbed, can I take a message?" she replied.

"No, I need to speak to him, it's urgent. Please put me through to the boardroom."

"I'll try but I don't think they'll answer, please hold."

The phone rang out several times and eventually a voice said, "I said no calls, what part of that didn't you understand?"

Shivers went through me. It was Rex's voice.

"Hi Rex, I'm sorry to disturb you, but it couldn't wait," I said.

"Well, what is it, be quick," he snapped.

"Well, I have some good news and some bad news, which do you want first?"

"Margot, what is it?" He sounded cross.

"Well, the bad news is you are turning forty on Friday," I said.

"And the good news?"

"You're going to be a father."

The line went dead.

"Rex, Rex, hello?"

I felt sick. I started crying, panic crept in. I paced the office trying to think what to do. What an emotional rollercoaster I was going through this morning, and it wasn't over yet. I tried to relax but my heart was at fever pitch. All sorts of scenarios were running through my head. I wanted 'the happy ever after' scenario obviously, but how could that happen? Someone in this love triangle was going to be terribly hurt, and it was most probably going to be me. Oh Lord, please help me.

Half an hour later my office door flew open and Rex came in, looking very flustered. The fact that he didn't take me in his arms and tell me how much he loved me told me what his mind-set was.

"Come to my office, we need to talk." As soon as he'd shut the door, he asked, "Are you sure?"

"Positive." I replied, very quietly.

"Are you sure it's mine?"

Physical pain I was used to, but this pain was indescribable. I stood up.

"WHAT? What the fuck do you mean is it yours? Who the hell do you think I've been screwing for these past two months; how dare you!" I shouted.

"Margot, keep your voice down," he said angrily.

"Keep my voice down, keep my voice down?" I began crying and pacing up and down his office, holding my head in my hands.

He came towards me and put his arms around me.

"Margot, please calm down and come and sit down." He poured us a coffee and sat next to me. "Margot, I told you it was purely physical. We can't have this child; I don't want children; I told you that."

"Oh, so this is all about you, is it? It's ME that's having the child, not you. What sort of a man are you? You said 'you loved me', but obviously you don't."

"Look I know you're upset but this would ruin my career and my marriage. I can't do that to her. I'll pay for the abortion, but you'll have to go overseas, it's illegal here."

"You can't put 'her' through it. Can you hear yourself Rex. You should have thought of that before you fucked me, shouldn't you Rex, and definitely you should have thought of telling me you were married Rex. But you wanted your cake, and you ate it, and now there's a problem, you expect me to have an abortion? The fact that you are even suggesting putting me and your unborn child through such an ordeal makes me feel sick. It's your answer to everything isn't it? You've got money, so you think you can just 'pay your way out. Well, that's not going to happen. If you don't want anything to do with the child or me, then so be it, but I am categorically NOT having an abortion."

I stood up, grabbed my bag and ran out of the office. I went to the ladies' room to clean my face up and then headed to the car park.

I drove around Johannesburg for a while trying to think what to do next. My phone kept on ringing and ringing so I turned it off. I drove to Sandton City Mall and parked the car. I sat for a long time and just cried.

Pull yourself together, came the little voice in my head. *Go and get your hair done and your nails and maybe a facial. Try and relax.*

I went to see Chris, who luckily had an appointment available. He gave me a coffee while I waited for him to finish with his client. Chris and I had become good friends over the years. He was gay, and he had often shared things with me about his life and he could empathise with my situation when it came to men. He tried to console me but I was inconsolable. I just cried and cried.

I walked around the mall aimlessly for hours. I'd never noticed before how many pregnant women there were. I kept imagining myself with a large bump and then I found myself looking at baby clothes and accessories.

I can do this alone if Rex isn't going to be around. I'd made my mind up. I was going to have this baby.

I went to the Sandon Hotel for a bite to eat and was about to order a glass of wine when I realised, *I can't drink alcohol now,* so opted for an orange juice. I sat for a long time just trying to sort things out in my head. I switched my phone back on and it started beeping with lots of missed calls and messages.

Margot, please call me.

Margot, I'm worried about you, please call me.

Margot, I'm at your house, where are you?

Margot, we need to talk, please come home.

'Home', a funny word that. Home. Where the hell was home? How many times had I set up home? I'd lost count. I must have left Jorgen a dozen or more times, living in communes, garden cottages, on friends' sofas trying to escape a beating. I started crying again and just couldn't stop. I stayed at the hotel until well after ten and eventually came to the realisation that, with nowhere else to go, I had to go back to Sunny Rock.

As I turned the key in the door, Debbie was standing in front of me.

"Oh my God, Margot, where have you been all day? Rex has been here three times; he's going out of his mind."

"Oh dear, what a shame, I'm going out of my mind too, thanks to him." And the tears came again.

"I take it Rex wasn't so happy with the news?" she said.

"Well basically he put the phone down on me and came straight to the office. He said I would have to have an abortion, as he couldn't put his wife through that."

"What! But he could put you through that ordeal? He should have thought of that when he was having 'purely physical relations' with you. God, Margot, what are you going to do?"

"I'm keeping my baby Debs. I thought I couldn't have children. There must have been something wrong with Jorgen after all, probably the heavy drinking; it lowers the sperm count apparently. I believe everything in this life happens for a reason, Debs. The reason I fell in love with Rex was to have a baby and that's exactly what I'm going to do. With or without him. I'm so excited, Debs. I'm having a beautiful baby."

Just then, the doorbell rang.

"No prizes for guessing who that is," Debbie said and promptly went upstairs to bed.

The doorbell rang again. I wasn't ready for this but I had to let him know that he couldn't buy his way out of this one. I opened the door and he stood there looking like a little lost child.

"I'm so sorry, I was in shock." He took me in his arms and held me tightly. We went and sat outside in the evening air.

"Where have you been all day, you had me so worried?" he said.

"I needed time to think and I knew if I came home, you would try and talk me around to your way of thinking, so I just stayed out. I'm keeping our baby, Rex. I didn't think I could have kids, but it's meant to be. Aren't you a little excited to be a dad?"

"I've had time to think and of course part of me is curious, it's just not what I had planned."

"Some things in life aren't planned; in fact, most things in life are just random happenings, but all for a reason, don't you believe that? I love you so much and even if we don't end up together, I will always have a part of you to cherish, forever."

"Okay, that's fine, we just have to take each day as it comes. I need time to think about how to handle this. Please, Margot, I need time. Let's go to bed, it's been a long stressful day."

"You mean you're staying the night?"

"I don't think you should be alone."

"So, you do care about me?"

"Of course, I care. Why didn't you say you'd missed a period?" he asked.

"I've missed so many times before so it was nothing unusual, I thought it was something to do with the cysts on my ovaries."

"When is the baby due, Margot?"

"I don't know exactly; I'll need to go to the doctor and have a scan."

"Okay. You can go in the morning before you come into the office. Come on, let's go to bed. This has been one hell of a birthday present Margot."

"It's one we'll never forget."

The following morning after breakfast I called the doctor and made an appointment for 09h00.

"Mrs Wilson, please go through to room 1."

"Good morning, Margot, you look well. What can I do for you today?"

"Good morning doctor. I'm pregnant and I need to know how far along I am."

"Well, that is good news. Congratulations. Go and take off your skirt and lie down so I can scan your tummy."

I went into the screened area and undressed and lay on the bed.

"Are you ready Margot?"

"Yes doctor."

"Right, let's have a look, shall we?"

He pulled the ultrasound scanner towards the bed and switched in on. He rubbed the contact gel on my tummy and then proceeded with the probe, making small moves around my abdominal area, pressing very lightly. It was very quiet until I heard the faint sound of a heartbeat, and it wasn't mine.

"There you go Margot, look on the scanner, can you see the tiny heartbeat?"

I started crying. "Oh my God, I'm overwhelmed Doctor. I never thought I would have children." I was sobbing. "Can you tell when the baby's due?"

"From the size of the foetus I'd say you're about twelve weeks pregnant Margot. That means the baby is due in February, around the fourteenth to be more precise. Okay, you can get dressed now."

"Well congratulations once again Margot. How does your husband feel about the baby?"

"Oh, he's beside himself with joy Doctor, just beside himself."

Chapter 10

The New Year Miracle

The following few months flew by and the pregnancy seemed to be going well until one morning, five months into the pregnancy, Rex and I were making love in his office when suddenly I started bleeding really heavily. I went to the toilet and huge clots of blood were passing into the toilet. I called for someone to come and help and Irene from accounts came running into the toilet.

"Oh dear, you've gone very pale, Margot." She looked into the toilet bowl and saw all the blood. "I'll be right back, hold on, Margot." She disappeared for a few moments and when she returned with Rex, quite a few people had come to see what the commotion was about.

"Get an ambulance someone, quickly." Rex dispersed the crowd and sat with me until the ambulance arrived.

Rex followed in his Bentley and waited patiently for me to be examined. The Doctor assumed he was my husband and called him into the office.

"Well, Sir, your wife has a placenta previa, which is very serious indeed. The placenta is in the wrong position, thus blocking the baby's exit, and if she starts bleeding, she could bleed to death in twenty minutes. She'll need to be hospitalised for the remaining duration of the pregnancy. Margot, we need to get you onto a ward and onto a drip. I'll call your gynaecologist. Dr Green, isn't it? He'll decide what to do. I know him well and my guess is he'll put you on a drug to stop any contractions which would cause bleeding. I'll leave you two alone while I get a ward sorted out."

"Doctor, is it okay if I take Margot home to get a few things? I'll bring her straight back."

"Absolutely out of the question, Sir. She has to rest. She's lost a lot of blood and if it starts again, well, it's too dangerous. The nurse will be with you shortly. Good day."

"Six months in hospital! Rex, what about the house? What am I going to do?"

"Don't worry about that, Margot, you'll still get paid and I'll make sure your part of the rent is paid."

"Debbie's just given notice, Rex; she's moving in with Danie at the end of October." I started crying.

"Look, don't worry about the house, Margot, I'll pay the rent. More importantly, you're going to need toiletries and lots of underwear and PJs. Can you phone Debbie and ask her to bring some things for you, I don't know what you need or where to find them."

Rex stayed with me the whole day with just a short break of an hour when he popped to buy magazines, flowers, chocolates and a Scrabble game. The matron in charge adored Rex; she said what a 'gentleman' he was. He visited every day and the matron bought us coffee and biscuits. "Just press the button if you need anything, Margot."

"Thanks, Matron."

During the second week of my somewhat daunting long stay, Matron Wilkes had finished her rounds and came to see me.

"Good morning, Margot, how are you today, apart from bored?"

"Not too bad, I feel fine but I am indeed really bored. I miss my home so much. It's like being in jail."

"Never mind, Rex will be here later to give you a game of Scrabble." She looked at me with a deep furrow in her brow. "Look, Margot, it's none of my business but I think you should know that there's a Mrs Charrington in reception asking questions about you. She wanted to know which ward you were in but I told her only family were allowed to see you and if she was family, she should know which ward you were in. Did I do the right thing, Margot?"

"Janet, her name's Janet. She's Rex's wife. It just happened, Matron, I fell in love. I've never felt such emotion as I did the day I first set eyes on him. It truly was a 'fatal attraction'. By the time I found out he was married, it was too late, I couldn't give him up, I was too in love, and he with me. What a mess." I started crying.

"Now, Margot, one thing you mustn't do is upset yourself; it's not good for the baby, do you hear me? I'll bring you a coffee. Now please calm down. Everything has a way of sorting itself out, believe me."

I smiled and wiped my face. "Thanks, Matron, please let me know if she comes back."

Rex visited a little later than usual and when I told him about Janet's visit; he didn't look too surprised. "She started quizzing me about things last night, I had to tell her about the baby, Margot. She's heartbroken. She was awake the whole night crying. I couldn't leave her this morning, she was distraught. I was late going into the office that's why I'm late coming to see you. I've explained to her that your pregnancy is complicated and she agrees that I can't just leave you to cope on your own. I'll support you and pay your rent and give you money and we'll have to reassess the situation when the baby's born."

"So, you're dumping me and your child as soon as she's born basically?"

"Didn't you hear what I just said, Margot? I'll be here for you and the baby."

"But you're not going to leave Janet? You're not going to be a father and stand up to your responsibilities?"

"Margot, my wife is my responsibility too, I told you all along that this affair was purely physical."

"Purely physical, really? Maybe it started that way, right up until you told me you loved me and started visiting my house at any time of the day or night, taking me away for long weekends. Why did you have to tell me you loved me?"

"Because I do love you, but I love Janet too."

"Oh! Of course, have your cake and eat it hey, Rex, typical man. You bastard."

"Keep your voice down, Margot."

"Keep my voice down! How dare you!" I shouted through the tears. "You're uncouth, do you know that? It's all about you, isn't it? What Rex wants; Rex gets. Well, let me tell you something, Mr Control Freaking…"

He leant forward to try and stop me from shouting, I picked up the jug of water from my bedside cabinet and threw it in his face.

"What's going on in here? The whole ward can hear you." Matron stood stern, eyes on Rex, the water dripping from his beautiful designer suit into puddles at his feet. "Rex, I think you'd better leave. Margot needs to be still and relaxed. Anything could make her go into labour and I thought I'd explained how dangerous that would be, for her and the baby. Please just go."

"Go on, Rex, go back to your cosy life and wife, carry on living and sleeping with her and seeing me up until your baby is born! No, I don't think so. I love you, Rex, we're having a baby. You have to make a choice, now."

70

He left the ward without a word.

On 25 September, my girlfriends Joanna, Penny, Debbie, Darleen and Vanessa came to wish me happy birthday.

"Hi Margot you're looking well, glowing in fact. How's the baby doing?"

"She's fine, but they've put me on a drip to stop any contractions. I can't believe you're all here. Thanks for coming, everyone, I really needed cheering up."

"Where's Mr Wonderful?" The room went quiet. They all looked at me questioningly.

"Well, we had a bit of a tiff, and he hasn't been to see me for a couple of months. I don't blame him. I gave him an ultimatum, oh and a jug of water, and he's obviously made his choice."

"Water! You love throwing things don't you, Margot?" Vanessa asked.

We all started laughing as I explained what had happened.

"I can just imagine his face, covered in water dripping down his designer jacket. What did he…" Vanessa stopped talking and I heard footsteps. I turned around to see Grant with a bunch of flowers in one hand and a gift bag in the other. He was in uniform, wearing a huge beautiful beaming smile on his face. "Hello, sweetie, how are you? Hello, girls, glad you could make it."

"So, it was you who organised this, oh Grant, you're such a star. Come here and give me a kiss."

The matron came in to see what all the commotion was about.

"Good morning, everyone. Please, if you could keep the noise down a little. Happy birthday, Margot." She was carrying the largest bouquet of red roses I'd ever seen. "These just arrived. I'd better go and find some vases, it's like a florist's shop in here."

She handed me the flowers and I took the small card and opened it.

Happy birthday Margot. I do love you. XX R. Another glimmer of hope.

"Are you going to open your gifts?" asked Penny.

"Yes, of course, let's see what delights you've bought me." I took the gift bag that Grant had bought. It was full shredded tissue paper and I rummaged around until I felt something small and hard in the middle of the shreds. I took the small box and opened it. A band of white gold, set with a continuous line of identically cut diamonds symbolising never-ending love, sparkled up at me.

"Oh my God, you shouldn't have, really." I took the ring from the small box and put it on my wedding finger. "It's beautiful, Grant, thank you."

"Hey, you're my wife, you deserve it." Matron Wilkes was standing in the doorway, a vase full of flowers in each hand, looking at me, with a 'thunderstruck' look on her face.

"Sorry to interrupt." She placed the vases down and took the roses from my bedside table. "I'll go and put these into water too, aren't they beautiful?" She walked off slightly embarrassed.

"Are you going to open the other things?" asked Penny.

There were lots of clothes for the baby, new PJs for myself, body creams, underwear, perfume, slippers and a huge cake. The bed was full of gifts.

The Matron came back with the flowers and placed them where she could find space.

"Could we have some tea and coffee please matron? I heard the trolley rattling down the corridor, we haven't missed tea break, have we?"

"No, I'll ask her to come back this way."

"Thanks very much."

Grant didn't stay too long; he'd just come off a long haul and needed to sleep. The girls and I gossiped and caught up for the next hour or so and eventually Matron came and said visiting time was over.

It was eerily quiet when they'd all gone. Matron came to see me. "It looks like you have a great circle of friends, Margot. I'm sorry but I couldn't help overhearing. You're married too?"

"It's complicated, really complicated. I don't even know where to begin, and I don't think you'd believe me anyway."

She looked at me. "I've seen and heard a lot of things in this hospital, Margot, believe me, nothing would shock me."

"Grant is gay. He adores me, but he's gay. That's all I'm going to say."

"I stand corrected, I am shocked. That's a first for me. It doesn't make any sense, but thanks for telling me."

"I'm really tired, Matron, exhausted, mentally and physically. I have no idea how this will all pan out, I just hope all goes well with the baby. If I lose her, I don't know what I'll do."

"When did you find out it was a girl?"

"Rex was worried because of his age; you know all forty years of him! He made me go for a trisomy test. He was worried in case the baby had Down's Syndrome."

"I see. It's quite a dangerous procedure you know, it could have caused you to miscarry."

"He wanted me to go for an abortion when he first found out, so now I'm wondering if that's what he'd hoped would happen."

"My dear girl, I notice he hasn't been to see you for a while. Maybe he's made his mind up!"

"That's what I thought until he sent the flowers, look at the card." I passed the small card to her.

"I've no doubt he loves you, Margot. He's a gentleman. He must be in turmoil too. Does he have children with his wife?"

"No, he said he never wanted children."

"He never wanted; what about his wife?"

"He said 'they' didn't want kids. They're both very career-minded. She's a bank manager. If they'd had children, I would never have carried on the affair, well, at least, I think… I don't know anymore. I love him so much, my heart aches. It's all such a mess."

"Now don't go upsetting yourself again. Try and get some sleep. Here, read your book for a while, maybe it will help you fall asleep."

"Thanks, Matron."

It was after three when I woke up. I was confused at first, couldn't fathom where I was. As I opened my eyes, Rex was sitting reading his newspaper by the side of the bed.

"Hi. How long have you been sitting there?"

"Half an hour or so. Did you know you snore?" He smiled and his blue eyes glinted with love. "I see you got lots of presents."

"Yes, it was good to see the girls. Could you pass me a glass of water please?"

He passed me the glass and as I moved my hand to take it from him, he saw the ring. "Where the hell did that ring come from Margot, it looks new?"

"I don't like your tone, Rex. Grant bought it for me."

"Grant! Why would he buy you a diamond ring, you're not 'man and wife' in that sense, you don't even live together. Is there something you're not telling me Margot?"

"Oh, here we go again. First you accused me of sleeping with Jorgen, now you think maybe the baby's Grant's! You're unbelievable, do you know that. Just go, go on get out; you don't love me, you just like fucking me and trying to control my life. Well, I've had it. Go on, get OUT."

Matron came running into the room.

"Not again, Rex, you have to leave. Margot needs to be calm. How many times must I tell you both?"

The day before New Year's Eve, my gynaecologist announced that he was going on vacation and told me that there would be a locum doctor in his place. Dr. Green had put me on a drug called Ipradol, to prevent contractions, from the first day I came into hospital. The locum doctor told me he was going to take me off this medication, as he didn't believe in stopping contractions. On 31st December 1987, at around 22h30, I went into labour and started bleeding. I was rushed to theatre and baby Sarah was born by C-section, six weeks early.

The matron called Rex and Debbie to tell them what had happened.

I was just coming around when I heard a voice. "Hey sweetie, it's a girl, she's so beautiful. She's like a 'mini' Margot, she has your big feet." Grant smiled down at me. "How are you feeling?"

"Like I've been chopped in half and I'll never walk again. Grant, how did you know about...?"

"I just got off a long haul and was on my way home when Debs called me and said you'd been rushed into theatre. I wanted to come and make sure you were okay, and to see the tiny miracle. She's in an incubator at the moment but she's fine. Here, I bought you a little something. Hope you like it." He placed it on the side table and bent over and kissed my cheek.

"I want to see her, Grant, can you ask the Matron to bring her?"

"Sure thing, of course. Hold on, I'll go and find her."

Grant and the Matron came back wheeling the incubator. She lay fast asleep on her back. She was so tiny that her nappy came up around her neck. She was perfect in every way, just very small, 2lbs to be exact, as big as a bag of sugar.

"Can I hold her please, Matron?"

"Let's just wait until she wakes on her own, it's best not to disturb her; she needs the rest. Can I get you a cup of tea? Are you hungry?"

"Tea would be lovely, thank you, but I'm not hungry." Matron Wilkes looked at Grant with a look that I couldn't fathom.

"Matron, you remember Grant?"

"Yes of course. Would you like a drink?"

"Yes please, coffee, black and no sugar."

"Just how I take it too." Rex was standing by the door. He came towards the bed and looked into the incubator. His eyes filled up. He bent over and kissed me on the cheek. "Are you all right, Margot? Sorry, I couldn't get here quicker, I was out at a party."

"No problem, I'm that glad you could make it. This will be a New Year to remember."

"Hello, Rex." Grant held out his hand to Rex. "Congratulations, she's beautiful." They shook hands but Grant could see that Rex felt awkward. "I'm really tired Margot, I just got in from Brazil. I'll come back and visit you tomorrow sweetie." He leaned over and kissed my forehead.

"Take care Grant. Thanks for coming and make sure you come back tomorrow. Promise?"

"Promise."

"Why was he here?"

"Because he cares about me."

"You're all so pally with him. You're not like that with me."

"That's because you're always so damn serious, talk about poker face! You should take the game up Rex. I'm totally and utterly exhausted so if you haven't got anything positive to say, then go home to Janet. Grant doesn't put any stress on me at all, or ask anything of me, he's just a dear friend." He just stood there looking at me.

Rex was hovering at the bedside when he noticed the package on the table. "What's this?" he asked picking it up and opening it.

"Perfume and body cream." He threw it on the bed.

"Well, it's more than you bought me. You should take a leaf out of Grants' book. Just a smile and a kind word would have been nice."

He turned around and fled from the ward.

A little later in the day, the Matron came to see me. "We need to try and get you up and about and walk a little. It will hurt, but the longer you leave it the worse it will be. Come on, try and sit up and put your legs over the side of the bed."

The pain was indescribable but with a little perseverance, I managed a couple of steps. I felt woozy and began to feel sick, so Matron got me back into bed.

"Well done. We'll try again in the morning. You should be able to go home in a couple of days. I'll go and fetch Sarah, let's see if we can give her some breast milk."

Try as I may, Sarah was too small and weak to latch onto my breast. The nurse bought me a breast pump to express milk which I gave to Sarah in a bottle. My breasts were like 'melons' and the more I expressed, the bigger they got.

On the fifth day of trying to walk, the matron said; "I think you're ready to go home Margot. You seem to be getting around just fine."

"Oh, that's wonderful Matron. I'll call Rex and tell him to bring Sarah's carry cot."

Matron Wilkes looked at me with sad eyes. "I'm afraid Sarah isn't ready to leave just yet. She'll need to be in hospital for another three to four weeks, maybe more. I'm sorry Margot, but we can't let her go until she's a good weight. We need you to come in every day and express milk for her, and you can spend as long as you like with her."

I waited for the Matron to leave before bursting into tears.

Chapter 11
Trouble at the Door

It was the first week of February 1988 when Rex and I went to collect Sarah from the hospital. Rex arrived with her carrycot and the Matron carried her out to the waiting car before handing her over to us. "Thank you for everything, Matron." Rex shook her hand.

"Good luck to you both, be happy."

Rex put Sarah on the back seat and I got in next to her.

"Fancy lunch somewhere? Any preferences?"

"Yeah, Rosebank Hotel out on the terrace." We found a shady place among the Jacarandas and Rex ordered a bottle of the very best Chardonnay.

"Oh boy this is going to taste so good. How long has it been? Cheers."

"Too long. Cheers." We both sat looking down at Sarah who was fast asleep. It felt so weird. This tiny new life. Another human to be responsible for.

"I've got something to tell you, Margot." *Oh dear, this sounds ominous.* "I've left Janet. I'm staying with a friend, you know Geoff? Well, it turns out he's getting divorced and he's moved into his own place. He said I could stay there for a while till we've sorted things out."

"So why don't you come and live with me Rex? It doesn't make any sense you living somewhere else!"

"Look Margot, I only moved in with Geoff last weekend. I think it's best until the air clears. Janet has been very ill. She collapsed at work and I had to go and take her to hospital."

"But surely, she wants you at home if she's unwell. None of this makes any sense, Rex."

"Well, like you said before, I keep on hurting you both because I can't decide what the hell to do, and Janet has had enough too, and she agrees I should have some time to myself to think. I'll come and stay with you every other weekend."

"And the other weekends? You'll be a single bloke around town with Geoff. Brilliant."

"Margot, please don't start a row. What would you like to eat?"

A couple of weeks later, on one of 'my weekends', Rex was in the bathroom when my phone rang.

"Hi, is that Margot?"

"Yes, that's me."

"This is Janet, we need to talk."

My blood ran cold.

"Are you there Margot?"

"Yes, I'm here. What do you want?"

"You must be a very special person for Rex to have had an affair knowing that as the Managing Director, he could have easily lost his job. I suspected something was going on but he only told me everything when you were rushed to hospital, when you were in the early stages of your pregnancy. I was once pregnant, Margot, but I never told Rex because I knew it wasn't the right time for him, and I got rid of my baby, for him, because I loved him so much. You can imagine my anger and heartbreak, when I found out about you, and that you were going to keep the baby. But still I stood by Rex and believed that he would do the right thing and end it with you."

"Did he also tell you that he wanted me to have an abortion? The thing is Janet, it was his choice to leave you, I gave him plenty of time to make his decision."

There was a long silence.

"What are you talking about Margot, he hasn't left me at all. Why would you think that? Oh, I understand. He's there with you, isn't he? That's the reason I'm calling you. I thought it was a little strange when he kept going away at weekends. Damn him."

"I have to go, Janet, Sarah needs feeding. Goodbye." I replaced the receiver.

Rex was standing behind me as I put the phone down. "Do you have something to tell me, Rex?"

"I didn't know what else to do, Margot. I didn't want to lose you."

"You actually took me to Geoff's house and got him to lie for you and you've been lying to Janet too! Okay, Rex, I'm going to make your mind up for you. Go back to Janet and leave me and Sarah in peace, I can't take any more. I'll let you know what maintenance I need and when I'm ready, you can come and see your daughter, if you want to."

The big strong man, always in control, broke down and cried.

"You can't have your cake and eat it anymore, Rex. I've cried all I can over you, enough is enough. Go home to your wife, I'm not your play thing anymore, and I'm not going to be the one with a broken heart. Goodbye."

With tears in his eyes, he turned to leave and the doorbell rang. He opened the door and found, for the second time, his clothes strewn on the front doorstep, but this time cut into small pieces.

Janet shouted, "He's all yours, Margot. Hope he makes you happy."

Rex physically broke down in a heap on the floor with his head in his hands, sobbing.

"She was outside all this time, on the phone, throwing my things on the floor."

He was inconsolable. I poured him a brandy and he downed it in one gulp.

I helped him to salvage what he could of his pile of clothes and binned the rest. I made us both a stiff drink and sat quietly with Rex while he sobbed.

We had a fretful night, with me up twice in the night with Sarah and Rex crying for most of the night.

Chapter 12

The Christening

Rex had been living with me now for about six months when I broached the subject of having Sarah christened in the UK. We agreed dates and I organised everything via my sister Carol in the UK, who arranged everything on our behalf.

"Why don't you go a few days before me, Margot, it'll give you time to catch up with your family and make sure all the arrangements are in place?"

"What about your family, Rex, aren't you going to invite them to your daughter's christening?"

He just looked at me. "Margot, my Mum will be distraught that I've left Janet. We were married for ten years and she knew I didn't want a family. So no, I won't be inviting them."

"There'll only be one christening, Rex. As long as you don't Regret it in the future."

Four days before the christening, I arrived at Heathrow airport. My sister and her husband John were there to pick me and Sarah up. At six months old, Sarah was still very small and I had her wrapped in a blanket and placed in the in small 'basket' part of the trolley.

"Where's Sarah? Where's Rex?"

"Sarah's right here." I unravelled the pink blanket. She was fast asleep.

"Where's Rex?"

"He's coming in a couple of days; he had a couple of meetings to attend. Not to worry, it gives us a chance to catch up. Hi John, how are you?"

"I'm very well thanks Margot. Congratulations. We never thought you were going to have any kids." He smiled.

"Me neither. Funny how things turn out."

The next few days were very hectic. Although all the christening arrangements had been finalised, Carol and I had to go up to Birmingham to collect Mom and Arnold. We did a round trip which took almost 4 hours, and when we got back to Surrey, John had cooked a lovely roast dinner. Thank heaven for John. The following day, the day before the christening, John took us all out to dinner at their local pub. We didn't stay out too late as we had an early start the following day. We'd been back at the house for about half an hour or so when the phone rang.

"It's for you Margot, it's Penny."

"Hi, Penny, how are you? Is everything okay?"

There was a slight pause.

"Not really Margot. I know it's none of my business but I thought you should know that Rex has moved out. I'm not sure where to, but I can guess!"

"When did he leave, Penny?"

"The day after you flew out. I thought maybe he'd gone on a business trip, but when he didn't come home for three days, I went and checked your room and all his belongings were gone, and he hasn't been back since. I'm so sorry, Margot."

I started crying. "Not to worry Penny, thanks for letting me know. I suppose he's right after all Penny."

"What do you mean Margot, right about what?"

"When we first got together, he told me 'I had some balls' for coming on to him. Well, he's right about that, because he definitely has no balls whatsoever. What an absolute coward. I've got to go Penny; I'm too upset to talk but I'll call you soon. Thanks again."

Carol came into the lounge when she heard me crying. "What the hell's going on now, Margot? What's the control freak done this time?"

"He's gone back to his wife. Nice of him to let me know."

"John, get a glass of brandy."

"I think she should have a glass of water."

"It's not for her, it's for me, you idiot."

"I'm okay you two. It was such a shock, that's all. Who's going to stand with me when Sarah gets christened tomorrow?" The tears turned into deep sobs.

"I will, I'll be godfather to Sarah. Don't worry, Margot, everything will be alright."

We'd just finished dinner and were in the lounge the phone rang.

"If that's Rex, tell him to go to hell."

81

"Rex, Margot said go to hell." She replaced the receiver.

The next day, my baby girl was christened, and as promised John stood with me. We went for a celebratory lunch, and I managed to not shed a tear. I don't think there were any left.

Carol organised lots of things for us to do to keep my mind off things. We went to a friend of hers who organised a 'Murder' evening. Carol and I dressed up as twin French girls who had been invited to a party on a yacht, where the murder took place. It was such good fun. She was such a good sister. She made sure we went out every day even if it was just for a cup of tea and slice of cake.

"What are you going to do when you get back to Africa?"

"Absolutely nothing. He's made his decision, again, and he can stay away from me. I'll go to court and have a maintenance order filed and that will be that. It's over. I hate him."

Friday came all too soon and it was time to leave London. Carol helped me with check-in. We were both in tears as we waved goodbye.

Chapter 13

Lunch at Kaldis

As I entered the arrivals' hall, I saw Robin.

"Hi, Madam. The boss sent me to take you home. Let me take the bags."

"Where is the boss, Robin?"

"He's at home with his wife, Madam, why?"

"Oh no reason. Thanks, Robin."

Robin helped me into the townhouse and bade me farewell. Penny was out in the garden reading the newspaper. "Hi, Penny, I'm home." She came running through the lounge to greet me, took Sarah from my arms and gave her a hug. "Did Rex get you from the airport?"

"No Penny, remember it's me who has the 'balls' in this 'triangle'. He sent Robin." As I looked around the lounge, I noticed a new dining table and chairs in the corner. "Is that yours, Penny?"

"No, Rex bought it for you, said he didn't like eating food from his lap."

"How ironic. He won't be eating off anything in this house again. Cup of tea penny?"

"You bet."

The following week, I found a crèche for Sarah and went looking for a job. It didn't take long before I found a job at a chemical manufacturing company as PA to the managing director, an English guy and ex-policeman. The salary was very reasonable, and coupled with maintenance from Rex, I would easily manage on my own.

Weeks went by and I began to feel more like myself again. If I wanted to go out, Penny was more than happy to baby-sit, and Debbie was always willing to take Sarah if Penny was unavailable. I made lots of new friends and one Saturday afternoon, while having a BBQ at my house with a few friends, the phone rang.

"Hi, Margot, it's me. Would it be okay if I could see Sarah?"

"No, it wouldn't be okay." I hung up. It rang again and I ignored it and when it had finished ringing, I took the phone off the hook.

Some while later, the doorbell rang. I knew it would be Rex at the door so I asked Joanna's boyfriend, Dave, to answer the door. I heard voices raised and went to investigate.

"Dave, who is it?"

"Some guy wants to talk to you."

"I'm not just some guy, mate, I'm the father of the baby."

I pushed Dave aside. "I don't care if you were God himself, you're not welcome here, Rex, so go away." I slammed the door in his face and double locked it. Eventually, he gave up ringing the bell and went away.

"He's got a bloody nerve Margot. 'I'm the father of the baby.' Who the hell does he think he is?" exclaimed Dave.

"He doesn't like to be told NO. I'm amazed he didn't break the door off its hinges. He's done it once before you know, when I locked myself in the bathroom. He's a total control freak, that's what he is, but he'll get the message eventually."

That night I had difficulty sleeping. Tossing and turning, trying to get Rex out of my head. I still ached for him. My heart was sore and so was my head, when I was woken the next morning to Sarah's crying.

"Hey there beautiful girl, come on let's go and make you some food."

I changed her nappy and headed for the kitchen. She was on solids now, well-mashed-up solids, and considering she had been premature, she was thriving. She had huge blue eyes and blonde hair and looked like her dad. The coffee machine had just finished its spluttering and gurgling when the phone rang.

"Hello."

"Hi, Margot, please don't hang up. Please."

"What do you want, Rex? I told you yesterday—"

"I know what you said but will you just listen, please. She's my daughter too. Margot?"

"I'm listening but I don't know why."

"Please can we meet somewhere, not at the townhouse, somewhere public, in the park or a coffee shop? I need to see Sarah."

"Sarah? Why all of a sudden, this paternal interest, you didn't even want her?"

"Margot this is difficult enough, just meet me, please."

"I choose where and when; you don't get to call the shots anymore Rex."

"Okay, where?"

"Kaldis coffee shop at midday. You can buy me lunch, see you later." I placed the receiver.

"You're going to see your daddy today, Sarah; well, 'we' are, both of us." Oh hell, I had a flutter inside, anticipation, nerves, wanting! "Open up, one more spoonful baby girl, well done." I lifted her from her high chair and headed upstairs. I ran a bath while I undressed Sarah and myself. "Here we go, look at all those bubbles, Sarah, are you ready? One, two, threeeee." She started chuckling and flailing her tiny hands and feet in the water. I sat her in her bath chair with her duckies while I had a quick shower.

I got to Kaldis ten minutes early and found a table at the front of the café near to the entrance by the windows. I felt safer where I could see lots of people, and besides I loved 'people watching', I found it fascinating. *What brought all these people to the mall today? To buy new clothes, a quick lunch break, a visit to the hairdressers, a job interview, an illicit meeting, an affair?! Or meeting the most controlling, good looking, sexy, father of your baby girl. DAMN.* I watched him as he walked towards the entrance, his eyes scanning the busy café. God damn it, my heart started pumping furiously as he approached the table. *Did he have to wear that blue stripe shirt and those tight jeans? Oh boy, I'm in trouble, again.* Sarah had woken up and was sitting on my lap.

He reached out and took her in his arms and held her at arm's length.

"Hey, Sarah, look at you. You look just like your Mum. Come and give Daddy a big hug." He drew her near and I saw his eyes water over slightly. He sat down and Sarah quite happily sat on his lap.

The waitress appeared and took our order. We sat quietly for a while doting on this small miracle of life that sat between us, who was smiling and banging on the table with a spoon.

"Well, this is awkward. I don't really know what to say to you, Rex. You wanted to see your daughter, so here she is. What now?"

"Margot, I thought I wouldn't feel anything but just the sight of you overwhelms me. I love you so much, it physically hurts." The waitress poured the wine and we both took a gulp.

"Really? Well, you've had your cake, and unfortunately you ate it all. Nothing left I'm afraid." I took another huge gulp. What I really wanted to say was *'I love you too, let's skip lunch and go back to my place.'* I was in turmoil.

I was just getting over this man and now this. He didn't come here to see Sarah, just as I didn't come here to make small talk, and pretend I didn't care anymore. The truth was I was still so in love with him; the need in me, the wanting, I wanted to rip his clothes off and feel every inch of his body, to kiss him and taste him. Another awkward few moments passed.

"Kingklip for you, Sir? Madam, our special salad of the day." The waitress placed the food down. "Anything else I can get you, Sir?"

"Yes please, another bottle of wine. Thanks."

Sarah was back in her carry chair and was fast asleep. We started to relax as the wine bottle slowly emptied.

"Dessert?" He looked at me and raised his eyebrows.

"You bastard, of course I want dessert. Do you?" His face said it all.

Once inside the confines of the townhouse, he pounced. All the pent-up sexual tension showing on his face. He pulled my top over my head and undid my bra, kissing me so hard, like a man possessed. Even if I'd wanted to stop this, I couldn't. The power of my arousal overtook all logical thought. We didn't even make it up the stairs. He unzipped my skirt, flipped me over on the staircase and started spanking me. "Have you missed me, Margot?" he said quietly. "Do you want me to fuck you, do you?" He spanked me again and he penetrated me.

"Go on, Rex, fuck me harder, smack me, harder Rex, harder. I love you so much, you bastard."

And so the affair was in full swing again. He came around every day for weeks and weeks but he never stayed over. At the weekends, I was left feeling empty and distraught knowing that he was with Janet. My friends told me I was crazy and deserved more from life but it was like some sort of fatal attraction, I just couldn't get enough of him.

I was sitting at my desk one morning when I realised, I hadn't heard from Rex for just over two weeks, so I called his office. "Good morning, can I speak to Mr Charrington?"

"I'm afraid he no longer works here."

"What? But he's the managing director. Where's he gone?"

"I'm not at liberty to say. All I know is he's moved to Durban… Hello?"

It took a while for me to process this information.

Durban! No. Durban? What the hell? So, he thinks he can just come around here and start the affair up again and then fuck off without a word? What a conceited asshole. No. No man is going to decide how MY life will be. How dare he?

I went through to speak with my boss.

"Mike, have you got a moment?"

"Yes, of course, Margot. Sit down."

"I need to leave, right now. Can you arrange for any money due to me to be paid into my account as soon as possible? I'm sorry I have to go back to the UK; it's my mother."

"Oh Margot, I'm so sorry, of course I'll arrange it immediately. Will you be coming back?"

"No, I don't think so. Thanks for being so understanding."

"Don't be silly, these things happen. I hope your mother gets well."

I collected Sarah from day-care, rushed home and searched online for places to stay in Durban.

Chapter 14

The Red Light District

I found a monthly rental 'hotel' near the beachfront for a really reasonable price. I had enough money to get by, and I knew I'd soon find a job and hopefully find Rex. I packed a couple of cases, jumped into the old VW and headed for the coast. I had to make several stops along the way as Sarah was sick from the long journey. I finally found the hotel which at least had a carpark.

The hotel was quite dark inside, more like a house that had been made into studio flats.

"Hi, I rang earlier and booked a month's accommodation. Mrs Wilson, Margot."

The man behind the desk looked at me and then at Sarah.

"You didn't say you had a baby!"

"Is that a problem?"

"Well, no, not really. Let me show you to your room."

The room was small but adequate. It had a small kitchenette and living area, consisting of a sofa and a coffee table, a small bedroom and bathroom. On the plus side, you could see the sea from the small window.

I unpacked a few things and freshened up, before putting Sarah into her stroller, and going for a walk along the promenade. I stopped at a small bistro café and had a quick bite to eat.

"Well, Sarah, how do you like Durban? Isn't it lovely by the sea? We'll go and buy you a bucket and spade, and we can build sandcastles on the beach. Would you like that?" While feeding Sarah and looking out at the people passing by, there were couples strolling along hand in hand, children running around excitedly. The smell of the sea air. It felt good.

I had to look twice. It can't be! Oh my God, it was Rex. Large as life walking straight towards me. Looking very out of place in his designer suit, shirt and tie on a promenade full of bikini-clad girls, men in shorts and flip-flops. He stood out like a sore thumb. He stopped within inches of the stroller. He raised his eyebrows.

"What the hell are you doing Margot?"

"What the hell are you doing, how did you know I was here?"

"Not difficult Margot. I received a call from my old company saying that a woman had called, I knew it was you. I called your house and Penny answered. Now, exactly where is this hotel?"

As we walked back towards the hotel, I asked him why he had left us without a word.

"Because I made my decision, Margot. I love you so much but you gave me an ultimatum and you made me choose."

"I see you still haven't grown a pair, Rex. The least you could have done was let me know what your plans were and not just disappear and go 600 kilometres away. How were you going to keep in contact with your beloved daughter? Who the hell are you to decide my future anyhow? How dare you? As long as you love me, I'll never give up, never."

We reached the hotel and I saw the look on his face. "Oh my God, Margot. Do you have any idea what this hotel is?"

"A hotel! Somewhere to stay until I get myself sorted."

"Christ. This is the red-light area of Durban. Don't you say a word, I'll handle this." We entered the reception area and Rex rang the bell. "Hello. There seems to have been a mix-up. My wife and I had a bit of an argument and she's not been feeling well lately. I've come to take her home. I'm sure you understand?"

"Yes, of course." The guy behind the counter looked terrified.

"If you could let us have the month's rent back, I'd be grateful."

"Yes. No problem, Sir."

"Margot, go and pack your things."

We walked along the promenade. "So now what, Rex? Where do you suggest we stay?"

"It's all arranged. As soon as I knew you were coming down here, I asked around at work. It turns out one of the directors has a garden cottage for rent. I paid up front for three months for you and Sarah. It's up on the hill towards Kloof, you'll like it there, you can use the pool, tennis court, etc."

"Wow. You really are organised when you want to be. Thank you so much. That will give me plenty of time to find a job. Are we going there now?"

"Yep, I've told them you're my sister, just in case they ask. Where are you parked?"

"Behind the hotel in a small private car park."

"Okay, I'll meet you here outside the hotel in ten minutes and you can follow me." He kissed me lightly on the lips and off he went.

Driving through the front gate, I knew it was going to be spectacular. There were rolling lawns, immaculately kept, surrounded by flower beds, tropical trees and plants, rockeries, ponds and waterfalls. Looking down the long garden, I could see a wall of pink, white and blue hydrangeas and nestling between them was a little cottage.

Rex took me up to the main house to introduce me to the owners. A very good-looking couple in their early sixties stood at the door.

"Hi Margot, welcome to South Africa. I'm Margaret and this is Hennie. I believe it's your first time here. And who's this delightful little thing?" She held her arms out to take Sarah, who quite willingly accepted the gesture. "Well, aren't you a friendly little girl? She's adorable, and those bright blue eyes. My, my, what a beauty."

"Her name's Sarah."

"Would you like to come in and have a drink, Rex?" Asked Hennie.

"Thanks Hennie, but I have to run, I'm afraid. I've got a few things to finish at the office. Is the cottage open Hennie, I'll just help Margot with Sarah and her bags."

"Yes, it's open. I hope you like it, Margot."

"Judging from the outside I'm sure it will be beautiful. Thank you so much."

We made our way down to the cottage. It had a lovely fitted kitchen with all the mod cons, a cosy lounge with huge bay windows overlooking the pool and a bedroom with en-suite bathroom.

"This is perfect, Rex." I flung my arms around his neck and kissed him. He pulled me closer and I could feel his erection instantly. "Oh God Margot, the launch sequence has started." He gave me that crazed manic look.

"I'm going to give you such a spanking, Margot, you're such a pain in the arse at times. Are you ready?"

"Oh yes, I'm ready."

And so here we were again; purely physical, of course.

Totally spent, we lay entwined on the bed, hearts beating rapidly, listening to Sarah as she lay in her cot gurgling away, playing with her toes.

I spent the next few weeks looking for work and during the second week, I was offered a job at an architect's office. Secretary to three architects, one of whom was the owner, based in downtown Durban in a beautiful large house designed by the architects. The owner, Koos, had a yacht, and on the Friday of my first week, I was invited on board for drinks.

"Koos, I'd love to but I can't. I have to collect Sarah from crèche."

"Well, why don't you go and collect her and bring her along?"

"Maybe another time, I've already made plans for tonight. Give me a little more notice next time."

"We normally get together on the last Friday of the month, pop it in your diary for next time."

"Will do. Have a good weekend everyone, see you Monday."

Apart from the three architects, there was an accounts lady, Gillian; a lovely young blonde girl, Chrissie, who worked on reception, who did photo copying, overload tying, all mailing in and out, managed petty cash and occasionally helped with filing. There was another young woman, Lizzy, a secretary to one of the other architects and from day one, she befriended me. We went out to lunch occasionally and on one such lunchtime, she said, "Just be careful, Margot, Koos is a bit of a womaniser, and I can already see the way he looks at you. Don't ever go aboard his yacht alone."

"Ouch, sounds ominous. Has he tried it with you?" I laughed.

"No, but there have been a lot of secretaries over the past two years."

"Ah, I see. Thanks for the warning."

The weeks went by quickly and it was coming up to my 35th birthday in September. My job was going well. I loved my garden cottage and I saw Rex three or four times a week, but rarely at weekends. Two days before my birthday, Rex called me. "Hi, Margot, don't plan anything for your birthday. I'm taking you out for dinner on Saturday."

"What about Janet? What have you told her?"

"Never you mind. The less you know the better."

"Hmmm."

Late Saturday afternoon Rex came around. "Hey, Margot." He grabbed me and pulled me close. "Oh my God, I've missed you so much."

"It's only been two days!" I replied.

"Only! I miss you so much Margot, I can't stand it."

"I know, I miss you too, want to know how much?"

He undid his zipper, and as soon as the 'beast' was free, he pushed me down to my knees, and grasping his cock in his fist, he began to rub it gently against my moist lips, teasing them open slowly inching further, and further in. I sucked until he could wait no longer. "Stand up, you bitch, and bend over." He took the belt from his trousers and twisted it around his hand, and spanked my buttocks. "Take that, Margot, and this." As the leather made contact with my skin, it made a 'thwacking' sound.

"Again, Rex, again."

As we lay entwined on the bed, catching our breath, we heard Sarah jumping around in her cot. "I'll get her, you go and shower and get ready." Rex jumped out of bed and went to fetch Sarah from her cot and bought her into the bathroom. "Hello, baby girl. Are you ready to take Mummy out for her birthday? Phew, you need changing."

We drove along the coastal road towards the Umhlanga Rocks Beach Hotel, which housed the famous Oyster Bay Restaurant. In much the same way that Sandton City in Johannesburg was rapidly becoming the financial centre of Johannesburg, Umhlanga was becoming the main economic hub of Durban. It was one of the fastest growing cities in South Africa. A very affluent area not just residentially but also commercially. Situated north of Durban on the coast with KwaZulu-Natal, which means 'place of reeds' in the Zulu native language, it also hosts the Gateway Theatre of Shopping, the largest shopping mall in the southern hemisphere.

We were shown to our table where we watched the clouds rolling over the ocean. The wind had started picking up and I could see forks of lightning zig-zagging behind the clouds. The thunder followed but was too far away and hardly audible. "What do you fancy to eat, the prawns here are amazing. Obviously, everything is freshly caught."

"I'll have prawns with salad." We were halfway through eating and had almost finished the first bottle of chardonnay when an almighty streak of lightning and clap of thunder passed right overhead. The lights went out. It was pitch black. Waiters came around and lit candles at each table and, during the minute or so that passed, the room became very still and quiet. Once our eyes had adjusted to the candle light, everyone started talking in whispers.

Rex managed to catch the waitress' attention and ordered another bottle of wine, and a few minutes later, she bought wine and another platter of prawns to the table.

The rain was now so torrential, we could hardly hear one another talk. It was two hours before the lights came back on and we'd managed to eat a third platter of prawns and another bottle of wine. "I'm going to have a coffee, do you want one, Margot?"

"Yes, please. Can I have a Cointreau as well?"

"Good idea."

When the waitress returned, she was holding a tray with the coffees and two bowls of ice cream. One of the bowls had sparklers alight and she said, "Happy birthday. Sorry for the hiccup with the lights, just nature doing what it does best. There's been flooding in some areas and the roads are closed, be careful on the way home. Can I get you anything else?"

"Just the bill please." Rex looked at the bill. "This can't be right. It says one bottle of wine and one platter of prawns. We had three of each!" He called the waitress over and she explained that anything ordered after the lights went out was on the house.

"Happy birthday to us." Rex was smiling.

We waited for the rain to ease off and enquired which roads were closed. Fortunately, as we were heading up the hill out of Durban, the roads were fine. It seemed to be the roads heading southwards that were having problems.

As usual the next morning, Rex was awake early. He bought coffee and croissants with a variety of fresh fruit and preserves on a tray. He placed the tray down beside the bed and went back to the kitchen. When he returned, he was holding a huge bouquet of red roses and a small gift-wrapped box.

"Happy birthday, Margot." I took the box from him and opened it quickly. Inside was a gorgeous gold bracelet of yellow meshed gold, with intermittent tiny solid gold crosses around it.

"Oh my God, Rex, it's lovely. Put it on for me." I held out my arm and he clasped it on. Just then, Sarah woke up.

"Oh, bless her. She's been so good she never wakes up in the middle of the night. Go and get her, please, Rex. What a perfect birthday."

We went out for lunch and spent an hour on the beach. We found a small pool in amongst the rocks where Sarah could sit and splash around.

"I wish we could be together all the time, love. I feel so lost without you."

"I know, Margot, it's not easy for me either. I'm at my wits end trying to live two lives but you know I can't leave her; she's only just getting over the last episode."

"Whose idea was it to come to Durban, Rex?"

"Margot, do we have to?"

"Yes, we do. I've held back for long enough. I shouldn't be scared to ask you questions. This is my life too and I need to know what's going to happen to Sarah and me in the future? I've just 'gone with the flow' as you call it for long enough. She's a year old in a couple of months." He stood up.

"We need to go. I can't do this right now."

We drove back to the house in silence. He helped me into the cottage with Sarah and kissed me goodbye.

Chapter 15

The Divorce Papers

I didn't hear from him until Wednesday morning, when he rang me at the office. "Hi, Margot, do you fancy lunch today?"

"Of course, what time and where?"

"I'll pick you up at twelve thirty."

"Okay, see you later."

We found a small bistro on the beachfront. We were looking at the menu when Rex looked at me with a rather worried look on his face.

"We have a problem. Janet found a dummy in the car. She knows I'm seeing you again."

"I don't know what to say, Rex. Is that why you were able to spend the weekend with me?"

"Yes. I wasn't sure if she'd just gone to a hotel or something but she's gone back to Johannesburg. She said she wants a divorce."

I put my menu down.

"How do you feel about that, Rex?"

"I don't really know. I suppose someone had to make a choice in this 'threesome'. I thought it would be me that made the decision but there you go, I guess the conundrum is solved."

I was speechless.

After a very quiet lunch, Rex dropped me off at the office and said he would call me later. I didn't hear from him for a couple of days and on Friday, I began to get worried. I called his office and was told he'd taken a few days off. I didn't want to push him or annoy him so I left him to sort his thoughts out.

It was the last Friday of the month, so I decided to take Koos up on his offer and go for a few drinks on his yacht with the rest of the staff. I collected Sarah from the creche and headed down to the harbour. We met on the quayside outside a little coffee shop as I didn't know which yacht it was.

"Hi, Margot, glad you could make it." Lizzy showed the way to the yacht. It was the biggest yacht in the harbour.

"Wow, I had no idea yachts could be this big. That's a serious machine."

"Yeah, I know. Koos is mega wealthy. He's also single, again. His second wife left him about a year ago."

"So, get in there then Lizzy, he seems to like you, a lot."

"I already have, but I think he's started straying again."

"Tell me more."

"Another time, too many ears on board. We'll go for lunch on Monday and I'll tell you all about it."

When I got back to the cottage, it was half past nine and Rex was sitting by the pool with a glass of Chardonnay.

"Hello, Margot. Where have you been?"

"Hi, Rex, I'm fine, thanks for asking."

"Margot?"

"What, Rex?"

"Where have you been?" He started to get angry and stood up and walked towards me, raising his eyebrows in a 'questioning manner'.

"I'm going to put something comfortable on and get a glass of wine, Rex. Do you want a refill?" He grabbed my arm and swung me around.

"My wife has left me and you weren't here when I needed you. I rang your office at five and there was no reply. I drove down and the office was closed. Where have you been?" he started to raise his voice.

"I'll be with you in a moment. Sarah needs changing and feeding." He followed me into the cottage and stood behind me while I filled my glass. "I've been for a few drinks with the people from the office. I haven't heard from you since Wednesday. When I rang your office, they said you'd taken a couple of days off. I didn't want to bother you. I thought you needed some time to yourself to mull things over."

"Where did you go for drinks?"

"On Koos' yacht." I took a sip of wine.

He knocked the drink out of my hand. "Koos' fucking yacht! Just the two of you?"

"Do not raise your voice to me Rex. You have no right. I've told you before he has drinks on board once a month for the staff and I think it's a lovely gesture on his part."

"I bet you do. And how much have you had to drink?"

"I don't like your tone, Rex. I'm not your property, or your wife, you have no right to talk to me that way." I began to feel frightened. "I think you'd better go, Rex." Sarah started crying. "Look what you've done now. How dare you raise your voice? Just go."

He went outside, taking the wine with him. I cleaned up the glass and wine and took Sarah to change her nappy. I heated her a quick jar of baby food and was sat feeding her when Rex came back in.

"I'm sorry. I'm not in a good place at the moment." Rex looked shattered.

"Feels like crap, doesn't it Rex? Now you know how I've felt for most of the time I've known you, with you going back and forth between Janet and myself."

"Do you want to come to my house tonight, Margot? We can have a BBQ?"

"Your house?"

"Yes, I don't want to be alone."

"Oh, how flattering Rex. What about all the nights I've spent alone, wondering what you're up to? If that's the only reason you want me there, because you don't want to be alone, then no thanks."

"Margot for God's sake. My wife has left me, and I'm trying my best to keep it together. Please, I love you. Please come home with me."

I stayed for the whole weekend and over the course of the next six weeks or so, I spent every weekend, and at least two days during the week, with Rex at his house.

After one particularly difficult long weekend with Rex, he announced that he had to go to Johannesburg on business for a couple of days, and arranged to see each other on Wednesday evening at his house.

When he got home on Wednesday, he seemed rather agitated. He came in, threw his jacket onto the kitchen table and got a beer from the fridge.

"Hello to you too, I'm good thanks, and yes please I'd love a glass of wine!" I said sarcastically.

"Sorry. Not a good couple of days. I was served my divorce papers yesterday." He handed me a glass of wine.

"Oh. I don't know what to say to you, Rex. 'Sorry' wouldn't be true. I'm just being honest. It hurts, doesn't it? I know only too well, even though it was me who divorced Jorgen, it still hurt like hell." I gave him a hug.

"Is Sarah sleeping?"

"I think so, I put her down about ten minutes ago. Why don't you go and pop your head in and see?" He was gone for a few minutes and when he returned, at least he was smiling.

"She looks so peaceful. I still can't believe I'm a dad. What's for dinner?"

"How about a braai. I've already made the salad and veggies so while you're lighting the fire, I'll get the meat ready."

He gave me a hug. "Good idea love, having a braai always seems to make me relax."

I didn't see Rex again then until the following Friday evening. When he got home, I was out on the patio with a glass of Chardonnay, watching Sarah playing in her sand pit. He got himself a beer and came out to join me.

"I had an interesting conversation with Hennie today, Margot." His eyebrows hovered for a split second.

"Oh yeah, what did he have to say?"

"That you'd moved out of the cottage Margot."

"Yeah, that's correct."

"He said you moved out last Friday!"

"I couldn't see the point in you paying for two properties. I'm here with you most of the time anyway."

"You should have asked me first; it wasn't your decision to make."

"I think we all know how good you are at making decisions Rex. Really. It's time for you to commit for once and stop 'pussy footing' around making excuses. Janet's gone and 'we', that is you and me and our daughter, are here, right now. What's it to be, Rex?"

"Okay, we'll see how it goes."

"Marvellous! 'See how it goes.' Well, I'll tell you how it's NOT going to go anymore. How hard can it be to tell someone you love them, and that you are very happy to be together at last? Go on Rex, say the words, go on, say it." He grabbed hold of me.

"Damn you, woman. I love you and I want you to stay." He kissed me.

"Was that so difficult?" I kissed him. "How long will dinner be Rex?"

"Not for a while yet, but I know what we're having for starters."

Chapter 16

The Teddy Bear

It was six weeks to Christmas and Rex announced that he'd invited his mother and sister over for the festive season. "Really! That's wonderful, Rex. Have you told them about us?"

"Yes, of course. Lucinda said she knew something was going on when I went over to see them last year. Remember the teddy bear I bought for Sarah? Well, I tried to say it was for my secretary who was pregnant, which was the truth. I just didn't say it was my baby. Lucinda knew I would never buy anything like that for a secretary and put two and two together."

"That's so funny, Rex. Women know these things. I bet your mum is so excited. I can't wait to meet them. When are they arriving?"

"23 December, for three weeks."

"That's marvellous, Rex, we'll take them to Kruger Park and maybe the Garden Route in Cape Town. It's a long way to come just to sit here in Kloof."

"Maybe. We'll see what they want to do."

"I'll get the rooms ready for them, we can move Sarah to the smaller box room."

"No, that won't be necessary; they can stay down in the cottage."

"You can't do that; they'll want to stay in the main house with us surely?"

"We all need privacy, Margot, they can stay in the cottage."

"Okay, you know best!"

It was the day of their arrival and Rex went to the Airport to collect them. I was a little apprehensive when I heard the large gates open and watched the Mercedes make its way down the driveway. I was holding Sarah in my arms, standing at the front door as they got out of the car. His mother, Lorna, got out first. With tears in her eyes, she came towards me and opened her arms to take Sarah.

"Hi, Margot, and hello, Sarah. I never thought…" She started crying.

His sister Lucinda was a beautiful slim blonde, big blue eyes, beautiful skin and very well-spoken.

"Hi, Lucinda, nice to meet you. How was the flight?"

"Long. But I'm used to it. I'm an air hostess."

"Wow. What a great job. Come on in, Rex will bring the cases in." Lucinda and her mum followed me through the kitchen and out onto the patio. "Would you like a cup of coffee?"

"Tea please. Not really a coffee drinker."

"Lorna, tea for you?"

"Yes please, milk, no sugar."

We sat out on the stoop chatting away while Rex unloaded the car. From day one, Lucinda and I got on like a 'house on fire'. She told me all about the 'teddy bear' episode and we laughed.

"Why is Rex putting our cases in that little building down there Margot?"

"Oh, we thought you'd like some privacy. It's a lovely cottage and right next to the pool. You can have an early morning dip."

"More like Rex wants 'his' privacy. No change there then." Lucinda looked at her Mum.

We spent the day at the poolside relaxing, getting to know one another. We splashed about with Sarah, had lunch, and of course cracked a bottle of wine. "It's a little early for wine, Margot!"

"Oh, for goodness' sake, Rex, they're on holiday, chill out, will you."

"Margot, come to my office." I saw the look on Lucinda's face as she turned towards me, then her Mum.

I followed Rex inside and went to his office.

"Margot. Lucinda drinks a lot, don't be offering them my alcohol. We'll take them shopping later and they can buy their own."

"What! You can't be serious, Rex." The look he gave me told me he was deathly serious.

I went back out to the pool and Lucinda was smoking. "Is everything okay, Margot?"

"Yes, it's fine. Rex said we need to go and do the Christmas shopping so not to drink too much, that's all. Do you want to come with us?"

"Yes, of course. Can't wait to go and have a look around Durban."

"The shops will be open late tonight so there's no rush. Can I have a puff of your cigarette, Lucinda?" She handed me her cigarette and just as I took a puff, Rex came out of the house.

"What the hell are you doing, Margot?" He rushed towards me, pulled the cigarette from my mouth, doused it in the ashtray and threw it down the garden, ashtray and all. "How dare you smoke, I won't have you smoking, Margot, and Lucinda, don't you dare give her another cigarette, do you hear me?"

His mother looked frightened.

"Rex, what are you doing son? You can't speak to Margot like that she's a grown woman. If she wants to smoke, that's her decision. Control your temper son."

"Don't you interfere, Mum. I can't abide smoking, you know that."

"Really son! You smoke cigars, what's the difference?"

"Cigars are totally different and I only have a cigar on special occasions."

"Well, this is a special occasion, Rex, so I'm having a cigarette." I went to take another from the packet.

"I forbid you, Margot, don't do it or Christmas is over."

"Suit yourself, Rex. Your mother's right. I'm a grown woman and if I want to smoke, I will." I lit another cigarette and Rex stormed into the house.

We heard the front door slam, the car engine revving and the gates opening and closing.

He forbids me! This is going into the 'memory bank'.

"Margot! I'm so glad that he's finally met his match. Good for you. It's about time someone put him in his place and stood up to him. Good for you. Cheers"

Lucinda lit up while I topped up the glasses.

"I guess he won't be coming shopping then. Cheers ladies."

We finishing our drinks, and drove down into the town centre. The shops were packed and it took us over an hour to get around the supermarket and by the time we'd loaded the groceries into the car, it was past five. There were queues of cars waiting to exit the car park.

"How about we go and have a sundowner on the beachfront while we wait for the traffic to thin out?"

"Great idea Margot, at least we can smoke and drink in peace."

"Hallelujah to that Lucinda."

102

By the time we got back to Kloof, it was way past eight, and there was no sign of Rex.

We unloaded the car and unpacked all the shopping. Lucinda had bought three bottles of gin, mixers and half a dozen bottles of Chardonnay. I put a couple of bottles in the fridge and the rest in the cupboard along with the large stash of liqueurs, spirits and bottles of red and white wine that Rex had. "I thought we'd have fish tonight, something light as we'll be having more than enough food over the next few days."

We heard the squeak of the gates and watched the headlights as they meandered down the large driveway. Then we heard the car door slam.

"Hi, Rex, where have you been?"

"Shopping, where else. Where did you think I was going, Margot? Someone had to do the shopping and you'd had too much to drink to be driving."

"Oh yes, of course, I'm not allowed to go shopping in case I spend too much money. Too late. We've been shopping and the fridge and freezer is full." I started giggling.

"What the hell Margot, what are we going to do with all this food and a spare turkey?" Now I could have given the obvious answer but thought better of it.

"It's not the end of the world you know. We do have a fridge-freezer in the utility room that you've never switched on. I guess today's the day. By the way, I'm not a mind reader. How could I have known you were going shopping. You just stormed out. Remember?"

"You've had too much to drink as usual Margot."

"Your powers of observation are incredible, Rex. Can I get you a beer?"

He knew he couldn't win.

"I'll get my own thanks. What do you want for dinner?"

"Kingklip. I thought we could have a salad and jacket potato with it, is that okay?"

"Yeah, lovely. You go and keep Mum and Lucinda company."

After dinner, while Lucinda and Lorna helped me to clear the dinner things, Rex went outside for a cigar.

"Another drink, Lucinda? Wine or G & T?"

"G & T, the wine gets a little acidic after a while."

I went to the cupboard to fetch the gin and couldn't find it, so I went outside to ask Rex. Lucinda sat next to Rex and lit a cigarette.

"Where did you put the gin, Rex? Lucinda wants a drink."

"I bet she does. She's had enough, and so have you."

Lucinda almost choked on her cigarette. "What! You know what Rex, me and Mum are on holiday. I bought my own gin and wine, and yes please Margot, I'd love a G & T."

"You can be such an 'ass' Rex, where did you put the gin?"

"Margot, come to my office."

"I suggest you go and sit in your office for the duration of the evening Rex. Lucinda and her Mum have flown out to see you and Sarah and it should be a joyful time. You are making it very uncomfortable to say the least. Go on, off you go. I'll find the gin myself."

"Margot!!!" he shouted, pointing to the door. "Now".

"How rude. Lucinda bought the gin for God's sake; you can't do that. What the hell's got into you son?"

"I said she's had enough." He didn't even look up.

"Okay, wine it is then." I said as I went into the house. His Mum was on the verge of tears. When I went back outside, he threw his chair backwards and banged his fist on the table.

"Margot," he shouted. "Don't push me. Don't talk to me like that."

"Like what, like the way you talk to me and everyone else? You don't like anyone to have an opinion, do you? Everything has to be your way or the highway. Well, let me tell you, Rex Charrington, not anymore." I filled the glasses and sat down, and left him standing at the kitchen door.

"Margot, come here."

His mother stood up and followed him to the kitchen.

"What the hell is going on, Rex? You've done nothing but be awkward and argumentative, and downright rude since we arrived. Are you ill?"

"WHAT! How dare you? Get to your cottage now, both of you, go on. Margot and I need our privacy."

I couldn't stand another minute of the bickering and I ran from the house, out of the gate, towards the large wooded area. I was terrified. I managed to find a thick bush and pushed my way into the middle of it and sat quietly. My heart was pounding.

I can't do this again? Why can't I be allowed to be me? Why does he have to control everyone?

I heard him say, "She'll be hiding in the bushes somewhere. She's got a problem. Always running away and hiding."

"Well, I'm not surprised, Rex. I don't know how she puts up with you. I'd want to hide from you too. Were you like this with Janet?"

"Leave her out of it Mum. Janet did as she was told, she never wound me up like Margot does."

"Come on, Mum, let's get back to the cottage and leave them to it."

I stayed where I was for the best part of an hour, and when I got back to the house, it was in darkness. I slept in the spare room with Sarah. Thank God she slept through the night.

The next morning Rex was awake at the crack of dawn and I could hear him in the kitchen making coffee. I could hear Sarah moving around in her cot so decided to go and 'face the music'. I picked her up and went through to the kitchen.

"Morning Rex?"

"Morning Margot. How was your bush adventure?"

I started laughing and couldn't stop.

"Hmmm. Glad you think it's funny, Margot."

"Never mind, let's just forget it. It's Christmas. I'll go and wake your mum."

I put Sarah into her highchair, put the kettle on and went down to the cottage. I knocked on the door and Lucinda stood at the other side.

"Lucinda, are you awake? Would you like some tea?"

"The door's locked, Margot, the bastard locked us in here."

"What! Wait there, I'll go and get the key." I stormed up to the house. "What the fuck, Rex! You locked them in the damn cottage? Surely that's illegal. There not prisoners for Christ's sake."

"Margot, your language."

"My language, my language? You're enough to make the Lord himself swear. Who do you think you are? Why did you lock them in?"

"Because we need our privacy, I don't need them snooping around."

"Snooping around! I think you're having a breakdown. Now give me the key."

He poured himself a coffee and went out and sat on the patio with his 'Financial Times'.

"Rex. The key?"

He reached into his shirt pocket, retrieved the key and threw it onto the table.

When I unlocked the cottage door, Lorna was sat with her head in her hands, sobbing.

"I don't recognise him, Margot. He always was a little weird when it came to 'privacy' but this is ridiculous Margot. I wish I'd never come here, but I wanted to meet you and my granddaughter."

"Oh dear, I don't know what to say to you both. I'm sorry for his weird behaviour, really, I am. I've left Sarah in the kitchen. Come on up, I'll make tea." I ran up the garden and was relieved to see that Rex had gone to his office. *Thank God for small mercies.* Sarah was happily playing at 'throw the cornflakes all over the floor'.

"What are you doing Sarah, that's not what we do with food is it? Come on, let Mummy help you."

Lucinda and her mum came up and we sat at the table drinking tea while I finished feeding Sarah.

"What are we going to do today, Margot, any plans?" Lucinda asked sheepishly.

"Not really, I've got a few last-minute things to wrap but that's all. Did you want to do anything?"

"Yes, get the hell out of here for a while would be good. If we're going to be stuck here with his 'Lordship' for the next two weeks or more, in this 'mood', I need a few hours' escape time."

"Well, I doubt there's any chance of that happening. If I tell him we're going out, there'll be another fight."

"Can we borrow the car?"

"Yes, of course you can. How will you find your way around, Lucinda?"

"It can't be that difficult. Once we get onto that main carriageway, it's a straight road into the centre. If I get lost, I'll ask someone to put me on the right road. Just write down the address. I've got your phone number just in case."

"Okay, if you're sure."

They looked at one another and in unison said, "We're sure."

"What would you like for breakfast, full English or fruit and yoghurt, or toast and jam?"

"We'll get something down in town but thanks, Margot." They finished their tea and went to get ready to go out.

Rex came out onto the patio and sat down with his newspaper.

Lucinda and her Mum came up to the house, dressed and ready to go.

"Have you got the keys, Margot?"

"What keys?" Rex looked up from his paper.

"I said they could borrow the car for a couple of hours. They want to go for a drive and have a look around Durban."

"What car?"

"Your lovely air-conditioned Mercedes, Rex, is that okay?"

Before he could speak, I laughed out loud. "Just kidding, Rex, I said they can borrow my old clapped-out Ford Escort, you know the one with no windscreen wipers, no indicators and no air conditioning and the huge dent in the side and back, you know the one?"

"They're not taking any car, Margot, we're not insured."

"It's my car and I said they can take it."

"I said NO."

"Oh, here we go again. 'Simon says this and Simon says that'. You know what, Rex, I'll go with them and then there won't be a problem, will there?"

"If you leave this house today, you won't get back in. That goes for all of you." He carried on reading his paper. We girls scarpered into the house.

"I'm so sorry. I have no idea what's got into him. Was he like this when he lived in the UK?"

"Pretty much." Lucinda and Lorna exchanged glances.

"Just let me go and get ready quickly, we're going out. I think we need to have a talk, some 'privacy' as his Lordship would say."

I went and showered and was getting dressed when Rex came through. "Going somewhere, Margot?"

"Yes, as a matter of fact, we are. Your behaviour is appalling, Rex. Your Mum is so upset. I'm going to take them into town for lunch and hope when we get back, you're in a better frame of mind. If you don't want us to come back, say so now, as your mum wants to book into a hotel. She said she hasn't come all this way to listen to us bickering and have you bully everyone. Well?"

"I'm sorry. It's not easy for me, you know. I can't stop thinking how unhappy Janet must be feeling, and I did that to her."

"Oh, so you thought you'd make everyone else unhappy as well. Great leadership Rex. Janet made her choice months ago, as did you Rex, I'm sure she's fine. Someone was bound to get hurt, we've all been hurt somewhere along this rocky road but treating me and your family like this isn't going to fix it or help in any way. We'll see you later."

Minutes later, as we drove towards the gate, I saw Rex in the rear-view mirror, hands on hips, watching us go. *Control freak.*

When we reached the beachfront, it was buzzing. Families and couples sitting in the many cafés and restaurants chatting away, children running around excitedly. We found a table and made ourselves comfortable. "Okay, order anything you like, on me." When the waiter came over, I ordered a bottle of Prosecco and fresh orange juice.

"I think we've earned it, don't you?"

Lucinda laughed. "Cigarette, Margot?"

"Why not. Now, Lorna, tell me about this son of yours."

"I don't know why he's like he is, Margot. When he was younger, he had everything he wanted. You know, being the only boy, he was spoiled rotten."

"Maybe that's where the problem lies! If he always had everything he wanted, and everyone running around after him, he expects that to continue."

"He didn't leave home until he was twenty-eight Margot, and that was when he left the country, so it can't have been that bad. He used to bring his friends from university around to dinner. He'd get me to do all the cooking and serving, then he'd lock himself and his friends in the lounge with a 'do not disturb' sign on the door, and he'd sit drinking and smoking cigars, like 'lord of the manor'. He treated me like the 'maid'. He worked hard, I'll give him that, always had a part-time job while he was studying. Did he tell you he used to work on the buses, a bus conductor? Can you imagine Rex running up and down the stairs all day on a bus, giving out tickets?"

"He must have been the most handsome bus conductor they ever had!"

Lucinda agreed wholeheartedly.

"Yes, he's a handsome man, I'll give him that." Lorna continued, "He did other part-time jobs, he loved money. He started off doing a printing apprenticeship, you know, and when he realised that printing wasn't going to make him 'rich', he took himself off to study business and economics at university. The next thing we know he's decided to emigrate to South Africa."

"Yeah, he told me how difficult it was when he first arrived, when he was living in Berea in downtown Johannesburg, looking for a job."

"Then out of the blue he came home and asked Janet to marry him and they both went back to South Africa. It took a while before he managed to get a managerial position but give him his dues, he worked his way up and eventually got to the top. You met him in his prime, Margot, and I can understand the 'attraction' from both sides."

"A fatal attraction, Lorna. I'll never forget the day I went for the interview. From the moment I clapped eyes on him, I knew I was in love. How stupid that sounds I know, but it's true. He overtook my whole 'being' if that's possible. I admit it was me that instigated the whole thing, though he didn't take much persuading. He kept telling me it was 'purely physical', until he told me he loved me, which changed everything. When I found out he was married, it was too late, I was in too deep and then when I found out I was pregnant, I was heartbroken when he said he didn't want a child and that he wanted me to go and have an abortion. I've never felt such pain. The whole affair has been soul-destroying at times for the three of us, not just me. I do believe he loved, correction, 'loves', Janet and me, and he must be in turmoil right now. Maybe that's why he's acting so strange, so controlling."

"Margot, he's always been controlling," said Lorna. "It's nothing new."

As we sat eating our lunch, there seemed to be some sort of commotion going on a couple of tables away. I noticed a black man sitting alone drinking. The restaurant was a 'whites' only area and two policemen approached his table. They grabbed the man and dragged him out of the restaurant and started beating him with a '*sambok*', a leather truncheon that they carried for protection. The guy was screaming for help as they hit him around the head and his torso. He fell to the ground and they carried on beating and kicking him. "Oh my God, Margot, what the hell's going on over there?" Lucinda was visibly terrified.

"I don't know but we'd better get out of here." I got the waiter's attention. "Can we have the bill please, and what's going on over there, that poor man?"

"He's been ordering mixers and has his own whiskey bottle in a bag. He's very drunk and apart from this place being a 'whites' only bar, it's illegal to bring your own liquor into a restaurant."

"Couldn't they have just asked him to leave? The beating seems a little harsh, don't you think? They wouldn't have done that if it had been a white guy!"

The waiter who was also black said, "Yes, Madam, I know, he shouldn't have been here, but that's the way it is. I'll get your bill, Madam."

"You two take Sarah and I'll meet you over by the kid's swimming pool." I pointed to the pool and off they went while I waited for the bill.

When I left the restaurant, the officers had dragged the man into an alleyway, out of sight of the diners, and were handcuffing him. He was splattered with blood, crouched in a heap on the floor. You know the really sad thing about this whole episode was that the officers beating him were also black. It was at this point that I realised the extent of the troubles that were yet to come in this glorious country.

The drive back to the house was stiflingly hot. Lucinda's face was rosy red from the heat and sweat was rolling down her face.

"I'm going to dive in that pool when we get back, the sweat is pouring off me. How do you cope in this car with no air con, Margot? Why won't he let you use the Mercedes?"

I just laughed and mimicked what Rex said:

'Oh, Margot, you haven't earned the right to drive my Mercedes.' "Whatever that means."

"Are you being serious Margot?"

"Deathly. The only time I get to drive the Mercedes is if he runs out of beer, or needs a lift to the airport, on one of his 'many' so called 'business trips'."

Lucinda gave her Mum a sideways glance, pulling a face that I read as 'oh dear, if only she knew'.

"Okay to two, what do you know that I don't?"

"Nothing Margot, really."

"If there's something I should know about, for the love of God tell me."

Lucinda looked at me, and again, the facial expression told me to leave it, she would tell me when we were alone.

"Never mind you two, let's just try not to annoy him, it's Christmas Eve."

By the time we got home, we were all sweating profusely. I clicked the remote and the gates opened. As soon as I turned the engine off, we piled out of the inferno.

"Right. Who's for a swim?"

Rex was out by the pool walking around with the net, fishing out dead leaves and insects.

"Hi Rex, we're back." I shouted down. "I'm just going to get my costume on. We need to cool off."

"Come on, Mum, let's go and get changed."

Lucinda's face was very red, and her blonde hair was wet.

I put my bikini on and stripped Sarah's nappy off and covered her with sun cream, put her little swim suit and sun hat on.

"Are you ready for a swim, Sarah?" We headed down the garden to the pool and, with Sarah in my arms, gently lowered into the cool water. It was bliss.

"Did you have a good lunch?" asked Rex.

"Very eventful, wait till I tell you what happened."

He put the net down and dove into the pool, coming up right next to me, shaking the water from his hair. He grabbed me and Sarah and held us close, giving me a big kiss on the lips. He took Sarah from me and started swinging her around in the water. She was shrieking with delight. *Must go to lunch alone more.* Into memory bank.

"So, what happened in town?" I told him about the awful incident and how upset his mum and Lucinda had been.

"Well Margot, it's going to get a lot worse. How would you feel to be treated that way? They're going to retaliate and you can't blame them. I've been here a lot longer than you have and it's getting worse. I fear the worst is yet to come. There's always been trouble in the townships between the many different African tribes but it's started to spill into the towns and cities. We'll have to be more vigilant. Robberies and car jackings are on the increase and women are an easy target. It's not safe to go out and about on your own. Always keep your car windows and doors locked."

"Yes, I know, Rex, I am vigilant, and by the way, they're not likely to car jack me are they. I couldn't give it away! Anyway Rex, don't discuss these things in front of your Mum. She was traumatised."

Lucinda and Lorna came out of the cottage. "Come on in, girls, it's lovely." Lucinda jumped in the deep end and Lorna used the stairs, carefully lowering into the water. Lucinda popped up from the depths.

"Oh, that's good. Hi, Rex, thanks for letting us go to lunch it was just what the doctor ordered. A bit of girly time."

He smiled.

"Shall we have a BBQ later, Rex?"

"Yes, I've taken out some chicken and sausage already. I'll prepare the veggies and marinate the chicken later. You just chill and enjoy yourself." He got out of the pool, headed up the garden and disappeared into the house.

Hmmmm What's he up to now I wonder.

"Can I get you girls a drink?" I asked.

"An ice-cold G & T with plenty of ice and lemon would be spot on Margot. Same for you, Mum?"

"Yes, please love."

"Coming up."

Rex was standing by the sink, downing a large glass of water. "Do you want to come to my office, Margot?"

"What?"

"For some dic…"

"What now? I can't just leave your folks out there, how rude."

"I bet Mum would love to feed Sarah. Give her to me, I'll go and ask them."

He picked Sarah up and went down to the pool.

"Would you mind feeding Sarah please Mum? I'm just helping Margot to prepare everything for dinner?"

"Of course, son, I'd love to."

"What happened to the gin and tonic Margot was going to bring down?" Asked Lucinda.

"Oh, okay I'll get her to bring them down."

"Thanks Rex."

I quickly made the drinks and took them down to the pool.

When I returned, I found Rex in his office, standing behind his desk. He'd taken his trunks off and he had a huge erection. "Come over here and bend over the desk, Margot, you need a good spanking, don't you?"

He pulled my bikini bottoms down.

The first smack echoed through the study. "You can't do that, Rex, they'll hear it."

"No, they won't, not with the water splashing."

"But they'll see the handprints."

"Then you'll have to put some shorts on, won't you, you dirty bitch?" He spanked me again and grabbed my hair, pulling my head back. "I'm going to give you the fucking of your life, Margot, are you ready?" Another slap followed, and another. I felt the head of his penis slowly edge its way inside me, growing bigger, as the slaps increased. He suddenly pulled out, turned me around to face him, pushing me down to my knees.

"Suck my cock Margot, suck, baby girl, suck." He flung his head back and cried out, "Oh my God, Margot, I'm coming, here it comes, here it co… Aaaahh." We sat on the floor for a few minutes to catch our breath.

"Do you feel better now, Rex?"

He smiled. "Oh yeah, much better. Go and put your shorts on, your backside's red raw."

Rex went out to find his mum walking around the pool, cradling Sarah in her arms,

"How long has Sarah been asleep Mum?"

"Not too long, ten minutes or so."

"Can you take her up to Margot, she'll sleep better in her cot."

"Okay."

While Sarah slept, and while we waited for the braai to be ready, we all sat around the pool chatting. "Christmas in the sun. I still haven't got used to it you know Lucinda; it just doesn't feel like Christmas without the snow and the cold."

"Well, I for one am not missing the snow one bit, are you, Mum?"

"No, I'm not. It makes a pleasant change. I could get used to it. My old bones don't like the cold."

We moved up closer to the house onto the patio. I was setting the table, ready for dinner, when we heard the top gate squeak.

"Someone must be lost. Are you expecting anyone, Margot?"

"No, I'll go and see who it is."

"No, you sit down Margot, I'd better go, you never know who it might be."

He was gone for about ten minutes and I was just about to go into the house to see if everything was okay when Rex called me from the kitchen doorway.

"Margot, come here."

"Yeah, what is it, who was it?"

"Grant. That's who. How the hell does he know where I live?"

"Did you send him away without even telling me he was here? How dare you! What if I'd done that to you if Janet had been at the door, Rex? How fucking dare, you?" I ran to the front door but it was too late, I just saw the red tail-lights as the gates closed.

"How does he know where I live?"

"He phoned me a couple of weeks ago on his way back from a long-haul flight, that bought him into Durban. He asked if I fancied lunch."

113

"Did you go, Margot?"

"Yes, well obviously, and before you start another row, I don't need your permission or approval either, I'm still married to him and he's, my friend."

"Friend? What did he want?"

"Just to see how I and Sarah were doing and to let me know that he had quite a bit of stuff of mine still at his house, and wanted to know if, the next time he was in Durban, he could pop over and drop them off. What did he say to you?"

"He dropped off your things. I've put them in the cupboard under the stairs. I don't want Mum and Lucinda to know he's been here. He also wanted to know when I'm going to him pay the money for the medical aid expenses incurred for Sarah's birth and your hospital confinement."

"Well, it was you who said it would be 'less complicated' for him, as my husband, to add Sarah to his medical aid, and that you were going to pay him back. That's almost a year ago, Rex. Did you give him a cheque?"

"No, I bloody well didn't and I'm not going to either. Like you said, his name is on the birth certificate; you are indeed married to him so he can pay."

"His name is on the birth certificate because you wanted me to get rid of her. I had no idea whether we would be together or not and you agreed it was easier and 'less complicated'. You bastard, you can't do that to him, Rex. Sarah's your child."

"She's yours too. You give him the money." Our voices were raised and Lucinda had come to see what was going on.

"Margot, are you all right, what's happened?"

"None of your damn business, Lucinda. Some privacy would be nice," snapped Rex.

"Rex, that's so unfair, she was just making sure everything was okay."

"Who was at the door, Margot?" Asked Lucinda.

"Like I said, none of your business; now go to the cottage and take Mother with you."

Lucinda turned on her heels in fits of tears.

"For the love of God, here we go again Rex." I said throwing my arms up in the air. "I thought you'd got rid of all your pent-up anger. Seriously! You are so rude. I'm going to see if they're okay."

I took a bottle of wine from the fridge and went after Lucinda.

They'd moved down to the poolside and Lucinda was trying to get her crying under control.

114

"He's such a miserable piece of work, really, Margot, you'd be better off without him. I don't know him anymore. Mum wants to change the flights and go home on Boxing Day."

"You can't do that, Lucinda, you've come all this way. You've only been here two days. No way. Why don't you go and stay at a nice hotel in Durban or go down to Cape Town? Oh dear, this is a disaster. Why on earth did he ask you to come over if he didn't want you here?"

Lucinda looked at her mum, she had an 'Oh dear' look on her face.

"What, Lucinda, what's wrong?"

"It was my fault, Margot. Janet called us when she finally left Rex and started divorce proceedings. She told us what was going on, about the affair and about Sarah. I called Rex and I asked if me and Mum could come and visit. At first he said no, but I called him three times and each time I made him feel bad, ashamed for not letting his mother see her granddaughter, and he eventually gave in."

"Lucinda, it's not your fault, love; your brother has some issues, he's never kept in touch, not even when your dad died. He didn't fly over for the funeral, his own father, and didn't even send money for flowers. Poor old Jo never even made it out to Africa, not even an invite, just like we didn't get invited Lucinda, we had to 'shame' him into it, and of course we had to pay our own air fares."

Now it was Lorna's turn to cry. *Merry Christmas everyone. If 'Scottie beaming you up' was a real thing, I'd be off.*

I poured more wine and had one of Lucinda's cigarettes. We sat in silence for a little while before Lucinda asked, "So who was at the door?"

"My husband." Lucinda almost choked on her fag.

"What! Good God Margot! Rex never said a word about you being married too."

"Rex isn't very good at 'life' in general, is he? He tries to keep everything hidden, like it's a sin or something in case people think 'ill' of him. You mustn't tell him that you know about Grant. He'll flip totally."

"So, you were married when you went to work for Rex? Did he know?"

"Yes, of course he knew."

I told them the story of how Grant and I had met and the circumstances of our 'marital arrangement'. Lucinda thought it was hilarious and didn't blame me at all, considering what hell I'd been through with Jorgen.

"Well, Margot, it's a good job you stand up to Rex, that's obviously why he's so attracted to you, someone with balls and not afraid to talk back at him."

"Yep, that's what he said the day I put my plan into action, the first time we… you know? His exact words were, 'Margot, you've got some balls.'" I even got a smile out of Lorna. Lorna went for a stroll around the garden. leaving Lucinda and I alone.

"While we're alone Lucinda, are you going to tell me this secret?"

"I'll tell you Margot, but you must promise not to tell him that I've told you."

"Okay, Mums the word."

"When you mentioned that he only lets you drive the Mercedes when he goes on business trips, it hit a nerve. The way he's been treating you, well, all of us. Business trips my arse. The last time he went away on 'business', he actually went on a cruise."

"How do you know that, Lucinda?"

"Because he asked me to get him a good deal, and I booked it. I'm an air hostess remember?"

"Which cruise? Where did he go."

"It was Carnival Cruise Liners, the Bahamas and Caribbean."

A cruise. I can't think straight. My head's gone all fuzzy.

"Margot are you alright? Margot, where are you going. Margot, come here."

I was having difficulty breathing, and my heart was beating so loud I could hear it thumping in my chest as I ran up into the house. I got to the toilet just in time before vomiting. I sat on the toilet for a few minutes trying to digest what Lucinda had said. What a total bastard. I knew his business trips were a little too long to be all business, but a cruise, alone, leaving me and Sarah behind. The door knocked. "Margot are you okay?" asked Rex. "Yes, I'm fine. Just had too much to eat. I'll be out in a minute."

116

Chapter 17
Christmas Morning 1988

After another restless night, in the spare room, I woke up to discover that Rex wasn't in bed. I could hear noises coming from the kitchen and went to investigate. *Had Hell really frozen over? Rex! Stuffing a turkey.* I went up behind him and put my arms around him and kissed his neck. "Merry Christmas, Mr Wonderful, you're up early. I was going to ask Lucinda to help me this morning. What a nice surprise. Thanks, baby."

He turned to face me. "I'm sorry, Margot, really, I am. I've been such a pain lately. Truth is, I would have much rather it had been just the three of us this Christmas. My mistake. Let's enjoy the day, shall we? What do you fancy for breakfast? We've got leftover sausages from the BBQ. We could have sausage butties and scrambled eggs, or do you fancy an omelette? I thought we could go for a walk after breakfast and get some exercise. It feels like I've got cabin fever and it's only been three days. Come here." He gave me a quick kiss.

Oh, dearie me, not another 'Jekyll and Hyde' episode.

"Good idea. I'll go and see if your Mum's awake and take them a cup of tea."

"No, Margot, let them sleep, they'll come up when they're ready and besides, I want to give you your Christmas present while the house is quiet. Come with me." He washed his hands and I followed him to the office.

"Wow! now I can't have an early morning swim. Look at the prints on here." I was inspecting the marks on my backside when I heard Lucinda and Lorna chatting as they walked up to the house.

"Rex your mum's awake, we'd better get dressed." I grabbed some shorts and quickly covered up. "I'll make some fresh coffee, see you in a minute. Oh, and thanks for my present, 'big boy'."

"Hey, Merry Christmas you two."

His mum and Lucinda came into the kitchen looking very cautious. "Did you sleep a little better last night? I know the damn monkeys are a nuisance but it's not every day you get woken up by a bunch of monkeys playing ball with a mango." I laughed.

"I was so exhausted after our eventful day yesterday, Margot, I didn't actually hear them last night. I could hear something scurrying around inside though, like paper rusting. Didn't you hear it, Mum?"

"No. I had a good night sleep thank goodness."

"Oh, that'll be the resident mouse who keeps me company when I'm doing my 'arty farty' things down in the cottage. He's harmless."

I saw Lorna's head shoot up. "Mice?"

"No, just the one, Lorna, and really, he's so cute. You're not scared of a tiny mouse, are you? There are much worse things here in Africa, you know. Rex found a snake under the cushions on the sofa not long ago. Not a big one but you never know if they're poisonous or not. It took him half an hour to catch it…"

"That's it, Margot, scare them to death, why don't you? Merry Christmas, Mum, Lucinda." Rex came in with Sarah in his arms. He gave them each a peck on the cheek and handed Sarah to his mum. "Not everyone loves nature and all its creepy critters as much as you do, Margot." Rex laughed, which was such a shock, the room went silent.

"Coffee, tea, anyone?" I replenished my cup while the 'dust' settled. I made Sarah her staple mealie pap with milk and honey which the maid, 'Precious' had introduced her to. I couldn't make it as good as Precious but she'd gone home for the holidays and wouldn't be back until the New Year.

"Okay, the turkeys in the oven and all the veggies are prepared, Christmas dinner should be ready late afternoon. Who's for sausage butties or omelette?"

The three of us looked at one another. 'Gobsmacked' as Lucinda would say.

As we sat eating out breakfast, I told Lucinda we were going for a walk and asked if they wanted to come along or stay by the pool. "I'm not a 'walker', I'd rather stay by the pool. Why don't you and Rex go and we'll look after Sarah?"

"Okay if you're sure, thanks, Lucinda."

When Rex and I got back a couple of hours later, we all sat out in the shade on the patio, waiting for the turkey to be cooked.

"Merry Christmas everyone." Rex popped a bottle of bubbly and filled the glasses.

"Cheers Rex and Margot, and thanks for letting us share your Christmas." Lorna lifted her glass and looked at Rex.

"Cheers, son, this is the best Christmas gift I've ever had." She had tears in her eyes as she sat with Sarah on her lap. "She's beautiful, just like her mother."

"Ah, thanks, Lorna."

"Does anyone fancy a game of Trivial Pursuit while we wait for the Turkey to cook?" Asked Rex.

"Oooh, Lucinda, you'll never beat Rex at that game." I said, "he's like a walking thesaurus."

"You're on Rex," replied Lucinda.

We cleared the table and set the board up. The game wasn't the English version, of course, it was the South African version, and I felt sorry for Lucinda, as obviously Rex knew more about South Africa than she did. I went and fetched another bottle of Chardonnay and the game commenced. It came around to Lucinda's turn and Rex read her question: "Which town in Natal was named after the Spanish wife of Sir Harry Smith?" Rex smirked at me. Lucinda thought for a few seconds.

"Natal, hmmm. Well, if he's a famous 'Sir', then she must be a 'Lady', then it must be Ladysmith."

Rex banged the table with his fist.

"You told her, didn't you, Margot? She couldn't possibly have known that."

"Rex, I did not tell her, I didn't even know the answer, you plonker."

"I'm not as stupid as you think, Rex. I'm an airhostess and I'm very well-travelled, probably more so than yourself. I don't need to cheat to beat you. Come on, it's your turn."

"I'm not playing with cheats." He threw the pack of question cards on the table and got up and stormed into the house. "Margot, come to my office."

Oh hell, Mr Hyde's back again.

"I knew it was too good to last. Just ignore him. Can I have a fag please Lucinda; if there's going to be another row, I might as well enjoy myself."

"Margot, did you hear me?"

"Loud and clear, Sir." I was feeling very mellow from the wine and the nicotine rush which had gone straight to my head. I was floating. "Well done, Lucinda. By the way, you shmashed it, and him. About time shomeone beat his shmug ass."

"Margot, you sound weird, you're slurring your words." Lucinda started laughing.

"It must be all that oraaange juice I had with the buubbly." That did it, we cracked up. We were all laughing hysterically when Rex came out and stood next to the table.

"What the fuck's so funny, are you laughing at me? Well, are you?" His face had drained of all colour. His mother stood up and turned to face her son.

"Rex, I've had just about enough of you and your despicable behaviour. It was a mistake coming here. Lucinda and I are going to get on the next available flight out of here. Rex, leave us alone. I mean it, go back into your office." Lorna stood her ground, staring right into his eyes. He turned and went back inside.

"Mum, are you alright? I've never, ever, heard you stand up to him before. That was incredible."

"This has been a long time coming, Lucinda, well overdue. I know he's my son, but really, he can't talk to people that way. I love him, he's my only son, but I DO NOT like him, I don't recognise him as my son; I'm ashamed of him. We're leaving."

"There'll be nothing open today, Mum, we'll just stay clear of him until tomorrow."

"Margot, come here."

"Don't go, Margot, I'm scared."

"He won't lay a hand on me, Lucinda. He wouldn't dare." I stood my ground and waited for the inevitable. He called once more and then the front door banged. We heard the car tyres screeching on the driveway, and he was gone. I felt my body relax, like I'd been given a sedative.

"Thank Christ for that. For the first time in four days, I feel at peace. Let's make the most of it." Sarah had fallen asleep in her highchair so I carefully lifted her out and took her and placed her in her cot. "G & T anyone? A little music perhaps, a swim, whatever you want to do."

"Any Beatles' music Margot?"

"Does a bear shit in the woods? You all come from Beatle land. Rex told me he used to go to the Cavern when the Beatles were just coming onto the music scene. I've got just the track, hang ten."

"*When I was younger, so much younger than today, I never needed anybody's HELP in any way…*" The music blared out onto the veranda and we were singing on the top of our voices. We knew all the words to every single track on the album. I smoked my brains and we got through half a bottle of gin.

The moon was shining so brightly, I could see it peeking through the blinds straight into my eyes.

"Wake up, Margot." Lucinda was sitting on the edge of the sofa.

"What, where am I?"

"You fell asleep on our sofa. I just heard the car, he's back."

"What time is it?"

"Two o' clock. What are you going to do?"

"Don't know. Let's see if he comes down here looking for me. Where's Sarah?"

"I went and fetched her; she's in my room in her carry cot."

"Why are we whispering Lucinda?"

"I have no idea."

"Oh my God Lucinda, do you think the Turkey's cooked yet."

"Oh shit, we should have taken it out of the oven, it'll be ruined. Should I go up and have a look?"

"Are you mad Lucinda! I think he's locked the doors anyway, but I wouldn't risk going anywhere near him right now."

"But I'm hungry, we missed Christmas dinner, can you believe it."

"Don't worry we'll have it later, or for breakfast if you like."

We started laughing so loudly that we didn't hear Rex open the cottage door.

"I'm glad you think it's funny Margot. The fucking turkey is crispy on the inside and charred black on the outside. The damn house could have burnt down."

"Well, you're the chef, not me. You should have turned everything off before you stormed out. Where did you go Rex. Oh, don't answer that, I really don't care where you went. Shut the door behind you there's a good chap, I need my beauty sleep."

121

Chapter 18

Happy New Year

My head was throbbing when I woke up, and I was sweating, profusely. The sun was streaming through the windows directly onto the sofa, and I'd forgotten to put the aircon on. I went outside and just fell into the pool. When I surfaced, I saw two hairy legs at the poolside.

"Good morning, Margot. How's your head?" Rex stood looking down at me with Sarah in his arms.

"Nothing a strong coffee can't cure." I got out of the pool and went into the cottage. "Lucinda, do you want a tea? Lucinda!"

"They're not here." Rex was standing behind me. "They asked me to drop them at the Holiday Inn in Durban. I think it's for the best, Margot, we need our privacy."

"Me, me, me, me. Do you know what, Rex! You're the most selfish, controlling, chauvinistic pig I've ever met. It's all about you. What you want, what you need, what you say, and God help anyone who doesn't comply."

"Before you say another word, Margot, I'm going to Cape Town for a few days. I need time to think."

"What! Let me get this straight! You've thrown your family out to fend for themselves, on boxing Day; you're going away for a few days and leaving me and Sarah alone too. See what I mean? Selfish to the goddamn core. Go on then, fuck off and give me some peace."

I took Sarah from his clutches and went up to the house and put her in her cot while I found the number for the Holiday Inn.

"Hello."

"Hi, Lucinda, it's Margot. Are you okay?"

"Yes, we're fine. Are you looking forward to going to Cape Town, that was unexpected, wasn't it?"

"I'm not going to Cape Town, Lucinda."

"Oh, why not Margot, we'll have fun?"

"What? What do you mean 'we'll' have fun. Are you and Mum going as well?"

"Yes, he's coming to fetch us later. He's paying for the flights too." My knees started shaking. "Margot, are you still there?"

"Oh yes, I'm still here. I'll call you back later." I replaced the received.

I knew he was standing behind me; I could smell him.

"Margot, I've made you a coffee; please, we need to talk."

"Nothing you could possibly say Rex could salvage the damage you've done this time."

"I'm sorry I'm not handling things very well. You have to remember I've known Janet since school days. She understands every bone of my body, and me hers. It's strange living with someone else. I just need a little time to adjust, that's all. I'm going to take Mum and Lucinda to the Cape for a couple of days. I feel so bad the way I've treated them, it's the least I can do. I knew I should never have let them come; I didn't want them to… you know… I told them no but Lucinda insisted."

"I know, Rex, she told me. The question is why can't Sarah and I come to Cape Town too, it's my holiday time as well?"

"Because there's too much tension between us and I don't have any energy left to fight. Just let me be with my family, just for two days. Please."

"Are they staying here when you get back?"

"Of course. I'll book somewhere for New Year's Eve. Somewhere lovely to eat. It's a pity Precious isn't here to look after Sarah, otherwise we could have made a real night of it. Mum and Lucinda have bought their return flights forward. They're going home on the second, which is just as well as we're both back at work anyway. Oh, that reminds me, will you be able to take them to the airport? I'll be in meetings all day."

"So, they came all this way to see you and to meet your new girlfriend and baby daughter, they've been traumatised by our continual fighting and bickering, and you're quite happy for them to go home three days early. No olive branch for them, I guess. Oh, by the way, yes, I'll take them to the airport, if I can borrow the Mercedes."

"No, Margot, you can't—"

"Then you'll have to take them yourself, Rex. Now if you'll excuse me, I'm going to get ready. I'm going out to lunch."

"Who with Margot?"

"None of your damn business Rex. Have a great time in Cape Town, without me."

On the off chance that Grant would still be with his parents on the farm, I called him. "Grant, are you still in Durban?"

"Ya, still in Durban. Did you have a good Christmas, sweetie?" Silence. "Oh! that good?"

"Ya, that good. Can we meet for lunch, Grant? I could use a friend right now."

"Suries, where and when?"

An hour later, Grant and I were sat on the beachfront in my favourite coffee shop. Grant had Sarah on his lap, bouncing her up and down on his knee.

"She's just like you, Margot. She has your little chin. She's so cute. Who's a cutie pie then, hey Sarah, yes you, you're adorable." He was a natural with babies. "What do you want for lunch; pizza, pasta, fish?"

"Lasagne with salad and some of those garlic dough balls."

"Me too, what about Sarah?"

"She can have some of my pizza if she's hungry. I fed her before we came out."

"Wine? Champers? Let's have a toast to Sarah's first birthday. I can't believe how quickly it went. A whole year. Well just a few days to go."

"In that case, bubbly it is. Thanks Grant, you always make me feel at ease. I don't have to mind my Ps and Qs with you." Grant was the opposite of Rex. Dark hair, even darker eyes, full lips and he understood women.

"So, what's up, Margot, not going so well with Rex?"

"I don't really want to talk about it, Grant. I'm exhausted. My brain is drained. I can't think straight just now. Tell me about you, Grant, what have you been up to? Did you get to spend the whole of Christmas at home or were you flying off to somewhere exotic?"

"Actually, I had to fly out to Mauritius just before Christmas, had three nights' stay over and I only got back yesterday. It was very festive at my resort. I was invited to dinner with a lovely German family and spent the day on their huge speedboat. I had no idea I could water ski; it was great fun."

"Wow, lucky you. I was in 'deep water' too, for most of the time, but a very different type of water."

"Glad you haven't lost your sense of humour. When we've finished lunch, we'll take Sarah for a paddle on the beach?"

"Yeah, what a good idea, just a pity I haven't got my costume."

"No worries, Margot, I know a secluded little beach where costumes aren't necessary."

Time spent with Grant was always wonderful. Would a life with no sex be so bad? *I must be having a breakdown, no sex!*

In no time at all, Rex and his family were back from Cape Town. They all seemed refreshed and I could sense no tension. As promised, Rex had managed to book a New Year reservation at the Umhlanga Rocks Hotel. *Good choice,* I thought.

While Rex read his newspaper and made a couple of calls, the girls and I talked about their trip to Cape Town.

"How was Cape Town Lucinda, was it windy as usual?"

"A little, but it was fabulous weather, not as humid as here. We stayed at the Victoria and Albert Hotel, and there was a craft market down on the waterfront that you'd have loved Margot. We found a little bistro and had lunch. It was lovely wasn't it, Mum?"

Lorna seemed very withdrawn, on her guard. She didn't speak much at the best of times and I'd noticed that when Rex was around, she spoke even less.

"Well, that's a first. Rex hates craft markets." I remarked.

"Oh, no, Rex wasn't with us. He said he had a few calls to make and we met him back at the hotel."

"Oh. What else did you all get up to?"

There was an awkward couple of moments of silence.

"Rex took us to a place called Camps Bay. Such a beautiful place Margot. Have you ever been there?"

"No, I haven't. What was in Camps Bay? Anything interesting?"

Again, there was a slight awkwardness in the air.

"It had the most stunning beaches Margot, and the most opulent houses were built up on the steep cliffs leading up to Table Mountain. It was actually very odd, but lovely. There were no high-rise hotels or apartments blocks towering into the sky along the coastline, only residential properties. So different from any other countries I've visited, and there have been many. The views are unspoiled. There was a quaint little village too, with boutiques and restaurants, where we had a quick bite to eat. It was lovely wasn't it, Mum?"

I'll never forget the way Lorna looked at me. A sorrowful look in her eyes. *Memory bank.*

"Good morning girls. Party time tonight. What do you want to do today? We can either chill by the pool and catch up on your tans, or…. no, I think the pool is best. While Rex is at work we can at least relax. We could even have a snooze later on before the festivities begin. Rex has booked a table at Umhlanga Rocks down on the coast. It's the best fish restaurant in the area, if not the whole of South Africa."

"Wow that sounds lovely Margot. I agree. Let's stay here. What do you think Lucinda love?"

"Yep, I'm easy. I don't really fancy walking around the crowded mall. It's too hot in your car anyway Margot, you really must try and get a new car next year."

"It shouldn't really be an issue Lucinda, should it? Rex has three cars in the garage and we know he'll never let me drive any of them."

"Where's the Birthday girl Margot?"

"The last time I checked she was still sleeping. I'll go and I'll put the kettle on, and check if she's awake."

"Hello Birthday girl. Can I hold her please Margot?"

"Yes of course, here you go."

I passed her over to Lorna and went to make the drinks, and gave Rex a quick call.

"Hi darling. Is there any chance you could pop to Woolworth and pick up a cake for Sarah's birthday please. I really don't fancy driving all the way into town just for a cake?"

"Yes of course. What are you girls up to"?

"Nothing much. We're going to stay by the pool and relax. Is there any chance you could come home early and join us?"

"Ya, I think I will. Let me know if there's anything else you need from Woollies."

"Okay, love you, see you later."

126

Before getting ready for our New Year party, we lit the candles on the cake and sang Happy Birthday to Sarah. Lorna and Lucinda bought her a silver bracelet with a small charm on it, and a couple of adorable outfits from Harrods of London.

Lorna and Lucinda were out on the patio, having a quick sundowner, while waiting for Rex and I to get ready.

Minutes later, Rex came out onto the veranda and said, "Okay ladies, I'm ready, let's go." We had a reservation for 20h00 and were shown to our table which was close to the stage, where a male singer was playing guitar and singing. He sounded like Neil Diamond and being fond of country music I was really enjoying his performance. As the evening progressed Rex told me to stop looking at the singer.

"What do you keep looking at him for? Do you know him?"

"Of course not! I think he's really good, don't you?"

"But he keeps on looking over at you too."

"Well Rex, I can't help that can I! When there's entertainment, people tend to look at the artists performing so what's your problem now?"

"I think you've had enough to drink don't you Margot? Drink up ladies, we're leaving."

When we got home Rex said "Come to my office Margot."

"Absolutely not Rex, the evening is still young and I'm going to see the New Year in with your mom and sister. If you want to go to bed, then goodnight."

We three ladies toasted the New Year 1988 in watching the shooting stars in the magnificent African skies.

The day of his families' departure soon came around. "What time are you taking them to the airport, Rex?"

"I told you I'm in meetings all day, you'll have to do it."

"That's fine Rex, where are the Merc keys?" I saw the anger in his eyes.

"Don't worry, I'll make a plan. See you later."

"Yep, see ya." I turned to Lucinda. "Well, this is our last day girls."

"Can I hold Sarah quickly before you go off to work, Margot? I might not see her again."

"Lorna! Whatever made you say a thing like that? I know it hasn't been wonderful but hey, you got a suntan, you went to Cape Town and you got to meet

Sarah, and hopefully the next time you come out, Rex and I will be more settled, well 'him' more so than me."

Lorna was crying as she held tightly onto Sarah. I could see she was distraught, deflated.

"I have an idea, Lucinda. I can't leave you here for the whole day. Your flight isn't until 19h00 this evening. If you drive me into work, you can borrow the car for the day and then… no, that's not going to work. I know, I'll call in and make some excuse, sod it, even if I have to take a day's annual leave."

"Margot, what will Rex say?"

"Quite frankly Lorna, I don't give a damn, I'm done worrying about what his Lordship thinks." It was the first time in two weeks that I'd seen Lorna laugh. "Put the kettle on, Lucinda, I'll go and call the office."

"Okay, all done, tea anyone?"

"What did you tell them?"

"I told them Sarah's unwell and has a temperature and needs to see the doctor. You're not allowed to take children to crèche when they're ill and I told them that Precious isn't back until tomorrow."

"Is she back tomorrow?"

"Hopefully tonight, I'm tired of washing up."

"You've got a dishwasher, Margot, why don't you use it?"

"You must be joking. If I turn that thing on, there'll be another row. Rex says it costs too much to run; water, electricity, fancy tablets, etc. It's never been used."

"You're kidding, right?" The pair of them looked at me, teacups suspended inches from their gaping mouths.

"Go and open the door, it's still got the tape on inside."

"We thought it was broken, what a tight bast… really, Margot. Well, that shows how 'educated' he is. It's a known fact that you actually save water and electricity by using a dishwasher. When you do it manually, we rinse first, just letting the water run down the sink, then either boil the kettle or put the emersion on to get hot water, normally it takes two bowls for washing and then rinsing again. Why did he have it installed if he's not going to use it?"

"It's not installed, it's just for show."

"Oh, my Lord above, Margot, are there any other little 'foibles' we should know about?"

"Plenty, but we're not going to waste our time on Rex. Let's go and finish our breakfast down by the pool."

"Could I have another cup of tea please Margot?"

"Of course. Lorna, do you want more tea?"

"Why not. Thanks Margot."

Chapter 19

Three Months Later

Things had begun to settle down at home and towards the end of February, I asked Rex if it would be okay if my family came over to visit. Rex looked perplexed to say the least and he asked, "Who exactly will be coming?"

"My Mum and stepdad, Arnold. I thought we could take them to the Drakensburg for a few days, and we have to go to the Kruger Park. It'll be nice to have a break ourselves."

"How long will they come for?"

"Two weeks minimum. It's such a long flight and there's so much to see. I think the end of March would be ideal, as it's still hot but not too hot."

"Ya, that's fine by me. Let me know when you've booked it so I can take a few days off."

"Great, thanks, Rex. I'm so excited."

Once Rex had left for the office, I called Grant.

"Hey, Grant, how are you?"

"Hi sweetie, how are you?"

"Excited. Rex has agreed to let Mum and Dad come out for a holiday."

"Really? What about the fiasco with his own family?"

"I know, but he won't be able to speak to my parents like he did his own, I won't allow it. By the way, I sent you the money for the medical aid bill. I'm sorry it took so long."

"It's not the money, Margot, it's the principal of the whole thing. Doesn't Rex have any morals? Anyway, I don't want to waste air on him. When are your folks coming? Any particular dates?"

"Any time towards the end of March or beginning of April, if possible, for two weeks."

"Okay, leave it with me; I'll get them sorted."

"Thanks, Grant, what a great perk; free tickets for family members as well. It's wonderful. Thanks again. Love you."

"You too, Margot, talk soon." The following day, Grant confirmed the flights, arriving on 26 March, 08h00.

On the morning of mom's arrival, I woke early as usual, and was busy getting Sarah ready when Rex popped his head into the bedroom, "See you later, Margot, have fun with your parents."

"Will do, love you."

I parked up and found my way to the spectators' lounge and checked the information board for their arrival status update. The flight was bang on time and as I watched the doors of the huge aircraft open, and people started disembarking, my heart rate quickened, as I saw Mum at the top of the stairs. I had to look twice as my sister Carol was right behind her.

Oh my God, has something happened to Arnold?

Carol was wearing a large white, wide-brimmed safari hat, and a tailored, calf-length khaki-coloured shirtdress. Her long dark hair flowed around her shoulders. Glamorous as ever.

There's our Joan, I thought to myself; she always reminded me of Joan Collins, perfectly presented, very glamorous and oh so very wealthy. Still married to John, an oil tycoon, better known as the 'JR' of Aberdeen.

I made my way down the escalator to the arrivals hall and waited for them to come through the big double doors. As soon as I saw them, I ran over to meet them. We stood for a while hugging each another, tears flowing down our faces.

"Mum, where's Arnold? Is he all right?"

"Yes, he's fine Margot. He insisted that Carol take his ticket, he knew how desperate she was to come and see you. He's down in Surrey helping John with the girls. God Bless him."

"I'll kill Grant, he never said a word."

"Good, he was sworn to secrecy."

"Where's Sarah?" Carol still had her arms around me. "Is she with the control freak?"

I smiled. "Don't be daft, he's at work. She's at home with the maid."

"Oh yes, I forgot you had home help, you lucky devil."

"We've got the whole day to ourselves. Come on, let's get out of here."

The drive back to the house in Kloof took longer than expected as we hit early morning traffic. As we pulled up at the main gate, I saw Sophie standing with Sarah in her arms at the bottom of the driveway, underneath one of the many Jacaranda trees which were just about holding on to the last purple blooms. I swung the gates open and drove through, closed them behind me, and drove down the driveway towards the house. As soon as the car stopped, Mum jumped out and Sophie passed Sarah to Mum.

"Hello. I am Sophie. Welcome to Africa Madam."

"It's so lovely to be here Sophie, thank you."

Once the car was emptied, we went out onto the patio where I had asked Sophie to put the Champagne on ice, together with platters of snacks.

"Oh my God, Margot, that view is incredible. Look at all those hills over in the distance. No wonder you love it here in Africa. You're so lucky."

"The views are colloquially called 'The Valley of a Thousand Hills', because that's how many hills there are estimated to be. Hmm, anyway, let's get the bubbly open and have something to eat."

"What a fabulous garden," said Mum. "Look at all those fruit trees. Is that a banana tree over there Margot?"

"Yep. We've got lychees, avocado, pawpaw and prickly pears too. Not that we get to eat much of it. Between the gardener, Sophie and the monkeys helping themselves, we don't get to eat much ourselves. Not that it matters, rather someone eats it than going to waste."

Mum loved gardening and when she saw the pink, red and orange bougainvillea cascading like colourful waterfalls around the cottage, she said, "Margot, it's like paradise, and that wisteria around the pergola is truly a sight to behold." She had a tear in her eye.

We stopped talking for a few moments while we sipped our champers.

"What time's Rex coming home?"

"He normally gets in around six thirty, but he said he'd try and leave a little earlier. We're having a braai."

"What's a braai?" Mum asked.

"It's Afrikaans for a BBQ. Cheers, here's to a fabulous couple of weeks." We raised our glasses and drank to the toast.

"Does the maid live in that lovely little cottage down by the pool Margot?"

"No, she has a separate flat at the side of the house. I use the cottage to do my crafting. I've cleared it all out for you two. I'll go and get the key so you can have a look, you'll love it."

"Why aren't we staying in the main house, Margot? Oh, I get it. I assume it's something to do with the 'control freak' that is Rex. I can hardly wait to meet him – NOT," Carol said, rolling her big brown eyes, before downing her champers.

"Darling, keep your assumptions to yourself for goodness' sake, let's meet him first," Mum replied.

"It's all right, Mum, she's right. He likes his privacy and besides, if need be, I can escape to the cottage with you two. It's a lovely cottage with two bedrooms but if you wanted to share, one has twin beds and an en-suite. There's a small kitchen area and, most importantly, a fridge freezer for drinks and ice cubes. Talking of which, let's get back to the bubbly."

We spent the day lazing by the pool, chatting away, trying to catch up on one another's lives. "I thought the maid's name was Precious? What happened to her?"

"She was Rex and Janet's maid in Johannesburg when they moved down here and she came with them. When Janet went back to Johannesburg, Precious wanted to go back too. Sophie's much better with the children. Precious was older and I don't think she liked me much, for obvious reasons. It was a little awkward at times, especially with Rex and me arguing so much."

"Arguing? Aren't you getting on then?"

"It was when his family came out in December, he acted really weirdly. Even his mother said she didn't recognise him. But I don't want to talk about that. I've already booked and paid for several 'excursions' for us. The first of which is tomorrow. We're going to the Drakensburg Mountains for a week. We're staying in self-catering chalets but there is a restaurant if we need it. We can take our own food and drink as well. If you think that view over there is amazing, wait until you see the Drakensburg."

Rex called to say that he would be a little late and asked me to get the braai ready. Mum and Carol helped me with the prepping, we set the table and lit the fire, ready for Rex to cook the meat. It was past seven thirty when we heard the gate squeak. Mum picked Sarah up and walked to the front of the house to greet Rex.

Rex apparently walked straight past Mum holding Sarah, came around the side of the house with his jacket slung over his shoulder, walked straight past Carol and said, "Margot, come to my office." Carol gave me a look.

"Did he just say, 'Come to my office'?"

"Ya, take no notice."

"Margot, did you hear me?"

"I'll just go and see what he wants. If I ignore him there will be a fight. Give me a few minutes."

"Yes Rex, what's up?"

"How dare you light the braai! You know that's my job."

I was confused and took a couple of seconds to reply.

"You told me to get the braai ready because you were running late, remember?"

"I said prepare the vegetables and meat, I didn't say light the fire."

"Oh! I'm sorry Rex."

I walked out of his office and went outside.

"Margot, come back here."

"Margot did you hear me?"

"Loud and clear; if you want to talk to me, you'd better come out here. We have guests in case you hadn't noticed, how rude of you."

"Oh my God, Margot, how awkward, shall I go and talk to him? Margot, what are you doing with the hose?"

"Rex is very upset because I lit the braai so I'm just going to put it out."

The fire hissed and splattered as I hosed it down. There was smoke and ash everywhere. Rex came running out of the house.

"What the fuck Margot, what are you doing. I thought the house was on fire."

"No Rex. I know how you enjoy lighting the braai so here you go, it's all yours. Do hurry up though, we're all very hungry, aren't we ladies?"

Carol and Mum moved away from the table and were standing looking on in total bewilderment. Rex lunged towards me, and for a split second, I thought he was going to hit me so I pointed the hose at him.

He could see in my eyes that I meant it, and stopped dead in his tracks.

"You infuriating woman." He shouted.

As he walked towards the house I said "You'd better change your clothes darling, otherwise your beautiful suit will smell of smoke."

Mum and Carol came and sat back down at the table. Carol grabbed the wine and topped the glasses up, then lit a cigarette.

"Can I have a cigarette please Carol?"

I helped myself to a cigarette and lit it.

"Cheers ladies, here's to a fabulous couple of weeks."

Carol took a couple of gulps of wine and a puff on her cigarette and quietly said; "Mum and I have bought him a lovely gift Margot. Should I go and give it to him, maybe it will help to diffuse the situation?"

"You reckon Sis?"

Five minutes later, Carol came back out and she was crying. Now Carol was a really tough cookie, very outspoken, and to see her crying, I knew we were in trouble. "What happened, what did he say?"

"I gave him the gift and he looked at the box and said, 'Oh no, not another pen set, I've got three of these.' He didn't even open it. I asked if I could use the phone to call home and let John know we'd arrived safely and he said absolutely no way. Then he said he thought it might be better if me and Mum went and booked into a hotel down in Durban." She was crying so much now she couldn't speak.

"Did he now? We'll see about that." I stormed into the house and said, "You total ass! You might get away with treating your own family like 'trash' but you don't get to talk to my family like that. We are going in the morning, with or without you, to the Drakensburg. Sleep on it. Are you going to light the braai Rex?"

"Get out of my office Margot."

"No problem."

When I got back outside, Carol had stopped crying. "Okay, we're going out to eat girls, just the three of us."

Mum rarely intervened when it came to matters of a marital nature but very quietly, she asked, "Margot, is everything all right, love? Why is he so annoyed, what did we do?"

"Nothing, Mum, it's just him, but don't worry, it's all sorted."

"I don't really want to go out Margot, I'm tired. Can't we grill the steak, it won't take long?"

"What a good idea Carol."

Once the meat was ready, Carol asked me if she should take a plate of food in to Rex.

"No way. If he's hungry, he can come out here."

We were in the middle of eating when he came out onto the patio.

"Margot, the Golden Girls is on TV, are you coming to watch it?" Mum spilled her drink.

"No, thanks. Like I said, we have guests, come and sit down and have some food."

"But we always watch the Golden Girls—"

"Rex, I said NO. Leave it."

He sat at the table and filled his plate, poured himself a glass of wine and said, "We'll be leaving early in the morning. It's a long drive to the Drakensburg. Make sure you're all ready by eight."

"Yes, Rex, we'll be ready." He tried to make small talk but both Mum and Carol were too frightened to speak. He finally gave up and went back inside.

"What a control freak Margot, he's like a poison dwarf." Carol took a large swig of wine.

We started laughing rather loudly and so as not to disturb him, we moved down to the pool. "I'll get another bottle from the fridge in the cottage; if I go into the main house, he'll insist that I go to bed."

Early next morning, the girls and I were up and ready by seven thirty. Rex put the cases, cooler box and wine in the car. We then waited an hour and a half for his 'Lordship' to have a bowel movement before finally getting into the car.

"Margot, do you mind if I sit in the front, you know how car sick I get. Is it mostly motorway?"

"No, that's fine, of course you can sit up front, Carol, and yes motorway for a long stretch."

"We're not going on the motorway, Margot."

"Don't be ridiculous, Rex, it will take twice as long not taking the motorway."

"I thought we'd go the scenic route; it's such beautiful scenery on the way up."

"More like you don't want to pay the motorway tolls."

"Rex, I'll pay the toll; if we go on winding roads, I'll be sick." Carol gave me a pleading glance.

"Well just say the word and I'll pull over, no problem."

136

After two hours of winding roads, some of which were dirt roads, Carol asked Rex to pull over. It was too late. Carol vomited all over the gear stick and on Rex's legs.

He finally came to a halt on the verge and got out of the car.

"Margot, can I have a word."

I got out and stood in front of him. "I told you she gets car sick. Here, use these baby wipes while I clean the car."

"She did it on purpose. I told her to tell me if she felt unwell. Damn her, look at my trousers."

"She did tell you, but you were going so fast it took too long for you to stop. No sympathy from me I'm afraid. Now let's get back on the road, we still have a long way to go and please, slow down."

We finally reached our destination. Carol looked green and was the first to get out of the car. Rex went to reception to collect the keys. He strolled over to the cabins and opened the doors. "Here you go, girls, just unload the car. I'm going to take a shower."

We watched him disappear into the cabin.

"Charming, what a gentleman. You're mad, Margot. He's an asshole."

We made several trips to and from the car, unpacked the cases and put the food and drink in the fridge. I changed Sarah and gave her a feed; took a bottle of wine and glass of ice cubes and we went and found a table in the exquisite gardens and surroundings vista. The view was outstanding. Rex was still nowhere to be seen. Carol sparked up and, as the smoke wafted past my nostrils, I suddenly fancied a puff. I took Carol's cigarette and had just taken a drag when Rex turned the corner.

"Margot, not this again. How many times do I have to tell you I won't tolerate you smoking?" He snatched the cigarette from me, doused it in the ashtray and threw the ashtray down the embankment. "Margot, I need to talk to you."

"Sorry, Rex, I'm resting after the long drive. Can't you relax for just ten minutes? We're going to order something to eat. What do you fancy?"

"We brought food with us, don't be wasting money."

Carol flipped. She couldn't retain herself any longer.

"I'm paying, Rex, and then we're going to take a nice long walk, after which we're going to sit and chill by the pool until dinner time. If you'd like to join us, that's fine; if you don't, that also fine but for Christ's sake stop ordering us around, we're on holiday too. Got it?"

He must have been shell-shocked. He never said a word, but if looks could kill, I'd be dead. He turned on his heels and stomped off towards the cabin.

"Oh my God Carol, Mum, I'm so sorry. He's doing exactly the same thing as when his family came out. My stomach's in knots already."

"Don't worry Margot, he won't talk to me like that again, I can assure you."

"Okay then, girls! What do you want for lunch?"

During lunch, I went and fetched another bottle of wine and some ice and put three bottles in the fridge in Mum's cabin and locked the door. Sarah was getting restless and Mum took her over to the small playground area.

"I'm so fed up with Rex and his constant interfering, trying to control everything. How do you put up with it, Margot?" Carol looked really annoyed.

"I suppose I've got used to it. I don't hear him half the time. You mustn't think he is acting like this just because it's you. He was exactly the same when his mum and sister were here at Christmas. I remember on Christmas day, I asked his mum and sister if they fancied a liqueur with their coffee. I went to get up and go to the drinks cupboard when Rex threw me a glance, directing me into the kitchen. He said, 'What the hell are you doing, giving them my expensive liqueurs?' You'll never guess what he said, 'That's for very special occasions, Margot, how dare you.' Obviously, I was flabbergasted and I said, 'Don't you think this is a special occasion, Rex? You know your mum and sister have come all this way to meet your girlfriend and baby daughter, you know, your mum's granddaughter. Is that not special enough for you, Rex. Are you expecting the queen to pop in one day, or maybe President Botha!'"

Carol and Mum were laughing so hard we didn't hear his footsteps.

"Margot, can I have a word?"

"Actually, I'm in the middle of something, Rex, if you don't mind. We can talk later."

"Margot. Now. Come with me."

Carol stood up. "Okay, Rex, what's the matter with you now? You're not at the office, or in a classroom full of kids; we're adults and quite frankly, we're sick of listening to your dull and threatening voice. Go away like a good boy and leave us the fuck alone."

I just sat looking straight at him. It went deathly quiet and just as I was about to say something, Rex turned and went back to his cabin.

"Anyway, going back to the Christmas episode, he lost his shit and grabbed me by the scruff of the neck, took the sopping dishcloth from the sink and rubbed it in my face. Then he threw it back in the sink. As he walked away, I snatched the cloth from the sink and threw it at the back of his head. Upon contact with the back of his head, it made a sloppy wet sound and I couldn't stop laughing. Luckily, Lorna came in to the kitchen just as Rex was about to pounce and managed to diffuse the situation. He still wouldn't let them have a drink so we took a bottle of gin and went down to the cottage, where I stayed all night."

"What an arse. Margot, have we really got to spend a whole week with this freak?"

"Afraid so. With a bit of luck, he'll be pre-occupied with work. He usually is, even on holiday. Always on the phone or computer. Damn boring freak."

It went dark rather quickly in the mountains and became quite chilly. I'd put Sarah to bed in my room, and left her with Rex, who was reading his newspaper, and went around to Mum's cabin. An hour or so later, there was a loud knock at the door.

"That'll be Rex," Carol said as she opened the top half of the barn door and looked straight at Rex. "Can I help you?"

He popped his head around the door and said, "Margot, it's late; are you coming to bed?"

"Late! It's eight thirty, Rex, I won't be long."

Carol shut the door.

An hour later, the door knocked again but this time when Carol opened up, he had Sarah in his arms.

"You've woken Sarah up with all the noise, Margot, come to bed, now."

Carol grabbed Sarah from his arms and just before slamming the door in his face, said, "If you come back again, I'm going to shout RAPE." She said the word RAPE rather loud, and he scurried away to his own cabin.

Sarah and I spent the night in Mum's cabin. The next morning, I woke with a really bad headache.

I put the kettle on before scooping Sarah from her cot and smothering her with kisses and hugs, before heading next door to change her nappy.

Mum and Carol were still in bed. "I'm just going next door to get Sarah's food and nappies, be back shortly."

I opened the cabin door. "Morning, love. Hello, hello?" *That's odd,* I thought. "Rex, are you in the bathroom?" I looked again and realised that his laptop, suitcase and toiletries were gone. I ran outside to the parking bay only to find the car was gone too.

I ran back to Mum's cabin, holding tight to Sarah. Mum was still in bed and Carol was making tea and coffee. "Hey girls, I've got some good news."

"What is it?"

"Rex has gone."

Mum looked up from beneath her duvet. "What do you mean he's 'gone'? You mean he's left us here in the middle of nowhere! Three women and a baby?"

Just then, Carol turned around, coffee cups in her hands and shrieked, "Oh my God, has he taken all the booze? Margot, please tell me he hasn't taken the booze."

Now in life, there are times when something really funny happens, and this was one of those times. Carol and I started laughing and just could not stop. We only stopped when Mum piped up, "How are we going to get back to Durban Margot?"

"Who cares?" Carol looked at me, eyes bulging with tears of laughter. "We're here for a week!" she continued. "With no 'Control Freak' and NO alcohol, nothing, nada." Carol and I cracked up laughing again.

"I'd rather starve to death than have no Chardonnay, Margot?" cried Carol.

We finally got ourselves composed and sipped our coffee.

"What are we going to do, Margot? Mum's right. There are no trains and I'm assuming no buses either. We're six hours from home."

"I'm going down to speak to the lady at reception, maybe she can help."

"I'm coming with you. Mum, keep an eye on Sarah?"

"Good morning. I believe Mr Charrington has checked out?"

"Yes, Madam, the he left very early this morning." The young girl smiled up at me.

"We have a bit of a problem. As you know we're booked in for a week and the boss has taken all the food and wine and I was wondering how far the nearest bottle store is from here?"

"Bottle store! Oh, Madam, there's nothing around here, the nearest small town is over eighty kilometres away."

"Do you have any wine that we can buy from you?"

"I'm afraid not, Madam, we don't have a licence to sell liquor, that's why you have to bring your own. But I might be able to help you. There's a conservationist arriving today, he's coming up from Pietermaritzburg, I could call and ask him to bring some in."

"Oh, thank goodness, that's great, thanks so much."

"One moment, Madam, while I find the number." She disappeared into the small office behind her and came back with a small book. Flicking quickly through the pages, she said, "Here it is, his name's Raoul." She dialled the number. "Hi Raoul, it's Sylvia. What time are you leaving Pietermaritzburg, I need a favour?" She looked up and smiled, nodded affirmatively and continued. "We have guests who've booked for a week and they've forgotten to pack the drinks. Okay, yes that's lovely, just hold on, I'll ask her."

"Okay, Madam, what do you need?"

Carol jumped straight in, "A dozen bottles of Chardonnay, two bottles of Gordon's gin and, do I need tonic or do you have them here?"

"We have all the mixers, Madam." Looking slightly embarrassed, Sylvia said, "You're here for six days Madam!"

"Yes, you're right, Sylvia, thanks. Double the order, it's going to be a long six days."

Sylvia's eyes widened; shock didn't describe the look she gave us. "Raoul, can you double the order please?" There was a slight pause. "Yes, three ladies! Yes. okay, I will tell them. See you later." She replaced the receiver and looked up. "Raoul will be here at lunch time, he's already on his way."

"Thank you so much, Silvia."

As we made our way back to the cabin, we were giggling. "Did you see her face when you doubled the order, what a shame! She's probably very religious as are most Afrikaans people, or else she's tee total.

We got back to the cabin to find Mum trying to get Sarah to walk. "You were walking at nine months Margot, she's fifteen months old!"

"Don't forget she was premature, Mum."

"Of course, I'd forgotten, but it shouldn't be long now, she can do a few steps holding my fingers."

"We got the drink organised Mum, some 'conservationist' is bringing it in later today."

"Oh. that's good. Thank the Lord Rex has gone, Margot. I couldn't bear another moment in his company; my stomach was in knots the whole time."

"Me too, Mum, now let's start this holiday."

We went for a long walk after breakfast, then spent a couple of hours by the pool before lunch. I was feeding Sarah when a park ranger approached our table. "Good afternoon, ladies. I'm Raoul."

"Raoul, please, will you join us for lunch? It's the least we can do for all your trouble, please sit."

"Thank you, I think I'll take you up on that, I've been on the road for hours and I'm ravenous. Shall I go and fetch a bottle of your wine?"

"If it's not too much trouble." Raoul came back with the wine and glasses and a tub of ice. "Hope you don't mind; I brought a glass for myself too?"

"Mind! Of course not, you saved our lives; well, you know what I mean. Raoul, I'm Margot, this is my sister, Carol, and my mother, Ida, and this cutie is my daughter, Sarah."

"Pleased to meet you all." Raoul was a muscular, six-foot-tall blonde with a broad smile and huge brown eyes. His hands were large and strong and 'dwarfed' the wine bottle as he filled our glasses.

"What work do you do in the parks Raoul; Silvia said you're a conservationist?"

"That's right. I specialise in snakes. I'm up here for a week to catch 'mambas' to take down to the zoo in Durban. We're going to try and get them to breed."

Mum shuddered involuntarily. Her worst nightmare was snakes.

"Snakes? There are snakes up here?" Mum asked.

"Oh yes, many snakes, and not just mambas."

"We'd better change the subject, Raoul, Mum's petrified of the things."

"Oh, sorry. I didn't think! What brings you here to the Drakensburg, you're obviously from the UK, right?"

"I live here, in Kloof, in Durban. I've been in South Africa for a few years now. My family are on holiday for two weeks and this is our first excursion."

"Fancy forgetting the wine. Cheers, ladies."

"We didn't actually forget the wine Raoul. I had a bit of an altercation with my other half and when I got up this morning, he was gone, wine and all."

142

"No way! I take it you came in two cars?"

"Actually, no, we didn't. On the upside, we've got six days to come up with a plan. We'll have to hire a car, I guess."

"The nearest town is an hour away, and I don't think they have a car rental place; it's just a small farming community."

"At this point, I don't really care; do you, girls?" They shook their heads.

"I'm going back to Pietermaritzburg on Friday, if that's any good, and if you don't mind travelling in a jeep, I'd be more than happy to give you a lift. It's not that far from Kloof."

"What a hero! That's so good of you, Raoul, are you sure it's no trouble?"

"You have no other options. I can't leave three damsels in distress can I, especially this little one? She looks just like you, Margot, beautiful." I felt my cheeks flush up.

"Thank you, Raoul." I went to raise my glass and realised it was empty.

Raoul jumped up. "I'll go and get another bottle, shall I?"

"A man after my own heart," said Carol, as he headed for the restaurant. "What a lovely guy. Now he's more your type, Margot; a fit ranger, with manners and a 'heart' apparently."

"Oh yes, I can just imagine the scenario, Carol. That would go down a treat, wouldn't it? Go away for a few days with my boyfriend and child, and a week later return with a game ranger!" I looked at Carol.

"You've done weirder things, Margot. Married a wife beater, twice; married a gay guy! Which reminds me, when are you divorcing Grant? I take it you and Rex are going to get married now you have Sarah?"

"Grant is being stubborn. He said he really loves me and he's waiting for me to go home." Carol went to say something. "I know, sis, don't say a word. He'll come around eventually."

Raoul came back with the wine and we sat peacefully enjoying the ambience and the conversation.

We didn't see much of Raoul until the day of our departure. Mum seemed a little quiet. "Is there anything wrong, Mum?"

"Where's he putting the snakes?"

"Oh, Mum, don't worry really, they'll be in a cage in the back of the jeep, relax."

Chapter 20

The Olive Branch

We arrived back in Kloof at around three. Raoul helped us to unload the car, and we said our goodbyes. As soon as he'd gone, I took my case into the bedroom and found an envelope on the pillow.

I opened it quickly and read, *'Margot, once again we're at loggerheads. I'm offering the olive branch, again. I'll see you later. Xx.'* I went down to the cottage to find Carol and Mum. "Read this." I passed the note to Carol.

"Olive branch! I know what I'd do with the olive branch, Margot. My stomach's in knots already."

Mum was sat on the lounger out by the pool, looking very sad.

"In that case, ladies, don't bother unpacking, I've had enough as well. Come on, girls, let's pack up the old Escort, we're going to finish this holiday in style, without Rex."

"Where are we going?"

"I've booked us into a game reserve in Umfolozi from Monday for a couple of days, so we can either book into a hotel in Durban for the weekend; sun, sea, and sand, and no Rex, or we can drive down towards Umfolozi and see if we can book in early. If not, we'll find somewhere else to go for a couple of nights. There's a lot of lovely places down there."

"Margot, are you sure, Rex's going to freak out?"

"Freak! Control Freak! I don't care, come on before he gets home. You've only got just over a week left. and we're going to enjoy it."

By the time we'd finished packing the car, the back end was almost on the ground. I locked the house up and off we went.

Two and a half hours later, we pulled into the reserve and were lucky enough to check into our A-frame retreat, which was on the outskirts of the reserve amongst the forest, two days early.

We parked the car in the shade and started to unpack the car. We'd stopped along the way to buy provisions and while Mum kept an eye on Sarah, Carol and I unpacked the car. Once the car was emptied, we set about making some lunch. "What did you do with the eggs, Mum?"

"On the breakfast counter by the microwave."

"Where, I can't see them." We looked everywhere. "Oh, never mind, we'll have sandwiches for now. Where's the bread?"

"On the counter."

"Where?"

"What's going on? I definitely put the eggs and bread just here!"

We heard a noise, something banging on the wooden roof. I went out to investigate and found the culprit. A monkey sat on the veranda banister with a slice of bread, chomping away. I closed the door so the monkey couldn't get in, and saw the notice: *'Beware of monkeys. Keep all food locked away and close all windows when out.'*

"Ah. They should have that notice on the outside of the damn door. Now we know."

We were all pretty tired after the number of miles we'd covered and didn't venture far that day.

The heat was stifling and being in a treed area, which attracted mozzies, we plugged in the mosquito repellents and closed the doors and windows and sat outside on the veranda with a glass of wine listening to the night chorus.

"I wonder what Rex is doing. He'll be furious."

"Oh my God, I've just remembered. He knows the itinerary; he knows this was the next place on the list. I think we should check out early on Monday and find somewhere else to go."

"But you've paid for this already?"

"I'm sure they'll understand when we explain the circumstances. Even if they don't reimburse me, I don't care. I just want a quiet holiday without Rex. My brain hurts."

Mum began yawning. "I'm pooped, girls, which room am I sleeping in?"

"Come on, Mum, I'll show you." There were three bedrooms, all very small. Sarah and I shared a room and Carol and Mum had their own rooms. Having had all the windows closed to keep out the night critters, inside was like a sauna.

In the middle of the night, I heard the fridge door open and someone glugging down water.

"Can't sleep either? It's so damned hot." I said as I watched Carol gulp a pint of water.

"It's not so bad in here with that huge fan light, why don't we sleep in here? Come on, come and help me." We hauled our mattresses into the centre of the lounge, right underneath the fan.

"Good idea, sis." We decided to have a glass of wine as we were wide awake now and were just getting comfy when Mum came through.

"I've seen it all now. What are you two nutters doing?"

"It's too hot in those tiny rooms, we couldn't sleep."

"Me neither. I'm going to join you." We got Mums' mattress and placed it in between ours.

The next morning, we heard someone knocking the front door. "Oh my God, that'll be Rex." I opened the door to find a smiling young girl.

"Good morning, Madam, I come to clean the chalet."

"Oh, good morning, what time is it?"

"It's nine-thirty, Madam. Should I come back later?"

"No, no, it's just, we had a bad night with the heat. Do come in." As she entered the room, she stood looking at the scene in front of her. Three mattresses strategically placed in a 'three armed' star shape, directly underneath the fan with three glasses and a bottle of wine and a mosquito coil burning away in the centre. It must have looked like some sort of ritual that weird foreigners get up to. "We couldn't sleep, it's so hot in those tiny rooms." I pointed to the fan.

"Oh, I see. Shall I leave the mattresses where they are, Madam?"

"Yes, you might as well, we can't sleep in those tiny rooms."

We sat out on the veranda with tea and coffee and Sarah eating her porridge, while the young girl cleaned up. There wasn't much to do and an hour later, I gave the girl a few rands and she was gone.

"Shall we go for a walk in the forest after breakfast? The bird life will be amazing, Mum. There should be lots of hoopoes. We had a family of them in the garden. Rex found them when he heard chirping sounds coming from underneath a piece of corrugated timber. When he lifted it up, there were five tiny babies, all sitting with their curved beaks open waiting for Mummy to bring food. The cutest things, about the size of a thrush when fully grown. They've got a light pinky brown body with black and white striped wings and a vivid pink crest. I believe they've been spotted down on the south coast of England."

"Christ, Margot, where do you learn all this sort of stuff?"

"Sorry, am I boring you?"

Mum intervened. "You're not boring at all, Margot. Your sister here is more interested in her hair and nails and what's 'in vogue', than what's going on around her. She wouldn't know the difference between and hoopoe and a hippo. You carry on, blondie."

"Charming, thanks, Mum."

"Moving on, folks. Who wants what for breakfast? I'm having cereals and fruit, toast and jam."

With breakfast finished, we locked all the windows and doors, strapped Sarah to my back in a baby carrier, and set off towards the forest. I'd packed a small bag with water, sandwiches and a couple of packets of crisps, food and nappies for Sarah and a pack of baby wipes and off we went. We were full of giggles, chatting away, venturing along the dirt trail. The terrain was dense and overgrown in some places and stepping over large rocks and twisted tree roots was quite tiresome. We stopped for our first break at around midday. We found a fallen tree trunk to sit on.

"Cigarette Margot?"

"Ya. Oh, just let me make sure Rex isn't watching!"

"Too funny Margot. I wonder what he's doing right now?"

"Shush, you two, can you hear that?" Mum sat precariously on the tree trunk, finger on her lips, with Sarah on her lap.

"What Mum? I can't hear anything except birds."

"Exactly. No 'Margot, come to my office; Margot, do this; Margot, how dare you smoke; Margot I think you've had enough to drink.' What a nightmare."

"I know, can you imagine if he'd come to this place? We wouldn't have slept on mattresses on the floor in the lounge, that's for sure!" Carol sparked up another cigarette. "Margot, we need our privacy, come to bed now."

"Oh don't, Carol, you're making my stomach churn." We sat for a good fifteen minutes. We had a glug of water and after putting Sarah back on my back, we carried on through the thicket. As we got further into the forest, the midges started biting the back of Mum's legs and she had little spots of blood trickling down her legs. The three of us were soaking with perspiration and Sarah had become restless. We'd been walking for a good three hours in total, including a few breaks now and then for a short breather or to take pictures. "Stop, you two, can you hear water?"

"Yes, it's coming from over there." Carol said, pointing to the left.

"Okay, let's head that way, we can have a swim and cool off."

The terrain became even denser and as I stepped over a large tree root, I forgot to look up, and Sarah's head bashed into an overhanging branch. She started screaming and a red mark was instantly visible on her forehead. I tried my best to console her. She was very hot, so I stripped her down to her nappy and gave her a quick rub down with a baby wipe. I fed her another jar of baby food and gave her a drink of milk, and she was full of smiles again. We followed the sound of the water and finally came to a clearing, and a large expanse of water. To our right was a large bridge that enabled you to get to the other side, under which flowed rapid waters. There was no sign of wildlife apart from birds, and the three of us stood at the water's edge with small waves lapping around our feet.

"What are we waiting for? Let's do it." The three of us stripped down to panties and with Sarah in my arms we waded into the cool water. "Oh, that's heavenly. So cool. Come on, Mum, duck down and cool off."

"It's colder than I thought it would be. You know I don't really like water. Let me take Sarah for a stroll and you two have a swim." She quickly put her clothes back on and I passed Sarah over. Carol and I lay floating on our backs and I could see Mum walking towards the bridge. Suddenly, I heard Mum screaming and running back towards us. "Get out of the water, girls, get out, crocodiles in these waters." In my panic to get out, I stubbed my toe on a rock and fell over. Carol grabbed my arm and hauled me up and we ran onto the muddy bank.

"What idiot didn't think to put the sign at the start of the trail warning people about crocs?" Mum was crying.

"Crocs live out of water too, you know, I'd never have ventured out here especially with Sarah if I'd known." I began to panic.

"Get dressed and let's get back to camp." Once dressed, we turned towards the forest.

"Which way did we come, Margot?"

"Well, when we came out of the forest, the bridge was on our right so... heck, I have no idea which way the camp is!"

We tried to find the trail but the terrain appeared to be elevating slightly, making it very difficult for Mum, and with Sarah on my back, I was exhausted. We found a place to rest and had the last of the water.

"Poor '*Joan*, you don't look so glamorous right now."

We laughed. Her mascara had smudged around her eyes, her cheeks were flushed and her hair was tangled and sticking out all over the place. "What the hell do we look like? How long have we been out here, Margot?"

"Oh my God, it's half past three. We've been walking around since eleven this morning. Now I'm worried. Any ideas?"

Mum said, "We can't be that far away from the cabin, I reckon we've gone around in a big circle. Let's just sit here, really quietly, and see if we can hear anything."

"Like what?" Mum was near to tears again, and covered in bites.

"Cars, there must be roads around the reserve or even through the reserve, rangers or something." We sat quietly listening.

"Did you hear that?" Mum whispered. "Listen, over that way." We sat straining our ears.

"Yep, I heard it, a car engine faintly rumbling over that way in the distance, definitely a car." We headed off in the direction of the car's rumble.

An hour later, we came to a dirt road with fresh tracks in the red soil. "Thank God. Which way?"

"Jesus, Margot, I have no idea. When we heard the water, we did a 'left, which would have taken us off the trail so my guess is we go right. Either way, we should eventually come out onto a main road. What do you think?"

"Okay, right it is, we don't want to be walking around out here in the dark."

Another hour passed. "I can hear a car." We stopped walking.

"Yep, it's coming from behind us." The car engine rumble got louder and when it came into sight, I ran into the middle of the road waving my arms. The vehicle pulled over and the driver rolled the window down. "Good day, ladies, what are you doing out here?"

"We're lost. We came out for a walk and lost our way."

"Where are you staying?"

"Umfolozi Nature Reserve." The guy turned and looked at his wife and back at me.

"Are you sure? We're on our way there and according to the map, it's another hour's drive!"

"Ya, I'm positive. We left the cabin before eleven this morning." He got out and opened the sliding doors of the camper. "Jump in girls. Have you had anything to eat today?"

"We had crisps and a sandwich. We didn't intend being out for so long, we just wanted to have a walk. Luckily though, I packed Sarah's two feeds and two bottles of milk." I saw him look at Sarah.

"What happened to her head?" The red had turned blue and a slight lump had appeared.

"I forgot to duck and she banged her head on a branch, I was too busy stepping over rocks and roots." He rummaged in the back of the camper and came out with bottles of water and a foiled parcel of sandwiches.

"Here you go, now let's get you back to camp."

When he dropped us back at the reserve, it was seven thirty. "Thank you so much."

"No problem, I'm glad we came along when we did or you might still be out there."

We watched them drive away.

"Wine, anyone?"

"I'm going to bathe Sarah first and give her a feed, she should sleep well tonight."

"She's not the only one, blondie. What a day that was!"

We sat quietly on the veranda going over the day's events, sipping wine. "I'm going to shower and hit the sack too." Mum went inside and half an hour later, she was fast asleep on her mattress.

"God bless her, she never complains. Thank God she saw that sign Margot!"

By nine o' clock, we were all fast asleep in our circle on the floor.

At five the following morning, the sun was blaring in through the windows, already hot and sticky, I got up to make a coffee.

"Margot, why are you up so early?"

"It's too hot to sleep. Do you want a cuppa?"

Carol and I sat out on the veranda listening to the morning chorus.

"What are we going to do today, Margot. We can't go walking again!"

"I was thinking the same thing. Maybe we should check out and find somewhere else to go. I'll go and have a word when we've had breakfast."

"Good morning, how can I help you Madam?"

"Lovely morning, isn't it? We'd like to check out today if that's alright. We had quite a fright yesterday."

"Oh dear, what happened?"

"Well, we went for a walk in the forest and came across some water with a bridge going across to the other side. We were cooling off in the water when my Mum came back screaming something about a sign that said 'beware of the crocodiles.' Surely the sign should be at the entrance to the walks. I had my one-year-old baby daughter with me, for goodness' sake. Anything could have happened. Oh, and another thing. When we arrived a couple of days ago, we couldn't figure out why our food kept on disappearing. We soon realised that, whilst unpacking the car, the cheeky monkeys had stolen our food. It wasn't until we shut the door and saw a sign that said; 'keep the door shut. Beware of monkeys.' Surely the sign should have been on the outside! They must have got in while we were unpacking the car."

"Oh dear, I'm so sorry Madam. I'll reimburse you for the two days, and cancel, at no charge, the remaining two days. Again, I'm sorry for the trouble."

"Alright, thank you. Have a good day."

"You too Madam, take care."

Chapter 21

Shaka Zulu Land

We didn't have any plans for the next couple of days. I'd booked us into the Kruger National Park from Thursday to Sunday and we had a very long drive ahead. We headed off on the main R68, out of the reserve. We'd been on the road for over an hour when Mum asked, "What's Shaka Zulu Land, Margot?"

"I've no idea. Why?"

"I keep seeing signs for it, sounds interesting."

"Okay keep looking and we'll go and take a look." We followed the signs for forty-five minutes when Mum said, "We've passed this spot before, I recognise that old dilapidated building over there."

"Ye, she's right, Margot, I think we've gone around in a circle."

"Well, I followed the signs so I don't know where we went wrong. Now pay attention, everyone, and we'll try again."

We followed the signs once more along the winding road. We were surrounded by hills, and there were no other roads except the one we were on. "Stop. On the other side of the road a few hundred yards back. I saw a huge signpost. Turn around and drive back I can't see what it says from here."

"Welcome to Shak Zulu Land."

"Hooray, we found it!" We drove a couple of hundred metres along a dirt road and came to a standstill when we saw a colourfully clad warrior standing at a huge wooden slatted gate. He had a shield in one hand and a spear facing the heavens in the other. "Welcome to Shakaland." His face and chest were painted with stripes of war paint, with fur wrist and ankle bands and an animal skin loincloth covering his manhood. His black skin glistened with sweat and every muscle on his body was perfectly sculpted as if carved from a block of ebony.

The warrior escorted us through the gates where we were greeted by a white woman. "Good morning, ladies. You look exhausted."

"We're lost. We've been driving around for hours trying to find this place, I think someone has turned the signposts around."

"Yes, we thought something had happened. All of our guests arrived late. I don't recall seeing a family with a baby in the check-in register?"

"Oh no, we were on our way to Kruger when we saw the signs for Shakaland and thought we'd have time to take a look around."

"You'll never make it to Kruger before they lock the gates. They close at dusk, you're about six hours away."

"For crying out loud, Margot, didn't you check how far it was?"

"I didn't envisage driving around in circles for almost two hours looking for this place, did I?"

The lady raised a hand. "Please, ladies. Let me show you to a hut where you can freshen up. As luck would have it, we have an empty rondavel. You're welcome to stay the night. No charge. It's not every day I get three women and a baby visiting, and English at that."

"That's fabulous, thank you so much."

The rondavel was huge. Well, for a 'mud hut', it was huge. It had a large four-poster bed draped with the essential mosquito nets to one side, and a partition of cane between two single beds, also with mosquito nets. Hand-painted depictions of cave men hunting animals adorned the walls. Through the small windows, you could see nothing but the forest.

By the time we'd finished showering, it had started to go dark. I could hear the insects just warming up their orchestra, the frantic chirping of mother birds feeding their babies, getting them into their nests before the light faded completely, when once again the day is given over to the night stalkers. There was a tap on the door. "I forgot to introduce myself, sorry, I'm Jackie. My husband and I have been running this place for three years. And you are?"

"I'm Margot, my sister Carol and my mum Ida, and this is Sarah."

"Nice to meet you all. I see you've freshened up. When you're ready, make your way over to the boma and come and join us for dinner."

"What's a 'boma', Margot?"

"It's a wooden enclosure, initially built to keep wild animals who are being transferred to other game reserves, while they check them over before releasing them into the wild. Nowadays all game reserves have them. It's a great way to relax after a game drive. Being totally enclosed it gives a cosy, warm, wind free ambience for guests, and keeps out predators. It's called; Dining under the stars. You'll see."

"Predators?"

"Stop fretting, Mum, just the odd elephant or lion may try and come in but the enclosure is built in such a way that when they get so far in, there's a false entrance and they get confused, and thinking there's no way out, they panic and turn around. So chill, we're going to have a blast."

"If it's anything like the 'blast' yesterday, I'll give it a miss."

"Ha-ha, very funny. Nothing like yesterday, I promise."

We could smell the barbeque as we stepped outside and, mixed with the smell of the bush, I was once again in my element. There were, surprisingly, lots of people in the boma, all seated on huge tables around a central bonfire. Some people were sat on logs close to the fire, enjoying the warmth, as a definite chill danced around once the African sun had set. Jackie came to greet us and showed us to a spot next to the fire. "What can I get you to drink, ladies?"

"Do you have Chardonnay?"

"Do I? Oh boy, looks like we have another thing in common."

"Why, what's the other thing, Jackie?" asked Carol.

"Independent women doing their own thing, no men around, just girls enjoying life to the full." We all looked at each other.

"When you bring the wine over, please bring a glass for yourself, we'll tell you a story!"

"Sounds ominous!"

We were relaying the events of the last few days spent with Mr Control Freak, when Jackie's husband came to join us. As he got closer to the fire, I gasped.

"Oh my God, it's Raoul from the Drakensburg, the ranger that rescued us."

"No way? It is too. What a coincidence."

I stood up to shake his hand.

"Three women and a baby! These are the ladies I told you about, Jackie."

"I gathered that; how funny. What a small world."

"I'll go and get a cold beer, be right back." Raoul returned and we sat chatting away for the next hour while the meat was cooking.

We were halfway through our meal when Mum noticed in the hills beyond the boma, dozens of small flickering lights, fireflies maybe? They appeared to be slowly descending down the hill, almost like a large glowing snake. It was dark now, pitch black. The light from the large open fire pit was more than adequate, and with candles on the tables and hanging lamps strung around, it was indeed very ambient and cosy. There was a slight breeze rustling in the trees and elephant grass surrounding the boma.

Mum whispered, "Margot, what are those lights coming down the hill, look over there."

"I'm not sure, maybe it's the natives out hunting or on their way home!"

Twenty minutes passed. Suddenly the ground beneath us started to shake. The wine in our glasses made slight ripples. Intermittent thuds that sounded like thunder became louder. Everyone fell silent, downing their knives and forks, wide-eyed and looking worried as the noise got closer, drums started beating and deep soulful male voices, chanting some sort of war cry, blasted out into the eerily quiet night. The ground started vibrating as the Zulu warriors entered the Boma. Native Zulu men of varying ages, wearing nothing but a loincloth barely covering their 'manhood', with decorative animal skin bands, decorated with beads, adorning their upper arms and ankles. They were all holding long spears in one hand and a shield made of either zebra or deer skin in the other. They continued stamping their feet into the red dusty earth. Once all the warriors were inside the boma, they made their way towards the centre, next to the fire. They stood in a row, and in unison, lifted their right leg high up into the air, way above their heads, then with all their force banged their foot down into the ground. The earth shook. They continued chanting, then repeated the sequence with the other leg as they made a circle around the fire. Their skin was glistening with sweat as they danced, with the light from the flames showing off their muscular buttocks each time they lifted a leg.

The guests were transfixed. Each warrior took his turn to come close to the tables and dance, before returning to the fire and continuing with the battle cry. This ritual continued, with each warrior engrossed in their own dance routine, before returning to the circle. In a split-second, and all in unison, the warriors stopped moving and chanting. They stood in a statuesque manner with sweat dripping down their muscular ebony-coloured skin. Their spears held high above their heads, and shields half covering their torsos. Silence. Nothing moving. No sound, other than the sound of the wild bush, and the crackling fire.

From the other side of the boma came the faint sound of native Zulu women, softly chanting in tribal ululation, growing louder and louder. From behind the tall elephant grass appeared young topless native girls wearing only a grass skirt, that didn't quite cover their buttocks. They too stamped their feet into the earth with the full weight of their muscular limbs and, approaching the guests, started shaking their 'booties' making the grass skirts dance and flicker in the firelight, showing off their round muscular buttocks beneath. Slowly moving forward even further, they started 'shimmying'. The men started banging their spears on the ground. As each of the girls congregated around the fire, they all dropped to their knees in front of the men. Silence. One by one, the girls took centre stage dancing to impress the warriors. They 'shimmied' and 'tweaked' in ways I never thought possible. They repeatedly raised their legs high, stamping their feet down onto the dry red earth with an almighty thud. It was like a can-can dance but with the added foot stomping. On their wristbands were tiny bells which tinkled in unison with the drummer's beat, and they were ululating wildly.

Again, in a split second, the drums stopped, the warriors stood perfectly still. The only sound was that of cicadas, and your heartbeat pulsating in your head. The natives walked silently to the exit and towards their village. The onlookers were sitting dead still, the silence broken only by the shrill call of a stray civet cat, hiding in the shadows, attracted by the smell of meat and dying embers, waiting for the scraps.

Applause erupted, followed by cheering and, although there were only twenty or so guests, in the still of the night, in the middle of the African bush, it sounded like Wembley Stadium.

Jackie told us the story of Shakaland where, apparently, the famous movie 'Shaka Zulu' had been filmed on this very location. The movie was named after an acclaimed warrior, King Shaka, who played an integral role in the identity of his people. The film was about this battle and after filming, all but one of the Zulu kraals were destroyed. The rondavel we were staying in had been especially built for the film director.

Most of the guests had now returned to their huts, leaving just a handful of us. We moved closer to the roaring fire, and listened as Raoul told us about life in the bush, and his many close encounters. "I have to admit," said Raoul, "in all my years as a ranger, I have never encountered three females and a baby, stranded in the middle of nowhere with no wine." We laughed and told them about our escapade and near-death experience with crocodiles, and getting lost in the bush.

"You should write a book, Margot, no one will believe it but you should write it, anyway. Tell us more about your escapades."

When we got back to the rondavel the native girl, who had been watching Sarah, had fallen asleep with Sarah next to her in her cot. "Oh Madam, I'm, sorry I fell—"

"It's no problem, thank you so much for sitting with her." I gave her some money and she smiled gratefully.

"Goodnight, Madam, if you need me tomorrow, please just ask Jackie to find me."

"Thank you so much. Goodnight."

With our tummies full, memories that would last forever, and extremely tired from the travelling and the heat and excitement, we all slept soundly. If there were mosquitoes, I certainly didn't hear them.

I was woken the following morning to the sound of people whispering loudly, "Come over here, you can see better, quickly." I jumped out of bed and ran to the window. There was a 'natural pool' amongst the umbrella thorn trees and I could just make out the shape of an elephant in the water, busily drinking. People had their cameras out clicking away as this majestic beast stood with not a care in the world. Suddenly she lifted her head, flayed her ears wide, and let out a long 'trumpeting' blast.

"What the hell was that, Margot?"

"Come and look quickly. Look over there by the huge tree, just behind the tree, can you see it?" The three of us watched as the baby calf stood between her mother's legs, suckling.

"That's why she was trumpeting, warning us to keep away from the calf. That's amazing to watch." I had tears in my eyes. Eventually the mother and her calf sauntered back into the bush. "Wow. You don't see that every day. Come on, let's go and get breakfast." Sarah was now awake jumping up and down in her cot.

The waft of smoke, sausages and bacon hit our nostrils as we entered the boma. Everyone was chatting excitedly about the visitors to the pool and Raoul was chatting to a group of people sitting drinking coffee by the fire. "We have a lot of visitors to the pool as you can imagine, but today, well, that was very special indeed. It's the first time that 'Nana' has brought her calf to see us."

"Do you have any problems with poachers in the area?"

"Good question, Sir, and I'm pleased to say that we don't have that problem. Poaching is more prevalent around the Kruger Park area."

"Have you ever seen a dead elephant Raoul?"

"Thank God, no, I haven't. Elephants are incredible creatures. They look after their elderly you know. When they become old and too weak to feed, they don't die gracefully of old age, they actually starve to death. Elephants have six sets of teeth over their life span, and when they've lost their sixth and last set of teeth, they can no longer strip bark themselves. The rest of the herd guide the elderly to softer marsh and swampland, where the pickings are easier for them to eat. When the old guy can no longer stand and, for many, dementia sets in, the herd guards him from predators until he finally dies and even after death, the family stays close to chase off scavengers. Elephants have been known to visit the bones of dead ones and pay respects for as long as the bones are there."

"A little like humans then, visiting the graveside of loved ones passed."

"Very much so, Margot, very much so. Anyway, enough of that, fascinating as it is. After breakfast, you'll be shown around the Zulu village and get a taste of some homemade delights and see the women making baskets and weaving blankets. Enjoy your breakfast and I'll see you back here in an hour's time."

As the tour began, we saw women sitting on the thatched rooves, busily fixing holes.

"As you can see ladies and gentlemen, the ladies are busy fixing any holes in the roof. Many tribes in Africa still live this way; the Bushmen of the Kalahari, for example. While the men are out hunting for the day's food, the women do chores, such as washing, the old-fashioned way in a tub and a wash board, just like my mum used to do back in the day. The young mothers of the tribes make bread and prepare vegetables, while the toddlers and babies are looked after by the elderly. The remaining girls and women make baskets and beaded gifts, such as earrings, and bangles to sell."

We arrived at a large thatched enclosure and were asked to sit and taste their local beer, which we drank from a ladle, made from a half coconut shell affixed to a long stick. At the far end of the hut were several warriors making spears and shields, and on the wall behind them, authentic shields which were used during the making of the film 'Shakazulu' were displayed, together with tribal masks and other carved items.

We finished the tour at around 10h00, and before departing for the long six-and-a-half-hour drive to the Kruger Park, we bought a few mementos from the gift shop, before saying goodbye to Jackie and Raoul.

"Jackie and Raoul, thank you so much for a most extraordinary two days. It's been an experience we'll never forget."

"It's been a pleasure to meet you all. Don't forget Margot, write that book."

"Maybe I will."

Before leaving, we hugged and shook hands, and Carol gave Jackie her telephone number and address, telling her that the next time they were back in the U.K., they shouldn't hesitate to get in touch.

I'd prepaid for all the excursions up to this point, and although we'd lost one night at the Kruger Park, the two nights spent in Shakazulu Land had more than made up for it.

Before entering the park, we stopped at Hazyview, a small town bordering the Kruger Park and bought groceries and wine. We arrived at the main gate shortly before dusk. We were greeted by a warrior, fully clad in his headgear of feathers and beads, and loincloth, and a shield in one hand and spear in the other. He welcomed us and gave us directions to Olifants Camp.

It took another hour before arriving at Olifants Camp. We checked in at reception, before being shown to our rondavel. We parked the now very 'dusty red' Escort and unloaded. "Look at the state of this car, Margot, inside and out. While you girls get the dinner on the go and see to Sarah, I'll give it a good clean."

"Thanks, Mum, you're a star. Come on, sis, let's light the braai." We prepared the meat and veg and lit the fire. I gave Sarah a quick bath and fed her and within an hour, she was fast asleep. Carol and I were sitting with a glass of chardonnay when Mum finally came to join us.

"You should have seen the crisp packets and chicken bones in the back of the car, bottles, plastic sandwich wrapper…"

"Chicken bones?"

"Yes, chicken bones. The ones Sarah kept hitting me over the head with. It kept her quiet, didn't it! By the way, don't they have funny tyres in Africa?"

"Tyres?"

"Yes, are you going deaf, Margot?"

159

"There's nothing weird with the tyres, they're the same as in the UK, rubber."

"Well, the ones on your car are made of hessian, there's no rubber, well maybe a little right in the middle, but the outside is 'hessian' looking."

"Oh my God, Margot." Carol got up and ran to the car to inspect the tyres. "Margot, come here quickly. Margot, there's no tread at all. Mum's right, you can see the hessian, on all four tyres. When's the last time you checked your tyres?"

"I've never checked my tyres, Rex's mechanic always does it."

"Margot, you've got to be kidding me, right?"

"Actually no, I had no idea."

"I don't believe it. When we leave here, we have to find the nearest garage and get new tyres. What if the police had stopped us?"

"We have traffic cops in Africa, not police, and they're about as interested as I am right now. Come on, let's put the meat on the braai."

The three of us sat sipping Chardonnay, the smell of wildlife in the air, smoke from the braai, cicadas buzzing when we suddenly heard an almighty roar. "Oh my God, what the hell, it came from over there." Mum pointed a few yards away where there was a fence securing a deep drop down to the Limpopo Riverbed and we went to investigate. We couldn't believe what we were seeing. There were hippos wallowing on the muddy banks, and 'blowing bubbles', or at least that's what it looked like they were doing. Zebra and deer were drinking, as were the giraffes, with their legs flayed awkwardly outwards with their long necks down between them to reach the water's edge. "Where are the binoculars, Mum?"

"You unpacked; how should I know?"

"Oh, never mind, we must remember to find them for tomorrow. It's going to be too dark to see just now, let's just watch while we can." We stood looking and listening to the wild African bush until the light faded.

"That was amazing, Margot, did you know our camp was right next to the river?"

"I'd like to say yes, but no, it was a total surprise to me too."

"What are those funny round things there?" asked Mum pointing to three large round objects on the BBQ. "Gem Squash. It's like a small marrow, but fleshier. I've put a big knob of butter in the middle with a little seasoning and wrapped them in foil. They taste lovely."

160

"Aren't you quite the little chef?" Carol said, as she sat with wine in one hand and cigarette in the other.

"Can I have a ciggy please sis?"

"Margot, I forbid you," she said it in a very low mocking 'Rex' voice.

"Oh my God, I wonder how Rex is. I haven't thought about him for days, thanks for that."

"Cheers, girls."

"Margot, you know when we came into the camp, at the main gate, did you see all those scars on the warrior's body? What were they?"

"It's called 'scarification'. It's an ancient method of tattooing."

"But what does it represent?"

"It means different things. For example, African women do it on their faces to 'enhance' their beauty; well, not so much these days because of the introduction of identity documents and of course AIDS, but primarily they used to do it to identify different ethnic groups, families and individuals."

"And how do they do it, do they go to a specialist to have it done?"

"No way, they use glass, coconut shells, a knife, any sharp object to cut into the skin carefully controlling the shape on each part of the body and face and then they put caustic plant juice into the open wound to cause blistering."

"Gross; surely, they get infections?"

"Yes, probably, but they have medicine for everything, they go to the *Sangoma*, the witch doctor."

"What did you do with the meat girls, that 'tough as old boots' stuff that they sold to us in Hazy whatever? It tastes amazing, and soft."

"Well, we just hammered it a little, then marinated it with red wine, herbs and seasoning. Shin beef is not as tough as you think, Mum, as you can taste."

"Anyway, Margot, back to the tattooing. What makes the scars so black, it's much blacker than the rest of their skin?"

"They rub the wound with charcoal pigment which makes the scar a dark colour to emphasise the shape."

"And we thought tattooing and piercing in the UK was horrific. It must be excruciatingly painful." Mum screwed her face up in disgust as I continued.

"A lot of the elder Africans still have the scars."

"How do you know all this, Margot?"

"Because I read a lot and watch numerous documentaries about the wildlife in Africa and the different tribes; it's fascinating."

"Well, who'd have thought it! Margot reading! I never saw you once at home with a book in your hand."

"No, she was always painting or drawing or sewing or making something, weren't you, Margot, always very creative?"

"Aww. Thanks, Mum, I got it from you. You taught me to draw and sew. Remember the day I sewed my first pillowcase, by hand, and sewed it to the tablecloth and when I stood up to show you, everything came off the table?"

"Oh yes, that was quite funny."

"Well, okay, 'Mrs Attenborough', how did the Kruger Park come into being?"

"It was established by President Paul Kruger, hence the name, back in 1898, but was only opened to the public in 1927. It was opened with a view to protecting wild animals, to let them live as natural a life as possible and I bet you didn't know that Gary Player's brother, you know the famous South African golfer, his brother Ian, Dr Ian Player was a game ranger, and in 1957, he pioneered the very first wilderness trails in the park and is known internationally for his work and involvement in conservation and introducing walking safaris during the 1950s and '60s." Carol's face was a picture.

"You're like a walking encyclopaedia, I'm impressed. What else do you know?"

"Well, if you're really interested, thanks to combining the Limpopo National Park in Mozambique, the Manlinil Pan Sanctuary and Malipati Safari in Zimbabwe and the Gonarezhou National Park into a transfrontier park, there are 20,000 square kilometres of land. However, there are border restrictions and you have to pay to cross each of the country's borders. There are very strict and effective measures in place for the prevention of poaching, which means that all cars are inspected upon arrival and departure from the park. Just in case you have a gun or any traps, or maybe the odd warthog or springbok in the boot of your car."

"So how come they didn't search our car on the way in?"

"Oh, for God's sake, Mum! Do we look like poachers?"

"Do real poachers look like poachers? Isn't that the problem, who can tell who is and who isn't?"

"Good question, actually. Let's see if they check us on the way out, want a bet anyone?"

"Okay, Carol, you're on, whoever loses the bet pays for the new tyres."

"You're on, Margot." We shook hands and I started praying they would check the car.

The following morning, I woke early with a terrible thirst and was fumbling around trying not to wake anyone when Mum said, "Margot, is that you, what are you doing?"

"I'm parched, where's that huge bottle of water?"

"On the floor under the table, why are we whispering?"

"Didn't want to wake Sarah." I found the water and poured two glasses when Carol came through.

"Me too, I'm parched!" We were busy glugging down the water in the darkness when we heard, "Mama, mama."

"Sarah just said 'mama'. Oh wow!" I switched the light on and Sarah was stood in the middle of her cot jumping up and down.

"I bet she wondered why we were all walking around in the dark, whispering. Idiots."

"Hey sweetie, did you sleep well? Come on, let's make you a bottle. You know what we saw last night, Sarah, hippos and elephants, we'll go for a drive later and see if we can find them again." I took Sarah and placed her on the bed with Mum while I made her bottle.

"It's so humid already and it's not even six yet. Is there a swimming pool anywhere?"

"What do you think this is, the South of France? We're in the middle of the African bush, so no, there's no pool, unless you want to take a dip with the hippos."

"Sarah's burning up, her vest is soaked through, the poor thing. Shall I take it off?"

"Ye, can do, take her nappy off too, I've got an idea."

We had a large cool box which was now empty so I filled it with water and took it outside and placed Sarah in it. Her little face lit up and she started splashing around and chuckling. "There you go Sarah, your very own swimming pool." We all sat and watched the sun rise over the Lebombo Mountains, a narrow range stretching from Hluhluwe in Natal in the south, to Punda Market in the Limpopo Province in the north, some five hundred miles long, while we waited for the coffee to brew. Once the sun peaked its head over the top of Lebombo, the land came alive. The morning chorus of birds began as the stalkers of the night who had now found refuge in caves, high trees, or bushes, with tummies full, tried to sleep through the hot daylight hours. "What's the plan today, Margot?"

"We'll pack a lunch, plenty of water and go on our own safari, Escort style."

Carol just looked at me. "In that scrap heap, bald tyres and no air con, are you mad? We won't last an hour in the heat."

"Well, what else do you suggest sis? We can ask at reception how much a guided safari is but it won't be cheap."

"I'm only going to be here once, let's go and find out, I'll pay."

"Okie-dokey, let's do it. But you do remember last night, that we have a bet going on, about the car being checked when we leave, and that's going to cost a bit."

"What makes you think you're going to win the bet Margot, there's no way they'll check the car."

"Okay, your money."

Carol and I ambled down to the reception to make enquiries about a safari tour.

"Good morning, Madam, how may I help you today?"

A cheerful young woman at reception sat behind a huge carved wooden desk, surrounded by antlers and animals carved from wood.

"We wanted to know the price for a day's safari, or half day, whatever."

"How many people will there be?"

"Three grown-ups and a baby."

"Certainly, Madam, what is your name?" I gave her the booking details and names and she found us on the computer. "I see you checked in a day late, Madam, did you have a problem getting here?"

"Yes, actually we were lost in Kwa Zulu Natal and ended up in Shakaland and were too late to make the gate before closing."

"Please wait here while I ask the ranger about the safari."

"Thanks."

When the lady returned, she had a ranger with her.

"Good morning, ladies, I believe you want to go on safari."

"Yes, we'd like to know how much it is and what is included, for example food and drink, etc."

"Of course. Betsy here tells me you were delayed in checking in due to getting lost. Is that right?"

"Yes."

"In that case, we can take you on a half-day safari, which will be quite tiring out in the heat, especially with a baby on board, and there will be no charge."

"Really, well that's so kind of you... What's your name?"

"Lucas, everyone calls me Luke."

"Thanks, Luke, do we need to bring anything?"

"Just yourselves. I'll swing by at eight to pick you up from your hut, just make sure you have hats and sun cream."

"Thanks again, Luke, see you later." When we got back to the rondavel, Mum had brewed the coffee and we told her the good news about the free African safari experience.

"Margot, I can't believe how lucky we've been, the people here in Africa are so lovely, so accommodating. If this had happened in the UK, there's no way you'd get any sort of compensation for checking in late, no matter what the circumstances were."

"That's why I have no intention of ever going home, Mum. I love Africa, really, I love it." I saw a tear in her eye the minute I said it, but it was too late, it was said.

"You always were a wanderer, Margot; first Denmark, then the USA, now Africa, I often wonder where you'll end up."

"I will end up here in Africa, Mum, there's nothing about Africa that I don't love. Don't you remember when I was growing up and people used to ask, 'What are you going to be when you grow up, Margot?' And my reply was always, 'I don't know yet, but it won't be here in the UK.' Well, this is it, this is where I'm meant to be."

"Yes, I remember you saying that Margot" Then the tears came.

"Oh Mum, no, don't cry, this is a happy time and being on holiday with both of you here in Africa is the icing on the cake. And it's not over yet. Come on, let's get ready to see the 'big five'."

"Big five?" asked Carol.

"God damn it, sis, don't you know anything about Africa?"

"No, but by the time I get back, I'll be able to teach the subject."

"Very funny. Now come on, seriously, I'll tell you about the big five as and when we see them."

At eight on the dot, Luke was outside in his jeep. "Come on, girls, let's go safari."

"Have you got the binoculars, Mum?"

"Yep, and hats, and sun cream and Sarah's nappy and bottle." We jumped into the back of the jeep, secured Sarah into her baby seat and off we went. "Good morning, ladies. Firstly, let me introduce myself. I'm Luke, and this is Bheki, my tracker for the day." Bheki, a young black man was sitting at the rear of the jeep holding a double-barrel 12-bore shotgun.

"*Sawubona*, Madams. I will be looking after you today while we track the animals."

"Bheki has been with us for four years and knows every inch of the park. We are in radio contact with other jeeps and once we get into the thick of the bush, we will receive the locations of the big five. You must remain in the jeep at all times unless accompanied by myself and Bheki. When we stop to look for animals, you must be quiet. Okay, let's go."

"This is so exciting, Margot, my heart's beating so fast. I hope we see elephants."

"I'm sure we will."

"We're heading first to the major watering hole not too far away."

"We saw the animals in the river last night, hippos and elephants were making lots of noise, it was incredible. We saw zebra and lots of deer too."

"You were lucky Madam; they normally drink further down river. The rains from a couple of days ago must have made its way down the mountains and filled the *wadi*."

"What's a '*wadi*', Margot?" Mum whispered.

"A dried-up riverbed that only has water when it rains a lot. Here in Africa, there's a lot of droughts, so invariably the rivers are bone dry, a '*wadi*'."

"Thanks, Britannica!"

"Ha bloody ha."

On the way to the water hole, we saw lots of impala racing through the thick bush.

"Look you two, we'll see hundreds of those. They're called impala and are only found in Africa and are easily identifiable by the black and white 'M' like the McDonald's 'M', on their rear end. Very apt as they are known as fast food for most predators."

"Luke, cut the engine," said Bheki. "Over there on the right, look ladies, a kudu, the Greater Kudu. There is another type of kudu, the Lesser Kudu but it's only found in East Africa. To tell the difference is easy. You see the thin white stripes on his back, you see, Madam? Well, the Lesser Kudu, although he is much smaller, he has many more stripes, up to fourteen, while this bigger one has only six or seven stripes."

Mum interrupted. "How do you know it's a male, you can't see their 'bits and pieces' from this far away?"

I cringed with embarrassment.

"Mum! Really?"

Bheki laughed. "It's okay, Madam, it's a very good question 'Mummy', and a valid one. As you probably know in the animal kingdom, and indeed the bird kingdom, the male species are usually the more beautiful of the species. Take the peacock for example, what could be more beautiful that to watch him open his 'fan' or 'train' of feathers. The secret to the brilliant colours in a peacock's tail is the tiny crystals within the feathers which act like a kaleidoscope, splitting light into the different colours of the spectrum. The peacock's brilliant 'train' contains over 200 shimmering feathers, each one decorated with eyespots. The male Indian peacock has iridescent colouring of blue and green on its head, neck and breast and are the most common. The males display their beautiful feather trains as part of their courting ritual to attract the peahens. It is only during the moulting season, when the males shed their train feathers that their grey quill feathers are more obvious. Female peahens lack the bright colours of the male and have a duller appearance which is common in many other bird species. Peahens are generally brown in colour with lighter underparts. They also lack the long upper tail coverts, but they do have some iridescent green colouring on their necks and of course both male and female peahen have crests on top of their heads which are also iridescent. I'm rambling. Sorry, Madam. In answer to your question, Madam, it is in this instance, only the male kudu has horns, and that is how you tell them apart. The horns are very distinctive also. You see, Madam, they are very large and curved." Bheki was in his element. You could see the love in his eyes and hear the enthusiasm in his words. He truly loved the animals and the bush.

We looked through the binoculars but were too far away for a decent photo. Luke started the engine up and we continued along the very bumpy dirt road. Eventually, we came to the watering hole. Luke pointed to what looked like a shack in amongst the bushes and trees. "We're going to have lunch over there. It's called a 'hide'. We can watch any animals that come to the water and because they won't be able to see us, they won't run away. We should be able to get some good pictures."

Apart from the many different species of deer, we were graced with the presence of a family of elephants, a handful of buffalo and a lone cheetah.

It soon came time to head back to camp and to think about getting ready for the long drive ahead of us.

We said our goodbyes to all the staff and headed for the main gate out of the park. The drive was hot and dusty and all the effort Mum had put into cleaning the car had been in vain. Before we reached the gate, it was covered once again in red dust. The barriers were down and a guard appeared from his little hut under a baobab tree. "Hello, Madam. Did you enjoy your stay?"

"It was fabulous, thank you for asking."

"And where are you going now, ladies?"

"Johannesburg. By the way, can you tell us where the nearest garage is where we can buy tyres?"

"Hazyview is the nearest town, you can get tyres there." He walked around the car inspecting the tyres. "Shish, I hope you make it to Hazyview. Your tyres are very bad, Madam. Do you have a spare wheel in the boot?"

"I have no idea."

"Then I will check for you." He went to the rear and opened the boot, removing the cases in order to get to the spare. He put everything back and came around to my window. "There is no spare wheel, Madam, and it is a long way back to Johannesburg. Please make sure you get new tyres and really, Madam, you should also get a spare wheel. It is an offence to drive without one. If those speeding policemen stop you, you will be in such bad trouble." I smiled to myself.

"Thank you so much for your help." I gave him a few rand and thanked him for his kindness.

He opened the barriers to let us through and waved goodbye. "That was very clever of him, don't you think, Carol?"

"What was clever?"

"Opening the boot on the pretext of seeing if we had a spare wheel. He was really looking for poached goods."

"Don't be ridiculous Margot, he was genuinely concerned and was doing us a favour."

"Oh dear, how naive you are. You have no idea how clever these people are. When you've been here as long as I have, you'll get to know how crafty they are. He wasn't likely to ask if we had anything illegal in the boot. Very clever. I'm impressed."

"If you say so, Margot." I saw the look on her face through the rear-view mirror. Not a happy bunny. She reminded me of Rex a little, couldn't bear to be wrong.

Chapter 22

The Truce

We stopped in Hazyview to get the tyres changed, and while we waited, I called Grant to ask if we could stay with him for a few days.

We arrived in Johannesburg a little after 18h00 and Grant was waiting with open arms at the door as we pulled up. "Hi sweetie. I thought your car was blue?" He chuckled that familiar way I loved as we hugged.

"You wouldn't believe we cleaned it before we left the Kruger Park, idiots. I should have known better."

"Hello Ida, Carol. Glad you managed to keep our little secret."

"Hi Grant, it's so nice to finally meet you." Carol gave him a hug.

"Leave the bags, I'll get them later. Come on through, I've got the wine on ice."

"Now that's more like it, lead the way." We followed Grant out to the poolside. "I'm going to give Sarah a bath and give her some food, it's been a long hot day and she must be tired."

When I got back to the poolside, they were discussing what to have for supper.

"I'm a little fed up of barbequed food Margot, can't we go to a restaurant?"

"Great idea, Carol, I know just the place. Everyone okay with that?"

I looked at Mum and she agreed.

"Let's go and get ready, I'm starving." Sarah was fast asleep in her carrycot by the time we got to the restaurant.

Grant thoroughly enjoyed the company during our two-day stay, especially time spent with Sarah. He adored her. Mum and Carol thought he was great, such a contrast to Rex and his overbearing behaviour. On Tuesday morning, we piled into the old Fiesta for our trip down to Durban Airport. I knew from previous drives down there for a weekend break that it was going to take six hours, at least.

When it came time for Mum and Carol to go through to the departure lounge, the tears came.

"We've had such a great holiday, Margot. Apart from a few hiccups at the beginning. It's been, without a doubt, the best holiday I've ever had and that's saying something."

Carol and her wealthy husband had been all over the world, and nine times out of ten they took Mum and Arnold with them.

"You're so welcome, I loved it too. Will you come again?"

Carol looked at Mum, "Well, maybe. I wonder if Rex would have been different if John had come along."

"I doubt it Carol, he's just an anti-social control-freak. Why? Does John want to come to Africa?"

"Yes, he'd love to. Maybe in a couple of years' time, but he won't be staying in the same house as Rex, I can assure you. We'll have hotels booked throughout."

"Maybe Rex will have learned his lesson after this time. I've rather enjoyed our holiday without him. He's always been the same, you know, very demanding and bossy and I don't like it much."

We all waved to one another as they went through to the departure lounge. I headed off to the car park with Sarah in her stroller, and tears flowing down my face.

As Sarah and I drove away from the airport, the reality of what was coming next hit me. I had to go and face the music with Rex. Driving up the hill towards Kloof, I started to get anxious, my stomach was churning over. I saw his Mercedes in the driveway as I approached, my heart started racing. I got out of the car and opened the gate. As I drove through, I saw Rex at the front door. I closed the gates behind me and drove towards the house. Rex came towards the car and opened the door. I had no idea what to say to him. I got out and took Sarah from her car seat.

He wrapped his arms around the pair of us and kissed the top of Sarah's head.

"Thank God you came back, Margot. I thought I'd lost you forever."

"I'm not sure that you haven't."

"Have you eaten?"

"No, I came straight from the airport. I wanted to… well, I don't know what I wanted to do, Rex. I have no idea anymore which direction our relationship is heading. Do you, Rex?"

"Let's go inside and I'll get us a drink. I bet Sarah's hungry."

He took her from my arms and I followed him into the house. It felt strange to be home. I was still battling with calling this my home. So much had happened, and after all, this was Rex and Janet's love nest when they left me and Sarah in Johannesburg, without a second thought of how I, we, would manage.

I bathed and fed Sarah and within the hour, she was fast asleep. I watched Rex as he stood at the braai, turning the meat and sipping his beer. Neither of us had broached the subject of my disappearing. However, knowing that I had a history of running away at the first sign of conflict, and Rex, being fully aware of this too, it was unlikely that either of us was going to start the inevitable war. Rex went into the house to fetch another beer.

"Margot, come to my office."

We made manic, wild love, and the matter was never discussed again.

The next six months went relatively smoothly between Rex and I. Maybe our time apart had made him take a good long look at himself and to figure out what he wanted from life.

Every other weekend, at least, we ventured to places old and new, including a re-visit to the Drakensburg. Just the three of us. We stayed in a hotel and made full use of all the amenities, including the gymnasium, jacuzzi, steam room and of course the pool. I made a visit to the spa, and had a facial and full body massage while Rex looked after Sarah. It was perfect.

"I love you so much Rex, and I'm so happy we are finally on the right track."

"Me too Margot, me too."

Chapter 23

December 1989

Our routine in Kloof was torn apart one afternoon in December, when Rex came home earlier than usual.

"Hi Rex! What are you doing home so early." I flung my arms around him and kissed him. He didn't really kiss me back or hold me.

"I've been fired."

I released my grip and took a step back from him.

"What do you mean fired? How can you get fired, you're the boss!"

"Margot, I'm the managing director of a large company, yes, but I also report to someone. I have no idea why, but I was asked to pack up any personal belongings and leave the building straight away."

"Oh my God Rex. Have you no idea at all why? Can I make you a coffee?"

"I need a beer, please. Thank God I'm only renting this house."

We sat out on the stoop discussing what to do next.

"Are we going to stay in Durban or move back to Johannesburg, Rex?"

"There are more job opportunities in Johannesburg. I'll have to start job hunting. I might even try and buy my own company to manage. I'm tired of reporting to other people."

"It's called a company buy out, isn't it? When a company's not doing so well and it gets sold on."

"How do you know about that sort of thing, Margot?"

"I haven't been a PA for all these years and learned nothing about business. Give me some credit."

"I'm impressed."

"Well, that's a first, Rex!"

"And what do you mean by that?"

"Oh, come on, Rex, you treat, or used to treat me like one of your employees. You certainly didn't treat me like a wife." He laughed that annoying artificial laugh.

"We're not married, Margot."

"Okay, partner then. It's just as well we weren't married, otherwise you'd be on your second divorce, and before you say another word, forget it. I can see this ending up badly."

It only took a couple of weeks for Rex to find a company in Johannesburg to go and take a look at and by the middle of January1989, all our belongings were packed and ready to be transported and put into storage. Then out of the blue came a request that blew my mind.

"Margot, it's going to be pretty hard going for us both to stay in a hotel, especially with the baby. I need my sleep, and with all three of us, even in a large room, it will be difficult. Sarah wakes up in the night and I can't be disturbed."

"Then we'll have to have two rooms, won't we?"

"But it might take months to find another house, you know how long it takes to buy property. It'll cost a fortune."

"Well, we'll have to rent another house for a couple of months then, won't we? Surely that would be cheaper than paying for a hotel for three months? In any event, just where do you think me and Sarah are going to stay, if not with you Rex?"

I was busting at the gut to find out where this was going.

"I thought you could go and stay with Grant. You said you were good friends, surely, he will be only too glad to help you." I smelt a RAT. A really big one.

"Oh, did you now? The last time I went to lunch with Grant, you went berserk! Now you want me and Sarah to go and live with him? Or crudely put, to use him again to your own ends. You really are something else, do you know that?" I got up and instead of taking my glass for a refill, I fetched the bottle and filled my glass to the top, keeping it handy for the next one. "Anything else up your sleeve I should know about, Rex?"

"Margot, this is difficult enough; please let's not argue."

"I'm not arguing, Rex. I'm so flabbergasted at your suggestion. I have no words. Are you sure this is what you want me to do Rex? How awkward it will be for everyone, for you to come to Grants' house to see me and your daughter, don't you agree?"

I rang Grant, and before I'd even finished the sentence, he said simply; "Anything Margot, anything for you and Sarah. Of course you can stay, for as long as you want."

Rex and I set off for Johannesburg the following morning, me and Sarah in my old Fiesta and Rex in his all singing and dancing Mercedes. It must have been hell for him to keep at such a low speed but my car didn't go past sixty. About halfway through the journey, I heard Sarah being sick and she started coughing and choking and I had to pull over on the hard shoulder of the motorway. With hazards blaring I pulled Sarah out of the car. She was covered in vomit and was soaking wet. I rummaged in the boot for a change of clothes and sat on the grass verge until she had recovered. Rex had been too far in front to stop and obviously he couldn't turn around on a motorway.

When I arrived at Grant's house, Sarah was asleep. I was hot, tired and very hungry. No sign of Rex. "Hey, sweetie, come on in," said Grant. "I'll get Sarah out of the car, you go and put the kettle on."

After Grant had unloaded the car, we sat by the pool and had a cup of tea and a chat. "You don't look happy, Margot. What's happened now?"

"I smell a *rat*, Grant, mark my words, all is not what it seems."

I told him what had transpired and giving Rex the benefit of the doubt, he said, "I can see his point, Margot. Living in a hotel for months on end isn't ideal, especially with a baby. You need space to breathe. How are you going to look for work if you're stuck in a hotel?"

"I suppose you have a point but what if we had no one to help us, we'd have had to make another plan wouldn't we? I just think it's very odd. We'd only just made up and got things back on track, and then this. I'm confused."

"No good worrying, Margot. You'll be safe here with me. Shall I light the braai, you must be hungry?"

Two weeks passed and I hadn't heard a thing from Rex, then, out of the blue, the phone rang. "Hello."

"Margot?"

"Yes. Who's this?"

"It's Janet. I wondered if you'd heard from Rex recently?"

"No, as a matter of fact I haven't."

"That doesn't surprise me. Look, Margot, he came to see me two weeks ago and asked me to go and look at houses with him."

I slammed the receiver down. It rang again.

"Janet, I don't want to talk to you or Rex ever again."

"Margot, please listen to me, don't hang up. Are you there, Margot?"

"Yes."

"I told Rex that the divorce is going ahead and to leave me alone. I just thought you should know, that's all. I'm a little worried that you haven't heard from him."

"He'll be too embarrassed and quite rightly so. Thanks for letting me know, Janet, and for what it's worth, I'm sorry for everything." I hung up.

When Grant got home, I told him about the call from Janet. "I told you I smelt a *rat*. That's why he wanted me out of the way so he could try and lure Janet back into his life. What a total ass. Do you know what Grant, I'll have the last laugh."

"Good morning, Pickfords Removals, how can I help you?"

"Good morning. My name is Margot Charrington. My husband and I have furniture in storage and we need to take some of the items. Would this be possible?"

"Yes, of course. I just need a few details. Where did you move from, Margot?"

"Kloof in Natal. We moved up a couple of weeks ago and we've found a small rental for the time being, until we're settled, so we don't need all the things."

"That's fine, Margot. It will be quite a job looking through the many crates but of course it can be done. Let me know what time you're coming and I'll have two of my men to help you sort through."

"Thank you so much. How much will it cost, please?"

"It'll depend on how big a truck you need. We can sort that out later."

"Super. I'll be there at eleven o' clock, and could you give me the address, please? Rex has all the documents locked in his office."

Grant was at work, on a long-haul flight, and wouldn't be back for a couple of days. I asked Jacob the gardener and his friend to take all Grant's old furniture from the lounge and stack it in the garage. Grant's maid, Josephine, took all the old dark curtains down and cleaned the white slatted wooden blinds and windows. What a difference just the sparkling windows made. Once the lounge was empty. Josephine cleaned and polished the beautiful parquet flooring, which, hidden by drab and tatty brown rugs, now took centre stage. With the sun beaming in through the windows, casting shadows of light across the floor, it looked very grand. I called my three helpers and gave them more tasks to do while I went and fetched the new furniture.

Chapter 24

The Big Reveal

I heard Grant's old Toyota Cruiser pull up outside and jumped up to go and greet him. "Hi, sweetie, what have you been up to today?"

He gave me huge hug and a peck on the cheek and followed me into the house. It took him a while to speak. He started laughing.

"Oh my God, Margot, what have you done? This place looks amazing. Where did all this stuff come from?" He went and sat on one of the huge four-seater, off-white sofas, hands crossed behind his head, still laughing.

"You were right, my furniture made the place look tired and dreary. I can't believe what a difference, and look at the floor, I had no idea how beautiful it was. This deserves a celebration." He disappeared into the kitchen and returned with a bottle of Moêt and two glasses. I could see Josephine and Jacob hovering outside trying to see what was going on.

"Grant, could we spare a glass for my helpers?" I pointed with my eyes in the direction of the garden house. "Sure thing, sweetie." He waved Josephine and Jacob to come into the house.

"Hi Jacob, would you like a beer or a glass of this?" He showed Jacob the bottle.

"Oh boss, that wine is too sweet, I would prefer a beer, thank you."

"Josephine, what about you?" She was crying.

"Oh boss, I never tasted alcohol before, I think it make me go crazy. I make a rooibos instead." Grant took his wallet from his back pocket and took out two R100 notes.

I whispered in his ear, "His friend helped as well." He took out another note and handed two to Jacob and one to Josephine. "Make sure your friend gets one of these, Jacob."

"Yes, boss, I will be sure to give it to him. Thank you."

"Oh boss, and Madam, you are so kind. Thank you. No white person ever offer me to drink before, I so very happy." Josephine started crying.

Grant chuckled, "Thanks for all your hard work, both of you, and you too, Margot." He gave me a quick hug. I heard Sarah chuckling away in her cot. She very seldom cried. "I'll go." Grant went and got Sarah. His face was beaming when he came through, and she was playing with his dark curly hair. "Look what Mummy did to the house, sweetie, doesn't it look great?"

Jacob and Josephine finished their drinks and bade us goodnight. "I've got something for you." He went and fetched his small cabin case from the hallway and took out a small bag. "There you go. I hope it's the right stuff."

"Juvena! Oh my God, Grant, it's the best stuff, how did you know?"

"It's not rocket science, Margot, I saw all the little bottles and jars on your dressing table." He started giggling. "Oh, there's another little something here." He took his jacket from the sofa and produced a bottle of Chanel No 5 perfume from the inside pocket. "Another little perk of the job. I get special discount off any items unsold on board."

The next thing that needed bringing into the twentieth century was Grant's dress sense. I took him into town on his next day off and got him totally rigged out, top to toe. Don't get me wrong, in his uniform, he looked like a movie star but *a lad bought up on a farm!* His preference was always shorts and takkies (trainers), which was fine for messing around the house and garden or working on old cars in the backyard.

I hadn't heard a word from Rex in over a month and so I decided to give it a go with Grant who cherished the ground I walked on, and he obviously adored Sarah.

Chapter 25

The Little Lie

Grant decided it was time to introduce me to his parents. They lived on a massive farm in the middle of Natal's agricultural band. "Not far to go now, sweetie, are you nervous?"

"No, not at all, should I be?"

"No. They'll love you, just like I do."

"Look at all those huge daisies, Grant, I've never seen them that big before."

"They're not daisies, sweetie, they're sunflowers." Grant was laughing. "My dad has acres of them, but the main crop is maize, corn! Maybe we'll get to go on the combine harvester, it's great fun."

"Does he have any cattle or sheep?"

"He sure does. He's got horses too, can you ride?"

"Never tried, but I'd like to give it a go."

"Ye ha, giddy up, girly." He put his foot down on the accelerator and we sped along the country lanes. *You can take the cowboy out of a ranch, but you can't take the ranch out of a cowboy!* I loved it.

"Grant, what are we going to tell your parents about Sarah?"

"Good question, Margot. They're simple country folk, they'd never understand the truth! We'd better tell them a little lie."

"Okay, Daddy you are then!"

There was nothing to worry about; his parents were delightful. When his mother caught a glimpse of Sarah, she started crying. "Why didn't you tell me I'm a grandma? She's your double, Margot, let me take her." She took Sarah from Grant's arms and held her close, kissing her face and head. His dad stood quietly smoking a huge cigar.

"Well, son, you kept all this quiet. Beer?" We all went and sat on the stoop which overlooked acres of farmland. His mum took a while to stop crying and

180

Grant and his father jabbered on in Afrikaans. I knew Grant had four brothers who supposedly worked on the farm and was just about to ask where they were when I heard the unmistakable sound of a tractor. I could see a huge machine in one of the fields churning up dust. "The boys are out harvesting. There's heavy rain forecast for Monday and you know what that means, Grant. It could have a catastrophic effect on crop damage. We'll need your help tomorrow. All crops need to be done by Sunday evening and I don't need to tell you how much work is involved."

"No sweat, Pa, been a long time since I drove the combine."

When the boys came in from the fields, they were covered in dust and crop debris. After a quick introduction, the boys went off to shower, then joined us out on the stoop for a sundowner, followed by a supper of succulent hand-reared steak, cooked to perfection on the braai by Grant. Everyone made a fuss of Sarah and she was passed from knee to knee. I didn't understand a word of Afrikaans and Grant tried his best to translate. It reminded me of early days with Jorgen.

The following morning at the crack of dawn, and I mean literally the crack of, Grant bought coffee and fresh-baked bread and conserves on a tray.

"Morning sweetie, it's going to be a long day. Do you want to come out on the harvester with me? Don't worry, Mum is looking forward to having Sarah all to herself."

His Mum packed us a couple of sandwiches and koeksisters, a flask of coffee and a few bottles of water.

By nine thirty it was already 28 degrees. There wasn't a cloud in the sky and apart from a small canopy over the cabin of the harvester, there was nowhere to escape the sun's rays. "Grant, I'm melting!"

"See those trees over there?" he pointed. "I've got a surprise for you sweetie."

"Oh ya, what is it?" He just laughed.

"You'll have to wait and see."

As we approached the cluster of trees, I noticed a huge tin cylindrical object in between the trees. "There you go, Margot, our very own swimming pool." There was a ladder affixed to the side of the huge tub. He cut the engine and helped me out of the cabin. "It's one of many water butts scattered around the farm and it's the only source of water on the farm. No rain, no water, no rain, no crops, too much rain can be a disaster as well as no rain." He stripped his clothes off. "What are you waiting for, there's nobody to see us."

I stripped off too, down to my panties anyway. He climbed up the steep ladder and waited for me at the top. We both sat on the side of the butt looking down.

"Remind you of anything, Grant?"

"It sure does, that seems like a lifetime ago. It was such fun at the Carnival, wasn't it? It's a good job there's rain forecast, she's quite low. Okay, after three. One, two, thr—"

"Hang on, how do we get out of here?"

"You'll have to stand on my shoulders, and... I'm joking silly, you should see your face. There's a ladder on the inside too. One, two, three..." It was a shock to the system, so cold but oh so invigorating. We splashed around for twenty minutes or so and had a quick drink and a bite to eat, before we dressed and got back into the harvester.

The heat became unbearable very quickly, and by midday, I'd had enough. Grant and I headed for the house. Sarah was in her baby bouncer seat on the kitchen table watching grandma bake bread and cookies.

"We were wondering how long you'd last out there. Come and sit down while I get you a nice glass of lemonade. It's hard work on a farm, non-stop from sunup till sunrise."

"I lived on a ranch in the USA for three months, a long time ago now. I know exactly how hard it is getting up at sunrise and working till dusk. It takes a certain kind of person. I used to look after the stray calves found wandering around in the mountains. They were adorable. I gave them all names, and in the morning, when I called them, they all came running down the garden for their breakfast."

"What took you to the USA Margot?"

"I was married at quite a young age. My husband was an adventurer and we travelled to lots of places, ending up here in South Africa. It was his childhood dream to become a cowboy, and when he was offered the chance in Idaho, he took it."

"How long were you married to him Margot?"

"For fifteen years."

I didn't tell her that I'd married him twice or the fact that he was a drunken, violent man. *God help me if she ever found out that Sarah wasn't her 'real' grandchild.*

We only stayed for three days as Grant had to be at work, another long haul to Brazil.

We promised we'd visit again when Grant had more time off.

We bade them **farewell**, hugged and cried again, and off we set for the big city.

Chapter 26

I was alone at home one evening when the doorbell rang. "Madam, it's someone to see you."

"Thanks Josephine, coming." With Sarah in my arms, I headed to the front door. "Jesus. Rex. What the hell are you doing here?"

"Nice to see you too, Margot. Are you going to invite me in?"

"Actually, no. I don't think it's a good—Rex, I said no." He pushed past me and headed for the lounge. He stood motionless for a few seconds, then slowly started looking around the room, taking it all in. "Very nice. My furniture looks good in here."

"Your furniture! It's the least you could do, Rex. I haven't heard a peep from you since we left Natal, not even a phone call to see if we had enough money to get by. Some father you've turned out to be. It's laughable Rex, also disgraceful behaviour for an 'educated' man. Palming your responsibilities off onto another man."

"How could you be so sneaky, Margot, taking things that don't belong to you?"

"Well, I've heard it all now. Me, you call me sneaky? Mr Control Freak extraordinaire. You definitely take first prize for sneakiness. Quite a conversation I had with Janet some weeks back now. What did you think I was going to do, come running back for sloppy seconds again? You'd better leave before I call the police, Rex."

"Go ahead, Margot, it'll save me the trouble." He sat down. "Got any beer?" He picked Sarah out of her seat and sat her on his knee. "Hello, Sarah. I've missed you so much." I saw his lips quiver slightly, trying to hold back a tear. I went and got him a beer and I sat on the sofa opposite him and sipped my wine.

"How's the new company, Rex? Did it all go through?"

"Yes, it's all up and running. It's hard work and quite a commute every day but at least it's all mine."

"Well done."

"Are you working, Margot?"

"Of course. I'm PA to a director of a multi-national company based in Bryanston. I've been there two months."

"Bryanston? It's a long commute for you from Benoni."

"I'm used to it."

"I see you've still got your old Escort. I thought it would have 'died' by now." He started laughing and then he realised that I wasn't.

"It died a long time ago, Rex, you just chose not to acknowledge the fact."

"Look, I know I've been unfair, Margot, it's not easy going through a divorce. The thing is, Margot, I love you, so much. You and Sarah are my world. Please come home." He was crying now.

"So, you're divorced now, Rex?"

"Yep. I got my Decree Nisi last week, which is part of the reason I'm here, Margot. Most of the things you took are Janet's, the cane and wicker bedroom suite for one and the two large sofas. She wants them back. I had no idea that you'd taken things until last week when the divorce was made final and I went to the storage place. I felt a right fool."

"I should have taken the leather Chesterfields and the mahogany bedroom suite, but I wanted to cheer the place up. I'm not keen on dark furniture. So, what are you going to do now Rex?"

"What time's Grant coming back?"

"He's on a long haul, not back till the weekend."

"Have you and him been having 'relations', Margot?"

"It's none of your damn business. How were your 'relations' over the last months? Yes, I thought as much. Silence says so much, don't you think, Rex?"

"I'm going now, Madam, goodnight."

"Thanks Josephine, good night. I'll see you in the morning."

Rex and I chatted and had more to drink and he ended up staying the night.

The following morning, I got up and made coffee and we sat out by the pool while I fed Sarah her breakfast.

"What happens now, Margot?"

"I guess you'd better have the furniture collected and maybe give me some money so I can buy some more. We can't sit on the floor, can we?"

"But we slept together last night Margot. Didn't it mean anything to you?"

"It meant the world to me, Rex, as I haven't had sex for weeks, so thank you."

"You mean you haven't slept with Grant?"

"Of course not. He's gay. I told you before we're just friends, but you are so jealous and judgemental you just can't see past the end of your damn nose."

"Well, why don't you at least come and have a look at the house Margot, you'll love it."

"For 'US'? You mean for you and Janet, but she told you to go to hell? Which is what I should be doing. But then she didn't have a child to think about, did she?"

"Margot, that's not fair. We almost destroyed her. We were married for ten years and she idolised me."

"It still doesn't take away the fact that I have to think about Sarah. Are you serious this time? Is your intention to act like a husband and a father or am I going to be your 'play thing' again until you get bored?"

"No, of course not. I love you so much. Please, just come and have a look. There's no harm in that."

The new house Rex had bought was magnificent; a lovely family home, in Douglasdale, near to Sandton in the northern suburbs.

"Do you like it?"

"It's rather big for one person."

"I didn't buy it for one person, Margot. This is our forever home." He pulled me towards him. As long as that 'magic' was there, I couldn't resist him.

Chapter 27

History Repeating Itself

We'd been in the new house for fourteen months and finally things were going extremely well between us. "I've got something to tell you, Rex, I'm so excited."

"Well, what is it, Margot?"

"No, Rex darling, I can't tell you over the phone, it's just too exciting, it's a celebratory kind of surprise."

"I'm not keen on surprises, Margot, just tell me."

"I'm pregnant. Hello. Rex, are you still there?"

"I'll talk to you later, Margot." The line went dead.

Two days later, I was going through the arrivals gate at Heathrow, baggage on a trolley and Sarah, now almost three years old, sitting on top of the cases.

"Over here." I saw Carol at the far side, waving. She came forward and picked Sarah up. "Look at you. Finally walking and talking. How was your flight?"

"Good as always. Thank the Lord for first-class and Grant."

"You look a little green around the gills, are you okay, Margot?"

"I'm a bit jet-lagged, that's all. I could do with a coffee. I must tell Grant that the coffee in first class is atrocious."

"It's so great to see you; where's Rex? I thought he was coming too!"

"He's flying out tomorrow. He had a business meeting he couldn't change."

"Why didn't you fly with him tomorrow so he could help with the luggage and Sarah?" And the tears came flooding. "Oh no, Margot, what the hell's going on this time? Every time you come to visit, there's a major fucking episode going on, normally to do with that control freaking man of yours."

"I'm pregnant, Carol."

"That's amazing, congratulations. How far gone ar... Margot? Why are you crying, Margot?" She put her arms around me and hugged me close. "Come on, let's get you home."

As we approached the house, John came out to get the cases and saw me crying.

"Oh, for the love of God. What's happened now Margot?"

"Let's get indoors first John. I'll go and put the kettle on."

"Margot. Is there something wrong with the baby?" asked Carol.

John looked up startled. "What baby? Is Sarah unwell?"

"No, John, Margot's pregnant."

"So why would there be something wrong with the baby?"

I managed to speak through the tears. "He wants me to have an abortion. I'm meeting him at a hotel tomorrow and we're going to a clinic in London."

I thought Carol was going to combust. She was livid, her eyes were bulging from their sockets, her whole face was red.

"Margot, are you totally stupid? Can't you see he's still controlling you? I can't let you do this, Margot. I can't. You'll regret it. Don't you remember what happened when you were seventeen, Margot?"

"Of course, I remember. It's something that I will take to the grave with me. But what's the point in having another child if he doesn't want one, Carol? He's only just about getting used to Sarah."

The following day, I took two over-ground trains, one underground train, and a taxi, to get me to the five-star hotel Rex had booked. He was waiting for me in his room. "How are you feeling, Margot?"

"How do you think I'm feeling? Apart from morning sickness, top of the fucking world."

"Margot, no need for that language. It doesn't become you."

"If that's the only thing that 'doesn't become me', then I'd say I'm doing pretty well. You on the other hand with a multitude of 'unbecoming' traits have no room to talk. Just give me the money."

He gave me an envelope.

"I've booked tickets to go to Athens for a few days. I'm flying out today, as I have some business to attend to out there. Your ticket's in the envelope with the money for the clinic. I'll meet you at the airport later on this evening."

"Really! How wonderful of you Rex. You think of everything don't you. Don't hold your breath."

When I arrived at the clinic, the waiting room was full of young girls. At thirty-six years old, I looked out of place.

"Mrs Wilson, can you come through please?"

I followed the nurse through to a ward with many beds. "Please undress and put your clothes in the cupboard and put the gown on. Oh, and take this pill. It's a sedative to calm your nerves a little." I downed the pill and undressed. A few minutes later, I began to feel drowsy and another nurse came in and sat on the chair next to the bed. "Mrs Wilson, I'm just going to go through a few things with you, if that's all right? Here at the clinic, we use what they call the 'suction method' and we are obliged legally to tell you that in a small number of cases, the procedure isn't always 100% successful."

"Sorry, what did you say?"

She repeated the words, and they were exactly the same words she'd spoken seconds before. "Let me get this straight; I've just flown thousands of kilometres, I've handed over £1,000, and it might not work? Is that what you've just told me?"

"I suppose that's the gist of it. But we are obli—"

"I'm only going to say this once. Go and get my money while I get dressed. Any quibble and I'll have this place closed down so fast you won't know what's hit you."

I couldn't face the train journey back to Surrey so I hailed a black cab. As I turned the corner into Carol's drive, she saw me through the kitchen window. I saw her drop whatever she was doing and she ran out to meet me.

"Margot, you look like a ghost, how come you're here, you said you'd be back late afternoon?"

I fell to my knees on the cobbled driveway.

"I couldn't do it, Carol, you were right, and I found out something mind-blowing."

I sat on the ground for at least three minutes crying, sobbing my heart out until I eventually found the strength to get up and go into the house. Carol made us a strong coffee and we both sat quietly for a while.

"What did you find out, Margot?"

"All those years ago, in that clinic in Birmingham. Do you remember I kept telling you and Mum that I didn't have sex with Jim again after the abortion. I was telling the truth, Carol. The nurse this morning, she told me that the 'suction method' used, isn't always 100% successful. That explains why, when the doctor examined me a second time and I was still pregnant, it was because the first abortion hadn't worked. How come the doctor didn't pick up on it, couldn't he tell from examining me that I was further along? All these years you've all looked at me as a liar. Why didn't anyone believe me?"

"Oh my God, Margot, this is major information. We should sue the bastards. It took you almost two years to pay off that debt."

"There's nothing I can do. It was years ago and I live in Africa, remember?"

"What did Rex say when you told him?"

"Rex doesn't know. He gone to Athens."

"What! Athens! What the hell for Margot?" Carol flung her arms in the air.

"He has some business over there, but God only knows what business. He said he'd booked it so that I can have a rest! His guilty conscience more like."

"He expected you to have an abortion and then fly alone to Athens? Margot, if that man shows his face here, I swear to the Almighty that I'll go for him."

"He's not worth it, sis. I hate him."

"What are you going to do when you get home, Margot?"

"I have no idea, Carol."

"Do you have any money saved?"

"A little, but even if I rent somewhere, I don't have enough for a deposit. I'll have to stay with him until I've saved up enough money."

"I have an idea."

She got the phone from the dining room. "Hi, Dad. Yes, all good, how are you and Ruth? I've got a surprise for you, Dad. Are you home tomorrow? Great, look forward to seeing you. No, I can't because then it won't be a surprise. Bye for now. Love you."

"We're off to Norfolk in the morning, Margot. Dad's never done a thing to help any of us kids, but I know for a fact that he has money. He'll be only too glad to help you."

The three-hour drive to Norfolk was a doddle compared with the long distances Carol, Mum and I had driven in Africa. On the way, Carol and I reminisced our travels of the past and agreed that our adventure in Natal was the best holiday we'd ever had and would never be bettered.

Dad's small cottage on the outskirts of Norwich was picturesque. I'd not seen him since I was a toddler and I didn't know what to expect. What I wasn't ready for was the fact that he was very ill. An alcoholic, not able to walk or move around, confined to a chair. When he saw Sarah, his face lit up. "I'm a granddad again. Now that's a surprise worth waiting for."

"Say hello to Granddad, Sarah."

"Hello."

"That accent is adorable. Come here and give me a kiss." Sarah went over and he picked her up onto his knee.

"Why are you in this chair with wheels, Granddad?"

"My legs don't work as well as they used to. Shall we go for a ride?"

"Oh yes, please. How fast does it go?" They got on like old friends.

While they enjoyed time together, Carol and I helped Ruth to give the place a thorough clean; it was filthy. We changed the bedding and bleached the bathroom upstairs.

The following morning, Carol and I sat talking to Dad and she told him about my predicament. "No problem, Bab, I'll give you some money. You need to get away from that bastard and look after your children." *'That's rich coming from a man who left his wife and three kids to fend for themselves!'*

Before we left the following day, Dad gave me two thousand pounds which he had stashed away in his bedroom somewhere.

John was cooking dinner when we arrived back at Langhurst.

"Any luck?" Enquired John.

"Yes, we got him to part with some money. Crafty old bugger had a pile of cash stashed away in his room."

"What's the plan when you get back to Africa, Margot?"

"I'll go and stay with a friend while I look for a place of my own. I have enough money now thanks to Dad, and I have a thousand pounds from Rex too. He'll never know I got the money back from the clinic."

"By the way, he rang here last night, wanted to know where you were."

"What did you tell him John?"

"I didn't, I hung up."

"Good. He's not worth wasting breath on."

On the morning of my flight out of the UK, John bade me farewell and good luck. I waited with Carol until it was time to depart. We arrived at Heathrow in plenty of time and had a bite of lunch in the VIP lounge.

"Margot, the next time you visit, can we please have some happy news?"

"I know, sis, I'm sorry. Let me get settled and you and John and the girls should come out and visit."

"We'd have come before now, but you move home so often we can't keep up. We're frightened that when we arrive, you'll have moved again. You're like a gypsy."

"Am I that bad?"

"Yes, Margot, that bad. You need to settle down."

We stood at the check-in desk and I could feel the tears welling up. Carol walked with me as far as she could.

"Now go on, before we start blarting again. Give me a big hug and kiss, Sarah. Look after yourself, Margot, and here, a little something towards your pot."

"Carol! Does John know?"

"It was his idea; here, take it. Use it wisely." I saw the tears well up in her beautiful brown eyes.

"I love you, sis. Thanks for everything."

"Love you too, Margot. Be safe." And she was gone.

Chapter 28

The Auction

I arrived at Jan Smuts Airport feeling rather sick. I felt drained, physically and emotionally. I waited at the luggage carousel until finally I saw my bright pink case coming around the bend. I sat Sarah on top of the case and we made our way to the final gate. There were crowds of people, many waving, some with signs held high displaying names and then I saw him. He was standing right at the front of the barrier, looking straight at me.

"Hello, Margot."

"Daddy, Daddy."

"Hello little one, I've missed you so much."

"I thought you were in Athens, Rex."

"I came to the clinic after you stormed out, but they said you'd gone."

"What else did they tell you?"

"Nothing, they said they weren't at liberty to divulge any information about their patients. They had no idea who I was. I couldn't even show them ID, your name's not the same as mine."

"What are you doing here, Rex?"

"What do you mean 'what am I doing here?' I've come to take you home! I knew what time you were getting in, Margot, why else would I be here?"

What choice did I have? I was exhausted, not an ounce of energy left in me. At six in the morning, who was I going to call to help me?

Halfway down the motorway, I began to feel sick, the bile rising deep from within. "Pull over quickly."

Rex hit the brakes and hazards and we came to a halt on the hard shoulder. We drove in silence the rest of the way home.

After feeding and bathing Sarah and taking a shower myself, we sat on the patio. I felt like I'd been on a roller coaster. "I'm going to bed, Rex, I'm so tired."

"You didn't go ahead, did you?"

"No, Rex, I couldn't kill my, our baby. I did it once before when I was too young to make that decision and regretted it ever since. But at thirty-six, I am quite capable of making such a decision, and the answer is no."

"Why the hell didn't you just say that before? Why did you go along with what I wanted?"

"Because I didn't want to lose you. I love you so much, Rex."

"Margot, I would have understood. All that money wasted and the trauma." He took hold of my hands. "What's another mouth to feed? It's not like the house isn't big enough. When is the baby due?"

"January."

"Right. Seven months before more sleepless nights. I'm joking, you have to admit I'm good at getting up in the middle of the night. Remember when Sarah had colic?" I smiled at him.

"I remember only too well. She cried for two hours and you paced the floor with her until the pain passed. You wanted to call an ambulance!"

"Wasn't that the night when we heard tapping on the bedroom window? That was so bizarre, when we opened the curtains and saw that owl in full flight pecking at the window, attracted by his own reflection in the glass. And we both said that we'd never see anything like that again and the following night he came back and did it again. What a pity we didn't get a picture, I'm sure people think we made it up." We both laughed.

On Saturday morning, Rex and I went into downtown Johannesburg. Rex wanted to go to an auction to buy a car for one of his senior managers. "This BMW looks nice. It's only had one owner and the mileage is quite low too. What do you think, Margot?"

"It's no good asking me, you know what you're looking for."

"I'll bid for it then."

"Really, how exciting, I like this auction vibe."

People were nodding and waving cards in the air as the bidding started. It all happened so quickly. "Great, I've just bought a car. Come on, we need to go to the office upstairs and sign the papers."

I followed him upstairs and sat in the small reception area while he dealt with the finances.

"Here you go, Margot." He handed me the keys. "You're okay to drive back, aren't you?"

"Are we taking it to the factory?"

"No, I'll get the guys from work to collect it on Monday."

"See you back at the house then."

The car was beautiful. A deep red convertible with a light tan interior. She drove so smoothly; the sound system was amazing and it had air con; it was awesome.

I parked the car behind Rex's and locked it. I could smell the fresh coffee brewing, as I went into the house, and saw Rex out on the stoop reading his Financial Times. "Nice drive, Margot?"

"Fab, really nice. Here, the keys." I threw them down on the table and went to get a cup of coffee. "You can keep the keys, Margot. It's yours."

"Really! Rex. Oh my God. I can't believe it. Really?"

"Yes, really. I'm sorry it took so long." He stood up and followed me into the kitchen. "Forget the coffee. Come to my office, please."

Rex never asked about the thousand pounds for the clinic and I never told him about the money I got from my family. In fact, Rex didn't even know how much I earned, or if I had any savings, and likewise I didn't know anything about his finances either. I broached the subject of buying my own house and although he looked a little shocked, he agreed it would be a good investment. I told him how much I'd saved and he was very impressed. "You can buy a decent house with that sort of deposit; which areas were you thinking of looking?"

"I'm not sure. It's all new to me. Do you think I've got enough money to buy something here in the northern suburbs?"

"I think so. Why don't we start looking?"

Over the following couple of months, we viewed several small houses in the area. One I particularly liked in Four Ways was a new build with two bedrooms, one-bathroom, open plan kitchen-diner and lounge with a decent-sized garden.

"I think this is ideal, Rex. I can easily rent this out. It's near to the schools and the mall and the highway."

"Let's go and see the agent then."

And that was that. I was now the proud owner of my own house. It felt good. There were lots of couples interested in the house and by the end of August 1990, I had tenants moved in.

Now five months pregnant, my bump was getting rather big to say the least. Unlike the pregnancy with Sarah where even at six months, you couldn't even see a bump.

I started to think about decorating the nursery. Two of the bedrooms were adjoined by a large white sliding door. Sarah slept in one of them and I decided to make the nursery in the adjoining room.

With the birth of another baby rapidly approaching, I thought it would be nice if Mum and Arnold could come out to South Africa for Christmas and New Year, to meet their new grandchild. Mum would be a great help around the house. I broached the subject with Rex and, to my amazement, he had no quibble in agreeing. I contacted Grant, who still wouldn't divorce me, and asked if he could get tickets for them. Again, I was dumbfounded when he agreed. He forgave me for leaving and said he was there if ever I needed him.

Grant called me later to confirm that Mum and Arnold would be arriving on the 22 December 1990.

Chapter 29
Annie

I stood in the arrival's hall waiting for the seven forty-five SAA flight from Heathrow. My bump was now huge and trips to the toilet pretty frequent. At last, they came through the doors with three cases stacked on a trolley. I couldn't run but slowly waddled over to greet them. "Hi, Mum, it's so good to see you." I gave her a big hug. "Arnold, how are you doing, how was the flight?" I gave him a peck on the cheek.

"There was a lot of turbulence so we didn't get much sleep. How are you? You look like you're ready to 'pop'."

"I am ready to pop Arnold, it's getting uncomfortable now. Roll on the seventh of January."

Mum asked, "Is she due on the seventh?"

"I'm booked in for a C-section. Apparently, I can't have a natural birth as I had a C-section with Sarah."

"Not long to go then."

"Just over two weeks and she'll be here. Anyway, let's get home and have a cuppa."

"How do you know it's another girl Margot?"

"Rex said he was worried, because of my age, and I had a Trisomy 21 test, to make sure the baby was okay and the scan revealed it's a girl."

"Isn't that when they take fluid from the womb?" Mum asked.

"Yes, it was fine. It didn't hurt or anything."

We arrived back in Douglasdale half an hour later. Arnold brought the cases in while Mum and I set about making a cup of tea. Mum pulled a handful of tea bags from her handbag. "Here you go blondie, good old Yorkshire tea. Bet you can't get that over here?"

"No, you can't, good old Mum. I haven't had a cup of Yorkshire Tea for years. Thanks, Mum. What other goodies have you brought?"

"Oh, you know. Just a few bits and pieces for the new arrival, and maybe a thing or two for you. It is Christmas you know."

"I wondered why you had three cases, you shouldn't have, but I thought you might go on a spending spree. At least anything you've bought from the UK will be different to anything I could buy here."

"I bought bigger sizes too. I know it's summer here so by the time winter arrives here, they should fit her just fine. I got some things for Sarah too. Where is she by the way?"

"At nursery school. She breaks up tomorrow until the end of January. It's the main Christmas summer holidays here don't forget."

"Of course. I can't wait to see her. The last time I saw her she had a huge lump on her head and she still wasn't walking."

"Now that was a holiday to remember. Did she tell you all about it, Arnold?"

"Yep, every little detail. I can hardly wait to meet Rex." He rolled his eyes mockingly.

"I know, he was an absolute nightmare back then, but he's changed. He's definitely mellowed." We all laughed, rather nervously.

The days that followed were 'textbook' happy families. Christmas was spent by the pool and really just relaxing while we waited for the new arrival.

On Sunday, 6 January, Rex took us all out to lunch at one of Rosebank's finest hotels where we ate out on the veranda in amongst the lush gardens. Rex looked so happy with Sarah sat on his knee for most of the afternoon.

Normally, at around three in the afternoon, Annie would either have hiccups or be kicking wildly inside me. Today, she was perfectly still. I was a little worried but didn't want to alarm anyone so I waited until we got home before mentioning it to Rex.

"I'm sure everything's okay, Margot. Surely the gynae would have mentioned things like that, if it was anything to worry about."

"Ya, you're probably right."

I was feeling rather tired and went to bed at around nine thirty. I didn't hear Rex come to bed. I was woken suddenly in the early hours, with horrendous pains in my back. I wasn't sure if it was wind or whether the baby had finally decided to have a good kick around. The latter turned out to be the case, but not with hiccups.

"Rex, wake up, the baby's coming, Rex." He put the light on. Mum came running through.

"I heard you screaming Margot. I knew there was something amiss at lunch Margot, you were so quiet and you hardly ate a thing. Rex, get dressed and get her bag for the hospital in the car."

"Oh Ida, these things take forever. It'll be hours before we see Annie. I'm going to put the coffee on."

I screamed so loud it made Mum jump.

"There's no time for coffee, Rex, we need to get her to the hospital now."

I was doubled over hanging onto the bedside dresser. The contractions were coming fast and furious but Rex wasn't going to be hurried. While the coffee brewed, he went and showered. He made himself some breakfast and casually popped into the bedroom every five minutes or so to see how I was doing.

"Rex, we need to go. Christ. My waters just broke, Rex."

It was eight thirty when he dropped me and Mum at the hospital and the contractions were mere seconds apart. Rex said he'd make his way to the office, and when the baby was imminent, he would come straight away.

I was taken straight into theatre for a C-Section, but after being examined, it was too late for that, as my cervix was almost fully dilated and the baby was coming.

"Mum, ask Matron to call Rex. My phone with his number, is in my handbag."

Rex was shown into the delivery room just in time to hear me screaming the place down. The gynaecologist, Dr Green, kept telling me to breathe deeply, and then push. I tried with all my might but I couldn't push any more. Rex was stood by Dr Green and had a bird's eye view of what was happening.

"Rex, could you go and get a cold flannel for Margot's head, there's a sink just outside this door." He came back with the flannel and I knew from the look on his face that something had happened.

"The head's almost out Margot, one more push and you're done, Margot. Come on, one more push."

Then this small bundle was placed on my chest. She was warm and wet. My little Annie, crying her little heart out.

I don't remember much else until I came around sometime later, with drips in both arms, an oxygen mask over my face, feeling as though my lower half had been split in half. Mum was sat by the bed on one side and Annie in a cot on the other side. "Mum. Is everything okay?"

"Yes, darling. You were so exhausted, you passed out. Are you feeling better?"

"A little. My vagina, Mum, is my vagina okay?"

Mum looked worried. "The doctor had to 'cut' you, Margot, the baby was in distress. You've had quite a lot of stitches." I could see the pain in her face.

"I'm never having sex again, never."

"That's what we all say. You'll live and you'll have sex again. I promise." She laughed.

"What's so funny?" Rex came towards the bed with a bunch of flowers and a huge box of chocolates, which he handed to Mum.

"Margot said she's never having sex again!"

"After seeing what the doctor did to her, I'm not sure I'll be having sex again either." He rolled his eyes in horror.

"I'm going to find the matron Margot; I want to give her these chocolates."

"Ida, you don't give quality chocolates to the staff." He went to take them from her.

"I bought them. I gave you the money Rex. I'll give them to who the hell I like." She snatched the box away from his grip.

Trying to deflate the situation I said; "Rex, aren't you going to say hello to your daughter, she's awake now." He moved towards the crib.

"God, she's ugly."

I thought Mum was going to smack him.

"She looks just like you, Rex, she's your double. Did you buy a new nighty for Margot, Rex?"

"She doesn't need a new nighty, Ida, I brought one of my old shirts. Here you go." He put the shirt on the bed.

"Rex! You saw what the doctor did to her nether regions. A shirt won't cover her adequately for God's sake. You can't have her walking around the ward uncovered."

"It's all females Ida, and it's only for a couple of days."

"Don't worry, Mum, I'll ask Joanna to bring one for me, she's coming to see me later."

"Do you want me to drop you back home, Ida, I've got to get to the office?"

"Don't worry, Rex, I'll ask Joanna to drop her back later." He gave me a quick kiss and looked into the crib and left the room.

"Good for you, Mum, that put him in his place. I won't be getting out of this bed anytime soon. This hospital gown is fine anyway, it's only going to get blood on it. I can hear the tea trolley, I'm parched."

"I'll go and find the matron and give her the…"

"Matron will be here soon Mum. She's dying to meet Annie."

Mum looked puzzled.

"She was the matron who sat with me for all those months when I was waiting for Sarah to arrive. She practically knows my whole life story, and, by the way, she adores Rex."

"She won't when I tell her what he said about the chocolates, stingy bugger." Mum glanced to the side table. "Did you move the chocolates, Margot?"

"No." I saw a look of disbelief in Mum's face and she was just about to say something.

"Leave it, Mum. He's got a problem. He has to have the last say, he has to 'conquer' all. You'd think he'd have higher-ranking priorities on his mind than who deserves the damn chocolates. He didn't even ask me how I was feeling."

It's amazing how a 'girly grapevine' works. When visiting time arrived, I was bombarded with the 'gang' bringing gifts from afar. I felt like a female Jesus, but with a very sore tushy. Joanna, Penny, Debbie, Jane my neighbour, Vanessa, and Miriam, the office manager from my current workplace, came to visit. As they stormed into the small room, I saw the matron hot on their heels. "I'm only supposed to let two in at a time so please keep the noise down. If one of you would like to come and help me fetch some more chairs, then I'll arrange tea and coffee for you all."

"Do you have any glasses Matron, we've bought some bubbly, and a knife to cut the cake and some plates, please." Matron Wilkes just smiled and said;

"How do you solve a problem called Margot? Just send in the girls."

"Do you know Matron, I've been asking myself that same question for years," Mum piped up.

"Girls, this is my mum, Ida. What question, Mum, what are you on about?"

"How to solve a problem called Margot? I've been trying for thirty-six years to fathom you out. Do you know girls, she's blazed a trail of heartbroken men across the globe, and still going strong." Mum teased.

Everyone started laughing rather loudly and the Matron pressed her finger on her lips.

What a lovely woman. I made a mental note to get her something really nice to say thanks for all her understanding and compassion.

"What's with the two drips, Margot?"

"I'll tell you another time, Penny, let's eat the cake first."

"Oh, that bad. Where's the new arrival?"

"They've taken her for a bath. I can't get out of bed yet; I can barely turn over so I don't know how I'm supposed to get out of this bed and walk."

"How's Rex? Was he here for the birth?"

"Oh yes! I don't think he'll be going anywhere near my vagina for a while. He witnessed the whole gory thing."

"Ya, right! I'll give it a week, tops, and you two will be at it like rabbits again." Penny threw me a look and I saw her cheeks flush.

"Well, if anyone knows that, Penny here does!"

Poor penny blushed crimson.

For the following five days, every afternoon, Rex came to see me and on two occasions bought Sarah along to see her baby sister. I was feeding Annie when they arrived and Rex put Sarah up on the bed next to us.

"Oh Mummy, she's so small. Can I touch her?" I nodded. She placed her small hand on her sister's head and stroked gently, then bent forward and kissed her cheek. "Hello Annie, I'm Sarah, your big sister."

On the fifth day, the matron came to tell me I could finally go home. I was so looking forward to a good night's sleep in the comfort of my own bed. Rex was at work so Joanna came to fetch us and as we pulled up to the front door, Mum, Arnold, Sarah and Sophie were waiting for me. Joanna helped me out of the car and I hobbled into the house. Sophie brought the carrycot and my small bag through to the lounge. I tried to sit down but the pain was still too intense. "Don't worry, Margot, I've got something to help you." Joanna produced a 'blown up' rubber ring.

"Yay, are we going swimming, Mummy?"

"No darling, not today." I sat on the ring and low and behold, it worked. It was still uncomfortable but bearable. Mum made everyone tea and biscuits and we sat for a while talking while Sarah just sat peering into the cot.

"When is she going to open her eyes, Mummy?"

"Soon, darling, very soon. You must let her sleep. Babies need to sleep a lot."

"Okay."

"Did you decide on a theme for the nursery, Margot?"

"Go up and have a look." Joanna went upstairs and I heard doors opening and shutting and she finally came down. "It's amazing, you're so creative Margot. How did you do that huge mural, surely not freehand?"

"I borrowed Rex's overhead projector and copied the scene onto a transparency, and hey presto, just had to paint the huge picture on the door."

"Still very impressive, Margot. I have to get back to work. Give me a call if you need anything, and don't be such a stranger, I hardly see you anymore."

"I promise as soon as I can drive Jo, we'll go for coffee. All of us."

"Ciao, see you later everyone."

Full of the joys of spring, holding a large bouquet of lilies and red roses, Rex came home a little earlier than usual. "Hi, darling, sorry I couldn't come and get you." He handed me the flowers.

"Oh, they're lovely, thank you. Will you put them in a vase for me, you need to cut the stems first."

"I'll do it, Margot, Rex probably wants to change out of his suit." Mum took the bouquet and Rex went upstairs to change.

After supper, I asked Mum if she would help me to run a bath.

"The matron said I need to sit in warm salty water to help soothe and heal my torn 'bits', and put this ointment on. Hand me those flannels off the little shelf Mum. The Matron also said to put a couple of hot flannels on my enormous 'melons', to ease the flow of milk."

Still barely able to walk or bend down I made my way to the bedroom. I was finished drying off and applying the ointment, when Rex came into the bedroom.

"Will you bring Annie up in her carrycot please Rex, and say goodnight to everyone for me. I can't manage the stairs again."

He sat on the edge of the bed.

"I've made the spare room up for you Margot. There's no point both of us having sleepless nights. You know I need my sleep, Margot."

"What? Are you joking? I've been looking forward to sleeping in my own bed for almost a week."

"Margot, you know the baby will wake up in the middle of the night and I need my sleep."

"Then why don't you sleep in the spare room? We don't have another bed anyway, only a mattress."

He looked at me rather sheepishly.

"Now you've got to be... you want me to sleep on a mattress on the floor? Which part of 'I can hardly move' don't you understand? Just getting up from the sofa is a major mission, Rex. Look, I'll show you." I stood up and lifted my nightdress up, turned around and bent over to show him what a state I was in. "Well, Rex, what do you think?"

"All the more reason you should sleep in the spare room, Margot. You're going to be uncomfortable and restless all night, keeping me awake too. Come on, I'll help you." He held my arm and tried to pull me out of the room.

"Don't touch me, Rex. Take your slimy hands off me."

Holding back the tears, I slowly walked out of the room and shut the door. Annie was fast asleep in her carrycot next to the mattress in the middle of the floor, nothing else in the room. I'd never felt such hate in my entire life until this moment. I went downstairs on the pretext of making a cup of hot chocolate and Mum followed me into the kitchen. "Margot, why are you crying? Are you in pain?"

"More pain than I thought possible, Mum." The sobbing started, tears rolling, nose running.

"What's he done now, Margot?" She handed me a piece of kitchen roll. "Come and sit down, I'll make you a drink." When I told Mum what had happened, she ran from the kitchen and up the stairs. I couldn't stop her. I heard her banging on his bedroom door. He didn't open it. When she came back into the kitchen, Arnold was sitting with me smoking and looking very nervous.

"The bastard won't open the door, doesn't have the balls to talk to me. What sort of man does that, Margot? Has he seen the state of you? How does he expect you to get up and down off that mattress, he's insane. There's not even a chair for you to sit and feed the baby. He has to come out at some stage and when he does, I'll be waiting for him."

"Ida." We all turned around to see Rex standing at the door. "It has nothing to do with you. I've explained my reasoning to Margot and that's all there is to it. Now keep your voices down, I need some sleep." He turned and went back upstairs.

The three of us just sat there.

"Mum, will you please go up and get Annie. She's in the room next to the main bathroom. I'll sleep on the sofa so at least I can get up and down to feed her." I sat sipping my hot chocolate, my head reeling. *Was I dreaming?*

Annie only woke once for a feed and a nappy change. Mum slept on the other sofa so that she could help me. I had no words to describe what I was thinking.

Rex didn't even come into the kitchen or lounge. He was up and dressed by seven and left with just a 'see you later' shouted from the front door.

"He won't see us later. Mum, we're leaving. Sophie will be in soon and she can help pack a few things. My house is empty at the moment. There's a new family supposed to be moving in, in February but I'll have to tell them what's happened. Thank God the car's automatic, I don't think I could press my foot down on the clutch." I started laughing. Mum started crying.

"What's going on here then?" Arnold stood by the door in his PJs.

"We're going to Margot's house."

We were in the garden watching Sarah in her little paddling pool when we heard the car pull up. "I don't want to see him, Mum. Tell him to go away." I heard them talking.

"What the hell's going on, Ida? One minute I'm a man with two kids, next minute I'm a bachelor. What's wrong with your daughter?"

"Nothing, Rex, I think you need to take a good look at yourself. You'd better go; Margot doesn't want to speak to you. If you can't fathom what's going on here, then I truly feel sorry for you. Goodbye." I heard the door close.

Chapter 30

The Proposal

Mum and Arnold extended their visit and stayed with me until the end of January. I went back to work in February and found a baby-minder for Annie, near to where I lived, and arranged 'after school' for Sarah in Bryanston until five thirty. At weekends I met up with my girlfriends, and at least every other weekend one of them would stay with me for the weekend.

Rex came to see the girls once a week and we went out for dinner most times. He begged me to go home, but I told him I was quite happy where I was.

It was towards the end of July and while reading the girls a bedtime story, the doorbell rang.

"Hello, Margot. Can I see the children?"

I let him in, and as he passed, I could smell his aftershave. It's amazing how smells can trigger an onslaught of emotions.

"I was just reading them a story." He followed me through to the girls' room. "Look who's here, Sarah."

"Yay, Daddy." She jumped off the bed and flung herself into his arms. Tears pricked his blue eyes as he held her close.

"Hey, big girl, what story are you reading?"

"Mia the Bee. Look, she's so pretty, Daddy."

"Coffee, Rex?"

"Got any beer?"

With the girls fast asleep, Rex and I sat in the lounge.

"How are you, Margot? You look well." He raised those brows and I could see those beautiful blue eyes staring at me.

"I'm doing okay and you?"

"Look, Margot, I need to know if we're together or not. I'm looking for jobs overseas, and it's quite a mission trying to fill out application forms not knowing where I stand with you. Am I a family man or am I free to do as I please?"

This wasn't a 'test' on his part, he was deathly serious.

"I want you to come home, Margot. I miss you and the girls. It's now or never. Will you marry me?"

Debbie, I'm going to marry this man, just you watch me.

He stared into my soul, then reached into his jacket pocket and produced a small box. He opened the lid to disclose a solitaire diamond ring.

What are you waiting for, this is what you've been dreaming of happening.

He leant over and pulled me up off the sofa and kissed me. And there it was. That spark, that fire in my belly. The next thing I know, he's pulled me down over his knee, and is spanking me.

"I thought you never wanted sex again Rex!"

"Do you want me to stop Margot?"

I moved back in with Rex the following weekend. Everything was rosy in the garden. Rex continued looking for jobs and came home a couple of days later, rather excited. "I've been invited for an interview for a job in Papua New Guinea. They want us to be there on 14 September."

"Wow, that's only six weeks away. It's a bit short notice."

"I know. We need to book the magistrate's court to get married. Can I leave that to you?"

"Why the rush to get married Rex?"

"I want you to come with me, as my wife. I love you."

I was rather taken aback.

"Wow. It's taken you long enough to get to this stage Rex, why the sudden urgency?"

"I just told you, I love you, Margot. What do you say?"

"Of course." I flung my arms around him. "I love you too. It doesn't leave us very much time to arrange the wedding though, and I want Mum to be there. She's never been to any of my weddings, and …."

"Margot, I don't want a big wedding, I thought we could get married at the Registry Office, just the two of us!"

"But Rex, I've never had a proper wedding, and as this will be the last time I get married, I thought…"

"Margot. Do you love me?"

"You know I do Rex."

"Then does it really matter where we get married?"

"I suppose not." I conceded.

"I'd rather spend the money on a lovely honeymoon. Wouldn't you?"

On the morning of the wedding on the 11 September 1991, Rex produced a document which he wanted me to sign. "It's to protect you and the children, Margot. While we're in Papua. You won't be allowed to work, simply because there is very little industry, and other than the shipping company that I will be working for, there are no other large businesses on the island. There are no shops or malls, no bars and restaurants. It's a very close-knit community and entertaining is done at home so there will be a lot of dinner parties. Obviously, I will buy you a car to transport the children to and from school and to go to the local market and things like that. I'll also be responsible for the house rentals here in South Africa. If anything goes wrong with tenants absconding or wrecking the place or if something major needs doing, I will sort it. I'm also going to pay into our UK pension funds, just in case we ever have to go back to the UK."

"Okay, that's fair enough, Rex. You sound sure you'll get the job!"

"They wouldn't be paying for us to go all that way if they weren't going to offer it to me. We'll go to the attorney's office this morning, before we go and get married."

"Oh my God, is this really happening? Getting married. I'm so happy, Rex. I love you so much."

"I love you too."

"Are the girls going with us to Papua?"

"No. Do you think Penny might come and stay here? She's the only one I trust with the girls. Sophie will be here to help her so the girls will be fine."

"I'll give her a call."

On the eleventh September 1991, we went to the solicitor to sign the agreement and two hours later were married. "By the powers invested in me, I now pronounce you man and wife."

I've got my man.

The following day we flew out to Papua New Guinea. I knew from the first day we met the big boss, that he and Rex would clash. From a rough upbringing in Glasgow, the small Scotsman, Logan, laid down the law. The flights and hotel were all paid for by the new company, but unbeknown to me, Rex had arranged to fly home via Mauritius, to spend a week on our honeymoon, at his own cost. When Logan found out about this, he showed his disapproval. They also had words regarding the choice of houses that we were given to look at, and when Rex enquired why there was such a 'quantum leap' in the difference between Logan's home and the basic wooden structures we were being offered, he simply said, "There's only one penthouse on the island, mate, and it's mine." I knew it was all over.

Chapter 31

The Honeymoon

The bumpy bus ride took us through vast sugar cane plantations, Mauritius' major crop, which took up a staggering thirty-six per cent of the island's seventy per cent of cultivated land. As space was so limited, they grew potatoes and vegetables in between the cane crops. I had no idea that the island grew and exported so much food, not to mention the tobacco fields. There were crops of bananas, tea, coconuts, peanuts, tropical fruits such as dwarf bananas, zatte (sugar apple), litchi, jackfruit and pomegranate, and they exported exotic flowers too, mainly anthuriums (arum lily). What I also learnt was that because of the shortage of land, rice, their staple food, and most other cereal crops, had to be imported.

As we drove further on, the roads became a lot smoother but very windy and hilly, then as the hill tapered the roads became smoother, and they were lined with huge coconut palms, with colourful exotic flowers scattered in between them. I saw the hotel towering in the distance. It was located amongst the remnants of a historic fortress and tropical garden. We were greeted with glasses of fresh juices before being shown to our bungalow by a young man wearing a very colourful tunic. Literally twenty footsteps away from the bungalow was white sands and crystal-clear blue seas. "Oh Rex, this is beautiful. I'm in heaven." Rex gave the young man a tip.

"Thank you, Sir, Madam, enjoy your stay. There is a cocktail deck right up on the peak overlooking the ocean."

"Thanks, I could do with a cold beer and some lunch."

We made our way up to the deck which overlooked spectacular views of the northern islands and the sparkling Indian Ocean. Constructed in the mid-eighteenth century, a French fort had been built using firebricks, lime basalt stone, hardwoods and metal, in order to defend the island against European nations, and the old canons they used were still in place along the ramparts, giving a unique colonial ambience to the place.

"This is amazing, Rex, I love you so much." I leaned in for a kiss. It happened every time I came within an inch of him, that fluttering feeling. He winked at me.

Each evening, Rex and I ventured to the outdoor dining area where they had live entertainment and invariably would end up going for a skinny dip before retiring to our huge bed. Each day, we tried something different; we tried our hand at skiing and wind surfing and we even tried the 'banana boat' which was hilarious. The highlight of the trip was a small cruise out to Port Louis. The sailing boat was laden with bright coloured streamers and cocktails and other drinks were served as we sailed over the waves towards the port.

We found a brochure on the table giving the history and information about Port Louis. Port Louis had been in use as a harbour since 1638. Only later in 1736, was it named in honour of King Louis XV, after it became the administrative centre of Mauritius under the French Government, and coupled with the fact that it was well-protected by the Moka Mountain Range from winds during the cyclone season, therefore being a good choice to house the fort and main harbour. During the seven years when the Suez Canal was inactive, Port Louis' activity increased and in the late 1970s, modernisation of the port helped maintain its role as the central point for imports and exports. In the late 1990s, expansion of the tourism industry to Mauritius saw the development of many shops, hotels and restaurants, making Mauritius what it is today. A thriving port known for its French colonial architecture and the famous Champ de Mars horse racing track. There were lively dining and shopping precincts, a huge central market full of hand-crafted goods and local produce, together with the Blue Penny Museum, which focuses on the island's maritime and colonial history and culture. Having read this tourist information, we couldn't wait to get to the port. We were to be very disappointed.

After disembarking, we had to get a bus into the centre of town. The bus dropped us slap bang in the middle of the bustling market area. It was unbelievably humid, flies everywhere, kids running around naked, the smell of human pee and faeces was rife. Inevitably, I needed the toilet and as we were too far away from a hotel, I had to use a local shop's toilet. When I opened the door and saw lots of ladies crouched down peeing into holes in the ground, their dresses covered in pee, dragging around their ankles, I caught the whiff of excrement coming from all directions. I saw one of the older women use her dress to clean herself. There were no facilities for washing hands and I left rather quickly, still in need of the toilet. Rex was standing by a fruit stall waiting for me and when he saw me, he started laughing.

"You don't need to say a word, it's written all over your face. We'll get the next bus back to the hotel. I'm not hanging around here for three hours for the return boat trip." We made our way through the bustling streets to the bus station and back to our hotel. Needless to say, we didn't venture outside of the hotel again and spent the remaining days of our holiday at the resort.

Chapter 32

Chartwell

Not long after we got back from Papua, Rex suggested moving a little further into the countryside. We looked at many lovely places but the one that we finally chose was a lovely house with ten acres of land, in an area called Chartwell. We had no problem selling our current house and within two months we'd moved into Chartwell.

Fortunately, Chartwell was still in the same catchment area for the girls to go to the same school. Sarah, now six, was looking forward to wearing her new school uniform and starting her first year at infant school. Annie, almost four, was starting pre-school, at the same school. I dropped them off each morning at seven thirty and collected them each day at one thirty and took them home to Sophie. The girls were in bed before Rex got home in the evenings and at weekends, Rex always had work to do in his office. We never went anywhere other than the shops and I began to get bored. I asked him several times if we could go out somewhere, even if it was just a ride out to one of the many outdoor lido and braai parks, just something different.

The response was always the same: "Oh Margot, we have a lovely garden and a pool and a tennis court, why do you want to go where there are lots of other people when we can enjoy the tranquillity here?"

I suggested maybe going to Sun City or down to Durban for a weekend, to the seaside. We never did anything exciting anymore. I was tired of asking so one Saturday morning, I told Rex I wanted to go to Sun City.

"Absolutely not, Margot. I have too much work to do."

"Well, I'm going. I'll take the girls and we can stay over and leave you in peace to do your ever-so-important work."

"I said NO, Margot."

"Sorry, Rex, I have a life too. I'm going."

Rex got very angry and started shouting. He grabbed me and pushed me towards the large bedroom window, then went to the bedside table and retrieved his gun. I was terrified and I mouthed at Sarah to go and tell Sophie to call the police. The girls ran down the stairs to find Sophie.

When Rex heard the doorbell ring, he rushed to the front of the bedroom and looked out of the window to see who it was.

"It's the armed police out there! Scurrying behind the trees with their guns poised."

I looked out and saw the policemen.

"Good, maybe they can calm you down, Rex."

Rex was in his dressing gown.

He put the gun away and said, "We're going to go down and tell them it was just a domestic squabble and that everything is all right. Margot, do you hear me?"

"You had a gun in your hand, Rex, in front of our children. I'm scared."

"I won't hurt you, Margot. If this gets reported, I will lose my job. Do you understand?" He took me by the hand a led me downstairs to the front door. "Remember what I said, Margot." I stood behind him as he opened the door. "Officer! Can I help you?"

"There's been a disturbance reported. Is everything okay here, Sir, Madam?" He looked past Rex and straight at me. Rex spun around.

"Everything's all right, isn't it, Margot?"

"Yes. We just had an argument, that's all. We're good, thank you."

Rex closed the door. The girls stood crying in the kitchen doorway, huddled to Sophie's apron. I saw a tear in Rex's eyes.

"Girls, come with Mummy, we're going to Sun City."

We got back the following day at around five. The house was locked and no sign of Rex.

"Where's Daddy?"

"I'm not sure, sweetie, he's probably gone to the shops. He'll be back soon, you know he loves a braai on a Sunday. Let's go and have a swim, shall we?"

I went and tapped on Sophie's door. "Hi, Sophie, what time did the boss go out?"

"He left yesterday, Madam. Not long after you went out."

"Oh! Where did he go?"

"I don't know, Madam, but he had a large suitcase with him. He was very angry, Madam."

"So was I, Sophie, so was I."

The following morning, Rex still hadn't come home. Sophie was in the kitchen fixing the girls' breakfast when the phone rang.

"Hi, Margot, it's Sandra. How are you?"

"Hi, Sandra! I'm fine."

"I just thought I'd let you know Rex has gone to the States on business. He called me on Saturday and said he would be away for two weeks, some urgent business deal."

"Look, Sandra, Rex and I had an argument at the weekend and I took the girls away for the night. When I got back yesterday, Rex wasn't here. He never said a word about going overseas, but then he never does. He always leaves it till the very day he's going. I feel as if I'm going out of my mind, Sandra."

"Ya, he's a very complex man Margot. Anyway, now you know where he is at least."

"Sandra, where exactly has he gone?"

"Florida."

"Florida! He hasn't any businesses in Florida, well at least nothing I know about."

"Look Margot, it's none of my business. That's all I know of where he went. Bye Margot."

"Bye Sandra."

Now I definitely smelt a rat. He didn't want to go away for the weekend, with me and the girls, he just wanted to relax, but now suddenly he's off on business! I don't think so.

"Riccardo, hi there. I'm sorry I'm not a work today but…."

"Margot! What's wrong?"

"I have a problem, a big one. I need to get out of here, are any of your houses empty at the moment?"

"Slow down, Margot. What's happened?"

"I don't have time to explain right now, please, can you help me?"

"Yes, of course I can help. You can come and stay with me for a few days. I live alone. My ex-wife took most of the furniture, so the place looks a little empty, but there's a double bed in one of the bedrooms and a single mattress on the floor in another."

"I had no idea you were married let alone that she left you! You never said."

"Why would I?"

He gave me his address and an hour later, as I drove up the long driveway towards the house, I saw Riccardo wave from the front door. I'd seen some large houses in my time but wow, this was something else. It had beautiful high arched windows with a front door large enough to accommodate a family of giraffes. Stepping inside the massive foyer of polished wooden floors, covered with red Persian rugs, I looked up to see a graceful banister that curved up towards a soaring second floor gallery. *Any of my furniture would look totally out of place in here,* I thought.

"Hi there, you must be Sarah and Annie, I'm Riccardo." He scooped them up in his arms and said, "This way, Margot, I've put a fresh pot of coffee on. Now come and tell me what happened, we can unload the car later." The kitchen was every woman's dream. Open plan with an island in the centre with a built-in six-burner hob. High stools surrounded two sides where he carefully placed the girls down. "Okay, what would you like to drink, Sarah?"

"Do you have rooibos please, with honey?"

"Coming up, and Annie, what would you like?"

"Orange juice, please."

"No coke, or sprite?"

"They don't have fizzy drinks; it's not good for them."

"What about some biscuits then?"

"No, thank you, Riccardo, do you have any strawberries or mango?" Sarah smiled at him.

"Well, let's see Sarah." He opened the fridge and peeked inside. "Hmm, no strawberries or mango, but I do have apples, bananas, and grapes; will that do?"

"Ya, I'll have a banana please."

"Annie, what would you like?"

"Grapes and apple."

"Well, what healthy girls you are, that's very impressive." He made the drinks while they were busy eating their fruit.

"Thanks Riccardo, for helping me out. I just need a couple of days to sort my head out and we'll be out of your hair."

"Hey, Margot, it's no problem really. It's nice to have some company and I love kids. Take as long as you need."

"I don't know what I'm going to do with the girls after school, Riccardo, they finish at one thirty and without Sophie to look after them, I…"

"Don't worry about that for now. My maid comes in three times a week and I'm sure she will be more than happy to work five days, even if she comes in at one, on the other two days. You'll have to pay her obviously. You'll get to meet her tomorrow; we can sort it out then. There's nothing majorly important going on at work; if they need me, they'll call. How about we get you all settled and go shopping, there's not a lot of food in the fridge. I eat at work and go out most nights, I don't like cooking; well, not for one."

"Looks like I can help you too then, I love cooking. What do you say we cook up a storm tonight? What do you fancy?"

"Can we have a braai, Mummy?"

"Fabulous idea, Sarah. A braai sounds perfect."

"Yay, is Daddy coming too?" You could hear a pin drop.

"Daddy's away in America, he'll be back in a few days. I bet Riccardo has a swimming pool, so you two girls can have a swim while Mummy and Riccardo do the braai."

"Have you got arm bands or do we need to get some when we're out?" asked Riccardo. The girls giggled.

"We don't need arm bands, silly billy, we can swim like fish, can't we, Mummy?"

"They can indeed. They could swim before they could walk. Can't wait to see what they'll be doing when they're sixteen!" *Sixteen. My God. Where will we be then,* I wondered.

By Wednesday, everything was sorted. I'd explained to Riccardo what was going on and he agreed with me, that he thought there was something fishy going on.

The bedrooms were palatial. Four of the six having en-suites, balconies overlooking the pool and landscaped gardens, which were set in two acres of treed grounds. We moved the double bed into one of the non-balconied rooms for the girls and I had the second largest room with en-suite and a mattress on the floor. *It made me think of the last time I'd slept on a mattress when Annie was five days old.*

Three weeks passed and I was enjoying the calm in my life. No confrontations, knots in my stomach, the anxiety had passed. I knew Rex hadn't a clue where I was, but he didn't call me either so I assumed he felt the same way as I did, totally fed up with arguing all the time, at loggerheads with one another.

At the end of the month with a hefty R10,000 cash in my hand, I told Riccardo I was going to look for a place of my own. "Oh, that's a shame; I was getting used to having someone here. I'll really miss you guys, especially the food. Back to cooking for one."

"You don't need me and the girls here cramping your style, Riccardo."

"You're not cramping my style, Margot, I love having the girls around; it livens the place up. I'd love you to stay, if you want to."

"Riccardo, it's a little weird to explain but working with you and living in your house, I need to be alone with my girls, to try and sort my head out. Does that make any sense?!"

"It's your call, Margot, but you are more than welcome to stay here for as long as you need."

While in bed that night, I weighed up the pros and cons of staying or moving. We got on well enough and he was at the office/casino most of the time; I had the run of the house. The girls loved it and they really liked Riccardo. I felt secure, I enjoyed the occasional evening if Riccardo came home and we all ate together. There was absolutely nothing sexual going on between us; we drank and laughed together, and if he could get time off at the weekends, he occasionally took me and the girls out! I decided to stay and see how things went.

Another month rolled by and the girls and I were happy. I hadn't heard a thing from Rex so I assumed he didn't care, and we were over. Riccardo announced that he was going down to Durban on business and would be away for the weekend. Even a 'house mate' had the decency to tell me in advance he was going away. Amazing.

On Sunday afternoon, Riccardo called me from Durban to tell me he had met the most amazing woman. "I'm bringing her home with me, Margot, I'm so in love with her. I've asked her to marry me."

"Wow, that's great news" Riccardo. I laughed and jokingly said, "You're not divorced yet, Riccardo, and you're already planning your next marriage, never a dull moment in your life hey." He laughed too.

"When you say it like that, Margot, it sounds bizarre, but surely my divorce should be through soon thanks to you."

"It won't be long now, Riccardo, the divorce papers were sent two weeks ago, so provided she doesn't oppose it, there's only a couple more weeks to wait then we can book your hearing date. What are you going to do if she does contest it?"

"She won't. I've been more than generous with the settlement and as there are no kids involved it should go through without a hassle."

"But what about all the rental properties, Riccardo, isn't she entitled to half of them?"

"She doesn't know about them. I bought them when we broke up two years ago and if she asks where the money went, I'll tell her I lost it on a bad deal, or gambling."

"Let's hope she signs the papers, you have a wedding to organise. What's the lucky lady's name?"

"Linda. She's half-Spanish, half-English."

"Where did you meet her?"

"I met her in Sun City a few months ago. She's a dancer there, you know one of those exotic show girls with all the feathers and masks, and legs that go all the way up to her… well she's stunning."

I laughed. "Good for you, Riccardo. It reminds me of when I met Rex; it was love at first sight, for me at least. It's funny how you just know, it's like a fatal attraction that won't go away. What time will you be back, I'll make sure the girls' toys aren't strewn everywhere."

"Don't worry about that, Margot, just be yourself and carry on as normal. Really, she won't mind a few toys around the place. I've told her the set up between you and I and she's cool with it. I think you two will get on famously. We'll be back around four, depending on the traffic. We can have a braai if you haven't already started dinner."

"I was going to make pasta, something simple but a braai sounds perfect."

"Would you mind checking that we have enough meat and vegetables etc., and charcoal?"

"No problem, I'll see you both later."

As Linda stepped out of the car, I could see the attraction. She was like something from a movie, a cross between Raquel Welch and Audrey Hepburn. He wasn't joking about the legs. She was wearing the shortest of shorts and a T-shirt, and her legs were beautifully sculpted, firm and tanned, as was the rest of her body. She had the deepest brown eyes and long dark-brown, thick, wavy hair cascading down her back and over her shoulders.

"Hey, Margot, this is Linda."

"Hi, Linda, it's lovely to meet you. Come on through, let's crack a bottle of bubbly. I believe congratulations are in order."

"Lovely to meet you too, Margot." She gave me a warm smile and a huge hug. I was old enough to be her mother.

"Where are the girls, I've missed them?" asked Riccardo.

"They're in the pool on that huge inflatable unicorn of yours."

When Riccardo went out to the pool, the girls got out of the pool and ran to him, arms wrapping around his legs. "Come and play 'Mr Shark' Riccardo."

"Mr Shark!" enquired Linda. "You don't mean 'doo du, doo du, doo du." She made the 'two-tone' noise of the terrifying music from the Jaws movie, whilst waving her hands around to look like shark fins.

"You know the shark game?" Sarah shrieked with joy. "You can play too, go and get your costume on."

The cork flew out of the champagne bottle and went into the pool. "Quickly, get that before the shark eats it, the first one to get it can have an ice lolly."

The girls both jumped back into the pool with a great splash while Riccardo poured the bubbly.

"Cheers, here's to life. Whatever it may hold. Never a dull moment around here;" I said. "You're so good with children Riccardo. The girls adore you." I saw Linda look at Riccardo, and for a split second, I thought I detected some sort of concern in her eyes.

Riccardo was smitten with Linda. The way he looked at her was amazing to watch. *I wonder if that's how I used to look at Rex.* I guess it must have been because I remember I couldn't sleep one night, and I sat up in bed watching him sleep. He'd woken suddenly and was startled to see me sitting staring at him. Funny how things change. It seems a long time since we even slept in the same room.

The following weeks went by with no hiccups. Linda would spend her mornings sunbathing in the 'nude' which disgusted the maid, and hours dolling herself up. She would come to the casino and either sit in Riccardo's office or at the gaming tables. Nine times out of ten, she would be sitting at the 'high rollers' roulette table and Riccardo and I would be in the office working. One of the 'pit bosses' came into the office one afternoon and said that Linda was getting a lot of attention at the tables.

"No problem, Dave, if she's keeping the punters happy and they're spending lots of money, that's fine." He laughed. Dave shut the door.

"Riccardo! You can't be serious. She's not a piece of meat to be auctioned off to the highest bidder. She needs to find a job, she needs independence like all people do." I was furious.

"Doing what, Margot? She has no qualifications other than dancing, mostly striptease! and she can make me lots of money doing what she's doing."

"Riccardo! That's disgraceful. I never had you down as a 'Pimp', and you certainly don't need the money so why would you do that to her, or anyone for that matter? I thought you loved her?"

"Margot, it's none of your damn business. Now run along and get me a coffee please."

This was no life for such a beautiful young girl, even an old girl. She spent most of her days, and all of her nights in the casino. I had to get her alone and speak to her. The next morning, after I'd dropped the girls to school, I went back to the house. Linda was in the kitchen making coffee.

"Hi, Linda, I could use a cup too. How are you? What time did you get in last night?"

"About two. I don't know how Riccardo does it. I'm so tired."

"How are you two lovebirds getting on anyway?"

We took our coffee outside and sat in the early morning sun. "Have you fixed a date for the wedding now that his divorce is final?"

"He's divorced? He never said a word. In fact, we don't talk much about anything, my life consists of sitting at the bar or the tables all day looking pretty. I feel like a prostitute. In fact, I think the next stage will be Riccardo 'pimping' me off to the punters." Oh my god, I was right.

"Linda, are you sure? That's one hell of an allegation."

"I'm sure, Margot. Several times he's let men talk to me and touch me while he's sitting right there. He says to them, 'Do you fancy a bit of her? It'll cost you.' And then he smiles at them and they just laugh, nervously, as if he's joking, but he's not. I'm too scared to say anything to him."

"I can't sit by and let him do this to you. Go and get dressed. We're going to talk to Riccardo." She flung her arms around me.

"I don't know, Margot, he'll be angry, he thinks he owns me."

"And there we have it. I didn't want to say those words Linda, but having been through a similar situation myself, I could see all the signs. Go and get ready. This has to be nipped in the bud now. You can't live your life in fear, and first and foremost, you need to 'have a life'. You're nineteen years old!" She smiled that beautiful innocent smile, flicked her long hair over her shoulders and went to get ready.

It should be her clicking her fingers and calling the shots. What a low life like Riccardo.

We pulled into the car park and I could feel the tension in Linda. "It'll be okay, Linda. Worst scenario here, I'll probably get fired, find a lovely townhouse and you can come and stay with me and the girls. If you want to, if the need arises."

"Really? You'd do that for me?"

"Ya. I think we'd make a good team. So, are you ready to go in there and be the 'boss'?" She just nodded.

I knocked on his door and we stepped in. "Morning, Riccardo, sorry I'm a little late, the teacher kept me talking."

"You're up early," he said as he looked up and smiled at Linda. He stood up and went over and kissed her. "You were sound asleep when I left. What's up?"

"Coffee, anyone?"

"Ya thanks, Margot." I went to the kitchen to make coffee. When I returned, the atmosphere had changed somewhat. Riccardo threw me a look. A look I had seen many times before. I put the tray of coffee down and stepped back a little.

"What have you been saying to Linda?"

Linda sat with her head down.

"Nothing untoward, Riccardo. She's very young and she's been thrown into this environment. It's rather scary for her, don't you think? She's used to the high life in Sun City, all the glamour and glitz, performing in front of all those people, being paid excellent money for it, having a life of her own. It can't be easy, suddenly without a job, no income, totally dependent on someone else for her every need. Look at her, Riccardo, she's a beautiful young lady, only nineteen

222

years old, her whole life ahead of her. She needs to get a job, be independent. That's normal. Humans need to have indep—"

He banged his fist on the table. "Shut up."

"No, I won't. I have a voice, Riccardo. I'm not nineteen, thank God. You're old enough to be her father, you should know better. You're 'grooming' her, aren't you?"

He opened the top draw of his desk. I saw something shine but it happened so fast I didn't even get the chance to move. I felt the air move as the flick knife passed my ear and twanged into the doorpost inches away from my head. His eyes were fixed on mine. Linda stood up and started screaming.

Riccardo pointed directly at her and said, "Quiet." The room fell silent. It was like slow motion. Nothing seemed real. The knife slowly stopped 'twanging'. I clapped my hands.

"And here we see the real Riccardo emerge. A 'crack-shot' with a flick knife, manipulative, charming on the outside but with a purpose." He stood up and came towards me.

"What are you going to do, Riccardo? Hit me, knife me, kill me even? You don't scare me. I've had bigger men than you for breakfast. I've lived a life of fucking hell, men beating me up, hospitalised more times than I care to remember, teeth knocked out, bones broken, nights spent in a police cell."

"You little shit," he spat the words out.

"The only shit I see, Riccardo, is stood right in front of me, stacked six feet high."

Two of Riccardo's bouncers had come in to see what the screaming was about.

"This lady is just leaving. Escort her to her car."

"I take it I'm fired then, Riccardo?"

He just looked at me.

"In that case, you'll need to pay me a month's salary. Cash as usual." He went to speak. "Before you try and talk your way out of it, we have a written contract, remember? I also have a copy of your divorce papers! I'm sure the authorities would love to get their hands on your 'books' too."

He left the room, slamming the door behind him with the bouncers hot on his heels, leaving Linda and myself looking slightly nervous.

"Remember what I said Linda. You have my number." Linda followed me out to the car. "You've got some balls Margot, talking to him like that."

"He's just a man, Linda, just a man. You'd do well to bear that in mind. Don't put up with him running your life, you have my number. Call me if the need arises."

"I will Margot. Wish me luck."

"I won't wish you 'luck' Linda because I can assure you, he won't change and you'll want out of that relationship."

Well, that went well, I thought, as I drove off trembling.

I got back to Riccardo's place and called Rex. "Hi, Rex, it's me."

"Oh my God, Margot, where the hell are you?"

"We need to talk, Rex. Can you leave work now or not?"

"Yes, of course. You've got a key, just let yourself in, Margot. Bye for now."

I packed up my belongings and headed for home. I made myself a coffee while I waited for Rex.

I heard the gates open and the Merc door slamming. He came out onto the patio and hugged me. A tear trickled down his cheek. That did it. I started crying and the next thing I know, we were hugging and kissing frantically. He took my hand and led me to his office.

"Oh my God, Margot, I love you so much. Why are you such an awkward bitch?"

He lifted my skirt up and pulled my panties down. I could feel him hard against me. In one swoop, he lifted me gently up onto the edge of the table, and thrust his hard erection inside me.

He stopped thrusting and withdrew his erection, turned me over, re-entered and started spanking me. It was all over in seconds.

"Well, hello to you too." We couldn't stop laughing.

"Where have you been staying?"

"I've been with Penny in Kensington. Her mum's house is huge." I thought it best not to mention Riccardo, not right now at any rate.

"Please come home, Margot. What do you think this is doing to the girls?"

"We've been through this a million times, Rex, there has to be a few rules. No, shush, don't interrupt. You have to let me have a life of my own too. You come and go as you please, and half the time you don't even tell me where you're going. But me! I have to account for every move I make. Not anymore, Rex. By the way, where did you bugger off to? When I got back from Sun City, you were gone."

"It doesn't matter now. All that matters is that you are home. You are going to come home?"

The girls and I moved back home with Rex and I started looking for another job. It didn't take long at all.

Chapter 33

You Have Post

I'd been working for Frank for almost two years now, and like Rex, he went away on business trips often. One Friday afternoon I received a call from Frank asking me to collect him from the airport. He'd been on a business trip to the Cape.

I parked up my BMW convertible and made my way to the arrivals lounge. Being a first-class passenger, Frank came through quite quickly. We made our way through the busy airport, towards the car park.

I opened the boot to the BMW and Frank threw his case in. He opened his door and after struggling to get in he said, "Where should I put my legs Margot, around your neck maybe. I didn't realise you had such a small car."

We both laughed, as he sat with his knees almost touching his chest, looking most uncomfortable.

"Anything happening at the office, anything that can't wait until Monday, that is?"

"No, it's been quiet, nothing urgent."

"Great, drop me at home in that case please." He gave me directions and off we went. "Give me forty-five minutes to shower and dress and I'll take you to lunch and you can give me a run down on what's been happening while I've been away. Meet you at the Italian in Four Ways."

"That's a nice surprise for a Friday afternoon. Thank you. see you later." We drank quite a bit during lunch and he started to get a little amorous, and started asking me things like 'What colour underwear are you wearing? What's your favourite position in bed? Is Rex a good lover?' I became very uncomfortable and just laughed it off and told him I had to go and collect the girls from school and wished him a good weekend. Over the coming weeks, he persisted in harassing me, embarrassing me with inappropriate questions and I had to literally tell him to back off as I wasn't interested in the slightest.

The following Wednesday, while Frank was out to lunch, I was busy filing and going through the post on his desk when I found an envelope with his name and *'Private & Confidential'* written on it. This was nothing unusual, and being his PA I thought nothing of opening it. It was a contract of employment offer for *my* job addressed to someone who worked in another department.

I put it back in the envelope and when Frank returned an hour later, I waited for him to sit down and went through to speak to him.

"Frank, have you got a minute?" I threw the envelope on his desk. He looked up at me startled. "Were you going to discuss this with me at any stage, Frank?" He didn't answer for a while.

"It's nothing to worry about, Margot. We're having a bit of a shuffle round. We've got a new guy from the UK starting next week and I thought you'd be better suited working for him. What do you think?"

"I think you should have asked me before offering my job to someone else. Is that even legal, Frank? And just as a matter of interest, what title does this new 'guy' hold?"

"He's our new Finance Manager."

"So not even a director then, so I'm being demoted too. What about my salary?"

"It will mean a slight cut but nothing major."

"Where is he going to operate from, Frank, there are no spare offices."

"He'll use the boardroom for a while and we can sort the rest out later."

"And where will my office be?"

"I thought we could get some partitioning and fix it up outside the boardroom for now."

"Oh, did you? So, I'm being demoted, less money and going to be sitting in the corridor?" He looked at me.

"Yes, Margot, I suppose you will be."

"When did you say this new director will be arriving?"

"Next week."

"Thanks for letting me know, eventually!"

Once back at my desk, I put my 'cogs' to work. I remembered that Frank had an 'arch enemy' in the form of an attorney. Bingo. I rang Gerhardt and made an appointment to see him the following day.

"How can I help you, Mrs Charrington?"

"Such a mouthful. Please call me Margot. I believe you know a Mr Frank Van der Merwe?"

"Indeed I do." The expression on his face told me all I needed to know.

"Okay Margot, what can I help you with?"

"I've been working for Frank for three years, and recently he's been harassing me sexually. I've told him I'm not interested which makes him try even more. Earlier this week, I found an Offer of Employment on his desk, for MY job, to someone else in the company. He came up with some cock and bull story about a British guy starting at the company, and that I would be better suited to work for him. Plus, I'll be having a reduction in salary and, wait for it, I'll be sitting in the corridor with a partition! I don't think so."

"Same old Frank. That's why we fell out. He tried his luck with my fiancé. Whatever you do, Margot, don't walk out. No matter how uncomfortable it becomes. You have a strong case of sexual harassment here. I will send him a letter and hopefully he will pay up."

"How much are we looking at?"

"R60,000. It's a serious thing these days. The last thing he'll want is for this to go public." Gerhardt smiled. "Just go to work as normal and sit tight, it shouldn't take long." He stood up and shook my hand and walked me to the door.

"Thanks a lot for your help Gerhardt."

The next day, the partitioning arrived, together with a new desk and a chair. Frank got two of the staff to help set it up outside his office, close to the boardroom. I sat in reception drinking a coffee and reading the paper while this was going on.

"Okay, Margot, your new office awaits." He had a big smirk on his face.

"Thanks, Frank." I smiled back and went and sat at my new workstation. I found a game on the computer and sat quietly playing when Frank called, "Margot, could you get me a coffee please?" I ignored him. "Margot?" He came out of his office and looked at me. "Did you not hear me calling?"

"I don't work for you anymore, Frank. Get your own coffee." I carried on playing my game. He looked bewildered for a moment, shook his head and went back into his office.

The day dragged on. The post arrived and when the young lady went to put it on my desk, I shook my head and told her to take it into Frank. A few minutes later, he stormed out of his office, and went straight to the PR office, slamming the door behind him. *So, you have post, Frank.* I smiled to myself.

An hour later, he returned to his office, collected his jacket and case and left the building. My phone rang. "Hi, Margot, Gerhardt here."

"Hi, Gerhardt. I know he got the letter. He was furious. What happens now?"

"PR will ask you some questions and you must tell them exactly what you told me. Nothing more, nothing less. And stay put. You have to go in every day until I tell you it's okay to leave, otherwise he will say you absconded."

"Okay, thanks again. Bye."

I arrived at the office the next day, bright and early, and as I passed his office, I could hear a couple of female voices whispering.

"Is that her, really?" I heard one of them say.

They chatted for a while and then one of them came out of the office. As she passed, my desk she gave me a dirty look. I went into Frank's office and Gloria, who had been Franks' previous secretary, was sitting at my old desk.

"Hello, Margot. How are you holding up?" I was slightly taken aback.

"I'm all right under the circumstances. What are you doing here?"

"The other lady he wanted to work for him declined so he's asked me to help out until he finds another PA." She looked sheepishly at me.

"You knew, didn't you, Gloria? He tried it on with you as well, that's why you were moved to another office? Did he demote you as well?" She went scarlet. "You don't need to answer, I can see it written all over your face."

"It's about time someone put him in his place. Good for you Margot, I wish I'd had the balls back then."

"You know I always thought it was odd. Whenever you had to come and see him, he'd literally 'pull you by your ears', like reprimanding a small child, belittling you. What boss has the right to do that? Why don't you join me? We'll take him on together. I'm suing him for R60,000. Don't let him get away with it, Gloria."

"I can't, Margot, I haven't got it in me."

"And that's exactly why he does it, because he knows that most women would just be too afraid to confront him. Come on, now's your chance to get even."

Try as I may, she wouldn't do it, but she did say if I had any problems with proving my story, she would come forward. Thankfully, it never came to that.

Before the week was out, Frank paid up and I was out of there. Sixty thousand rand richer.

Chapter 34

You Stupid Woman

Once again, I was unemployed. I decided that I'd had enough of working for male chauvinists and maybe do temporary work for a while. If only I'd thought of this sooner. I didn't really need to work full time, as I had enough money put by, and relished the thought of some time to myself. I didn't tell Rex about only working part time. Why should I? He never told me anything.

It was mid-February 1998 when I received a call from the agent who looked after my rental home in Bryanston. "Hello, Margot? It's Carl Botha. How are you?"

"Hi, Carl. I'm very well thanks, and yourself?"

"I'm good thankyou Margot. I'm afraid I have some bad news for you though. Your house in Bryanston. The tenants have absconded, and taken all your furniture, fixtures and fittings, doors, basically everything they could move, they took."

It took a while for it to sink in. "Have they wrecked the place too? You know I've heard of people having braais indoors, painting graffiti on walls, etc."

"No, nothing like that, thank goodness. There is no kitchen, nothing at all, all built in wardrobes, light fittings, all gone. Thankfully, you are insured so hopefully the pay-out should cover the cost of everything that's missing. I'm not so sure about the cost of labour to reinstall everything. You'll need to check that out."

"Is the house secure, any broken windows?"

"That's the main reason for my call, Margot; although the house is locked up and as far as I know all the windows are fine, I would suggest you get the locks changed immediately, just in case they come back or even worse give the keys to squatters."

'Damn it' I thought, Rex told me to get references for them but they seemed such lovely people, a family with three children to look after. I knew the rent was a little low but I felt sorry for them. They were a family from Nigeria trying to make a new life for themselves. The husband, Benjamin, had a good job in the bank, or at least that's what he told me. Rex is going to be furious.

While I sat with my Chardonnay waiting for Rex to come home, I remembered what he'd said about the contract I'd signed when we got married and went to Papua, something about his being liable for anything untoward happening with any of the rental houses, and about paying into our UK pensions, in the event that we ever had to go back to the UK.

The children were in bed when he got in. "Hi love, how was your day?"

"Same old. And you?"

"Everything was going fine until about an hour ago. I got a call from Carl, you now the guy who oversees my house."

"Oh yes. What did he want?" He went and got himself a beer and we went and sat out on the patio. I followed him out.

"The tenants have done a runner and taken just about everything they could move. Including doors, carpets, fixtures and fittings…" He raised his eyebrows and gave me that look as if to say, 'I told you so'. "I know I should have listened to you and got references. But I didn't. Carl reckons the insurance will pay out for the goods, but not the 'labour' required to put it all in place, and the locks need to be changed too."

"Hmm, that could be expensive for you."

"What do you mean 'expensive for me'?"

"It's your house, Margot."

"But what about the contract you made me sign when we went to Papua, about you—"

"Yes, I know which contract, but I didn't take the job in Papua, did I? It was only in the event of anything happening while I was the sole bread winner in Papua, but that's not the case now, is it?"

I just looked at him trying to think of something to say.

"Are you being serious?"

"Yes, Margot, deadly."

"Now you wait a minute, Mr High and fucking Mighty, a contract is a contract, that's what it means; it can't be changed after the wedding. ANC, Ante Nuptial Contract, signed and agreed before the couple tie the knot."

"I think you'll find that I'm right, Margot. Now, what's for dinner?"

"Dinner, you bastard." *And here we are again, happy as can be, everything is wonderful, for him but not for me.* I sang along to the 'ditty' using my own lyrics. I stood up and stormed into the kitchen to fetch the wine. "Go and get the contract, Rex, and show me, go on."

"It's at work locked up."

"Ya, I fucking bet it is. No worries, Rex, really, no worries." I took my drink and headed down to the poolside.

Why would he lock it away at work? Because there's something in it that he doesn't want me to see, that's why. That's why he hovered over me when it came to signing, telling me not to waste time reading it through, he'd already told me what was in it. And I believed him because I loved and trusted him. I'll show him. Watch me, just watch me.

I slept in the spare room; well, I tried to sleep but I kept on going over and over in my mind what he'd told me. The next morning, I was up and out before seven. He tried to talk to me but I ignored him. I went to Kaldis for breakfast, and waited for eight 'o' clock, before ringing the lawyer.

"Hennie, Mrs Charrington here, how are you?"

"I'm good, thanks. What can I do for you?"

"I need a copy of the ANC I signed back in 1991, 11 September."

"No problem, I'll get it ready for you to collect at reception. Is there anything else?"

"No. Thank you." At half past nine, I had the envelope in my hand.

I only needed to read the first paragraph to realise that it had all been a lie. *'Expressly NO ACCRUAL system, whatsoever, IN THIS MARRIAGE.'* I read on and there was absolutely nothing about Papua New Guinea, or the rental house, or the pension. The basis of the agreement was: 'IF YOU LEAVE, YOU LEAVE WITH NOTHING.'

I went straight home and turned on my computer. I filled out online all the necessary documents to conduct an unopposed DIY divorce. This was the final straw for me. Rex was going to be single again. It didn't take long to complete the documents. I drove into downtown Johannesburg to the Supreme Court, then waited in the queue to be allocated a case number. I then drove to the sheriff's office in Sandton, paid the small fee for 'Service of Documents' on Rex, and told the sheriff it would have to be an early morning delivery, preferably before seven.

A week later, the doorbell rang very early in the morning. Rex was in the shower. I heard Sophie answer the door. Sarah came running upstairs shouting, "It's a policeman, Mummy, he wants to talk to Daddy."

Rex came out of the bathroom asking what all the commotion was about.

"The sheriff's downstairs to see you, Rex. You need to collect your divorce papers."

"What? Margot, you're such a stupid woman, you'll never divorce me." He casually sauntered out of the room, whilst putting his gown on, and headed downstairs.

When he returned, he threw the unopened envelope onto the bed and started laughing. "Stupid, stupid woman." He finished getting ready for work and didn't say goodbye when he left. He slammed the door so hard the house shook.

All I had to do now was wait ten working days, and hope that Rex didn't oppose the divorce, then I could simply book a date for the hearing, which only I had to attend.

While I waited for the ten days to lapse, I put my house up for sale. Because it had been 'stripped' of all fixtures and fittings, I knew I wouldn't get much for it, but anything was better than nothing.

The ten days finally passed, and Rex hadn't even mentioned the divorce papers, and I'd heard nothing from the Court. I drove once again to the Supreme Court to book a hearing date. Before the end of July 1998, we were divorced. Rex was none the wiser. I kept the Final Decree Nisi safely hidden, and just sat tight and bided my time.

Weekends had always been difficult with Rex. All I wanted was a couple of hours to myself to go shopping and maybe meet up with the girls for a coffee, preferably without the hassle of the children, but this was far easier said than done.

I woke early as usual on Saturday morning, as my internal six o'clock alarm never switched off. With the sunlight streaming into the bedroom, the bird song and the traffic from the motorway rumbling in the distance, I rolled over and cuddled up to Rex, who was already awake reading the Financial Times.

"Shall we go to Sandton City, Rex? We could have breakfast at Kaldis?"

Rex didn't even put his newspaper down. "Margot, I work extremely hard and deal with people all day long, I just want peace and quiet at the weekend. I have work to do, sorry."

"Okay, I'll give Penny a call and see if she fancies breakfast and a catch up." I jumped out of bed. "Do you want a coffee, Rex?"

"Yes, thanks."

I went downstairs and put the kettle on, then went out onto the patio and rang Penny.

"Hi, Penny, how's it going? Are you busy this morning?"

"Oh hi, Margot, I was just thinking about you. How are you and the girls?"

"The girls are fine but, as for me, I'm dying to get some relaxing time alone without them. Do you fancy going to Sandton for a coffee and a catch up?"

"Sounds great, what time?"

"I'll pick you up at about half past ten, is that okay?"

"Yep, can't wait, see you later."

"Okay, see you in a while Penny."

I hung up and turned to go back into the kitchen to make coffee, only to see Rex standing by the patio doors.

"What do you mean, 'some relaxing time alone without the girls?'"

"Well, it would be nice once in a while to be able to go and sit quietly, and have a grown-up conversation with my girlfriends. I can't remember the last time I went and tried anything new on, it's impossible with the girls around. It's not fair on them either. How boring it must be for them, listening to grown-ups talking, and being told to sit still and not talk."

"Yes, I agree they are quite demanding Margot, which is why I would like you to take them with you. I told you, I have to do some work."

"But Sophie's quite capable of looking after the girls, Rex. I need some alone time too."

"Margot, Sophie does her best to keep them occupied but she has housework to do and they keep coming to my study. I can't work with the constant interruptions. Let's not go through this again," Rex argued.

"Well, sorry for you, Lord Charrington. When's the last time you even saw the girls, or spent some quality time with them? You could take a couple of hours out of your busy week and be a father. You don't see them at all durig the week because by the time you get home, they're in bed. It's becoming more obvious that you don't want to spend any quality time with your daughters, or me for that matter. Why don't you just get a bed put in the office, then you won't have to come home at all. Today, I am going to the mall, alone, with or without your consent. You can look after your daughters or ask Sophie, that's what she gets paid for."

I was standing at the sink when he said, "Margot, I won't have you speaking to me that way. I said you're not going out unless you take the girls with you, is that understood?"

I was washing out the coffee jug when I snapped. I turned and threw the jug of water and coffee slops over Rex and watched as the brown liquid dripped down his face and onto his dressing gown. We were both frozen to the spot and, momentarily, Rex had rage in his eyes. Oh my God. I had seen that look so many times before with my first husband.

Rex leapt forward and grabbed me around the throat with one hand, raising the other in the air with his fist clenched. I kicked him in the shins and he released his grip. With one pounce, like a raging lioness, I stuck my claws into his face, just missing his eye, and dragged my nails down his face to the corner of his mouth. Blood surfaced and trickled slowly down his cheek. He raised his hand to feel the blood, then moved towards the mirror in the dining area and looked at himself in disbelief.

"Oh my God, look what you've done to my face! I can't go to work looking like this, like I've had a cat fight with my wife. I'm the boss for Christ's sake. I have over four hundred employees; what will they think when they see my face scratched to pieces?"

We glared at each other.

"Is that all you're worried about Rex, your face and what your colleagues might think? Well, Mr. Control Freak, let me tell you what I was thinking about thirty seconds ago, when you had your hand around my throat, and your fist clenched high ready to punch me. I wasn't thinking, 'Oh dear, my poor face'. Do you want to know what I was thinking, do you? Well, I was thinking that I've been down this road before, Rex, and although I'm not sure which is worse, the mental abuse you dish out or the physical abuse I endured for years, but just to let you know, if you ever raise a hand to me again so help me God, I will wait for you to go to sleep and I will cut your crown jewels off, do you hear me? I will never let a man hit me again, not ever," I spoke the words in such a chilling tone that Rex turned on his heels and fled from the room.

I heard the back door open.

"Good morning, Madam," said Sophie, with a beaming smile on her face as usual.

"Hi, Sophie, how are you?"

"I'm very good thank you, Ma'am, are the girls awake?"

"They were sound asleep when I got up, but maybe they're playing in their room. Please can you go up and see what they're up to and get them some breakfast. You know they love your mealie pap with fruit and honey."

"Yes, Ma'am."

"Oh, by the way, Sophie, I'm going out this morning and the boss has work to do; could you please make sure the girls don't disturb him? You know what he's like."

"Oh yes, Ma'am, Sophie knows what boss is like," Sophie replied, with a more serious face.

Sophie gave me a look which confirmed she had heard our altercation. I put another pot of coffee on and went outside to sit on the stoop. I could hear the familiar sounds of the cicadas' high-pitched buzzing, the crickets' intermittent tweaking of their back legs and the mosquitoes' continual humdrum buzzing.

I could also hear the light *chug chug chug* of the pool cleaner, known simply as a 'creepy crawly', as it made its way around the pool, swallowing leaves, dead flies and debris from the bottom, keeping the water crystal clear. Two grey-crested louries were singing in the nearby strelitzia bushes, and the hoopoes with their long-curved beaks were extracting nectar from the flowering prickly pear trees. The two-acre garden was enclosed by a tall hedge of bamboo which hid the electric fence surrounding the property. It had felt alien at first, 'living behind bars' so to speak, but over the years it had become a way of life and I didn't notice the bars anymore, but I realised that I was in a kind of prison anyway.

Sarah and Becky came bouncing out onto the stoop with their swimming costumes already on.

"Hi, Mummy. Sophie's making us mealie pap. Can we go and have a quick swim first, please?"

Just then, Rex came out with a coffee and sat at the other end of the table.

"Oh, Daddy, what happened to your face?" asked Sarah.

"Daddy cut his face shaving. Go and give him a big kiss and make it better," I said, as I went to pour myself another coffee.

When I came back outside, Rex and the girls were down in the pool splashing around noisily, with Rex pretending to be a shark chasing them.

"Ma'am, the girls' breakfast is ready."

"Okay, thanks Sophie."

I shouted down to the girls, who quickly came running up the garden and went inside to get their breakfast. Rex was reading his Financial Times when the girls came out ten minutes later dressed in their 'Pocahontas' costumes and asked Daddy if he would put the tepee up for them. Rex looked over the top of his paper at me.

"What a great idea," I said. "Daddy loves playing that game, don't you, Daddy?"

He put his paper on the table and followed the girls down to the playhouse to get the tepee. Once the tepee was in place, he started chasing them around the garden. He was wearing his 'Pocahontas' necklace, which the girls insisted he wore, and with one hand over his mouth, the other holding a plastic axe, he starting whooping like an Indian warrior and chased them down the garden to the wooded area.

I happened to glance at the newspaper on the table and saw the headline *'Black Widow Murder in London. Man arrested.'* Staring back at me was the face of Riccardo and next to it a picture of Linda. I picked it up and started reading.

'The estranged wife of London hitman has been found dead in "safe house". Linda Russo was shot while under police protection. It's believed that whilst serving 20 years for accessory to murder, her estranged husband, Riccardo Russo, found out where she was living and, hired someone to kill Linda, because she gave the crucial evidence that had him convicted.'

My heart started palpitating, I could hardly breathe. I threw the paper down and went inside to get a glass of water.

When Rex finally came back up to the stoop, he was red-faced and gasping for air. He picked up his paper, caught his breath and took a sip of cold coffee.

"Would you get me another coffee, this one's gone cold."

"Margot, did you hear me?"

"Loud and clear, Sir. Get it yourself. I'm going to get ready, I'm picking Penny up 10h30. I will have my alone time, Rex."

He threw his paper down, and standing up gripped the twelve-seater table with both hands, and flipped it over. It crashed over the side of the veranda, rolling several times down the sloped garden, before collapsing in a heap just short of the pool. I carried on drinking my coffee, never flinching. Sophie was standing at the sliding glass doors, looking out with eyes wide and questioning. Rex threw her a look, and she quickly disappeared inside again. He retrieved his paper and walked silently into the house.

I finished my coffee and went upstairs to get ready to go to the mall. As I passed the study, I heard Rex on the phone.

"Okay Geoff, see you later mate."

I popped my head around his office door and said, "Going somewhere Rex? What will you tell Geoff happened to your face?"

"I don't like your tone, Margot," he replied.

"Really. My tone? I don't care much for your tone either, Margot this and oh Margot that, I just asked if you were going somewhere, that's all."

"I'm going to play a round of golf with Geoff."

"Well, don't forget to take the girls with you, will you? There's a good chap, they're no trouble at all, remember!"

He didn't even look up and in less than half an hour, he was gone.

As soon as he was gone, I went to the girls' room.

"Hey, you two, how do you fancy going to the Carousel today?"

"Yay, Mummy, will you buy us a teddy bear and some sweets and can we play in tumble town, and please can we go on the horses that go up and down?" They were both on their feet jumping up and down, clapping their hands.

"Of course! You can have anything you want today, but you mustn't tell Daddy where we're going, okay? It's a secret. Now come on, let's get you dressed."

"Sophie, have you seen my car keys by any chance?"

"No, Ma'am." I went to the study and checked the drawers. No keys.

I went to pick Penny up and off we went. The Carousel was a large gambling and entertainment centre, about a two-hour drive from Johannesburg. It had a large crèche and play centre which the girls loved, and as its name implied it had a huge carousel with beautifully painted horses. It had been months since I had been there, and I was looking forward to a few hours of uninterrupted gambling.

It was well after six when we got back to Johannesburg. I dropped Penny off and headed for home feeling a little anxious. As I pulled into the driveway, I looked about to make sure there was no one around, then clicked the remote to open the gates. I drove in and clicked again and waited for them to close before getting out.

I pulled up next to Rex's car on the driveway and felt a lump in my throat.

Oh dear, another altercation coming up, I thought to myself.

Rex was out on the stoop, standing over the braai with a beer in his hand.

"Daddy, look what Mummy bought us," shouted Becky as she ran towards him with a Pink Panther toy, bigger than she was.

"Wow, he's huge, isn't he? Where did she get him from?"

Before I could stop her, Sarah shouted out, "The carousel, Daddy, we went on the horses and played in tumble town, and we had popcorn and burgers and chocolate milkshake."

"Wow, that's awesome, girls. It looks like you've shared your milkshake with your clothes." He laughed. "Why don't you go and put your Pocahontas costumes on while Daddy makes you some supper? We've got sausages and chicken."

"Yay, this has been the best day ever," Sarah yelled as they ran into the house.

Rex took a sip of his beer and turned to face me. "You took my daughters, through a township. to a gambling joint?" He was seething.

"Well, you didn't want to take them with you so I took them out for the day," I retaliated, "and you heard them, they had a great day. Don't be so melodramatic, Rex, it's no big deal. We were perfectly safe."

He threw his beer all over me.

"Have you any idea how dangerous it is to be driving around these days, especially through rough townships, a woman alone with children, in a car that's not exactly safe. It has a fabric roof, which I assume you had open."

"Well, hallelujah, Jesus has risen again. You finally agree that my car is unsafe, but you needn't have worried. I know you think I'm 'stupid' but believe me, I'm not. You took my car keys, so I took the Bentley."

Almost choking on his beer, he said, "You did what? You took my fucking Bentley through a township?"

I walked off into the kitchen and retrieved a beer for myself. "You know what they say Rex, if you can't beat 'em, join 'em. How does it feel?" I raised my beer to him. "Cheers."

He walked past me, through the house and out of the front door. I followed him and watched through the window as he circled the car, inspecting every inch.

"What a total dick," I whispered under my breath.

"What's a dick, Mummy?"

I turned and saw the girls sitting at the top of the stairs. "I said tick, Sarah, tick."

"Oh, you mean a lunatic."

I couldn't stop laughing, as I thought how apt the word 'lunatic' actually was, and ran up the stairs to hug my innocent girls. 'From the mouths of babes' – how beautiful innocence was.

The front door opened and Rex stood at the bottom of the stairs, looking up at the three of us. We stopped laughing.

"Margot, come down here NOW."

The girls fled to their rooms.

"I'm going to bathe the girls and get them ready for bed, they've had a very busy day and they've eaten far too much for one day. Come to think of it, I'm not hungry either."

"Come down here NOW!" he shouted.

"No, you come up here, you're the one who wants to talk all of a sudden. This is the part where you normally walk away and lock yourself in your office, and do you know what Rex? I suggest you do exactly that before one of us gets to the point of no return."

He raced up the stairs three at a time. I stood my ground. He was standing so close, I could smell the garlic on his breath. He looked like a man possessed, with ugly stubble, a huge red welt down his face and his eyes looked dull, with dark circles underneath. He let out an almighty wail as he punched the wall behind me.

"You fucking infuriating woman, get out of my sight." And he went back downstairs.

I bathed the girls, then made them a warm drink before reading them a bedtime story. Annie lay huddled with Pink Panther and Sarah with Jonathon, a knitted toy that the neighbour had given her. It was past eight now and I decided to have an early night and read my book. As I lay in bed in the spare room, I wondered if the weekend could get any worse.

I was woken early the next morning when I heard the girls playing and giggling outside. Rex was laid out on a sun lounger next to the pool, reading his newspaper, presumably having a look at how his stocks and shares were doing. I went downstairs, poured a coffee, and, as the table was still just piled in pieces, decided to go down by the pool as well.

"Can I have my keys back, or can I use the Bentley again?" I waited.

"Don't push your luck Margot, you haven't earned the right to drive my Bentley, or my Mercedes for that matter."

"What the hell is that supposed to mean? 'I haven't earned the right!' I'm sick of hearing you say that. Come on tell me what that actually means. Can I get you some fish Rex?"

"What! Fish?"

"Yes, FISH, to go with that fucking huge chip on your shoulder?"

Rex sprung from his lounger and took a step towards me, rage in his eyes. Before he got close enough, I stuck my foot out and tripped him up, and he went flying into the pool. When he finally surfaced, I didn't know whether to run or stay put. I chose the latter. He hauled himself out of the pool and strode towards me.

"So, what does that mean Rex, explain it to me."

He walked towards me and stood right in front of me. I remained seated.

"Well, I'm waiting."

"Get out of my sight woman before I do something I'll really Regret. Your keys are in my Dior suit."

First stop, as always, was Kaldis coffee bar for breakfast. Breakfast at Kaldis was the best: a basket full of toast, croissants, Danish pastries and soft boiled eggs with soldiers. The girls loved going there because the staff made such a fuss of them. They had marshmallows in their hot chocolate, and they were allowed to have an ice cream each instead of having to share one like when Daddy was there.

I got shoes for the girls but gave up trying to look at clothes and decided to take the girls to the movies instead. After the movies we headed back to the car park and after several attempts, I finally got the car to start. As I approached the exit barriers, the African security guard in his blue uniform and flat cap stood ready to open them.

"Good afternoon, Ma'am, please would you switch off the engine while I do a spot check?"

"No, I won't turn off the engine, it's just taken me ten minutes to get it started and I don't want to get stuck here," I replied.

"I need to do a spot check, Ma'am, and I won't open the barrier unless you let me do the spot check."

"Really? You're not going to open the barrier?"

"That's correct, Ma'am."

"Okay, so don't open it."

I put my foot down, full throttle on the gas pedal, revved the engine and drove straight through the barrier, which flew over the top of the car, narrowly missing the guard by an inch or so. The look on his face through the rear-view mirror was hilarious. I chuckled to myself. "Silly sods, give them a uniform and they think they rule the world."

When we reached home, Rex's car was still parked outside the garage, meaning he hadn't been out. I parked up next to the Merc and went inside.

As I stepped into the hallway, I saw dots of blood on the floor leading down the long corridor towards the kitchen. I held a finger over my lips, telling the girls to be quiet. As I entered the kitchen, I could see Rex standing outside with a glass of brandy in his hand. When he turned around, I saw that he was splattered with blood from the waist down with a large congealed mess around his lower legs and his hands covered in blood.

"Oh my God Rex, have you been shot?" I screamed and instinctively ran towards him.

"No, I haven't been shot." He held out his arms and I collapsed into them. We hugged one another tightly for a few moments.

"Mummy, what's happening, why is Daddy all bloody?" asked Sarah, who was crying.

"It's all right, darling, come here. I want you to be a really brave girl and go upstairs and play in your room with Annie while Daddy and I have a little talk. Can you do that?"

"Yes, Mummy."

"What the hell happened?" I asked, once Sarah was gone. "Why are you bleeding?"

"Calm down, Margot, it's not my blood."

Rex began to tell me what had happened. Apparently while he'd been sat reading his Financial Times, a gunshot had gone off very close by and, with me and the girls' due home at any moment, he'd run out to the front drive to see if he could see anyone or anything. There had been no sign of anyone, so he'd opened the front gate, and, walking slowly along the hedgerow, towards the neighbour's house, in the direction where the gunshot had come from.

Rick and Jane, who lived next door, had recently had a new baby and Rick was away on business in America. Rex saw Jane's car in the driveway, the gates closed and there was no sign of anyone. He moved further along until he saw Jane at the kitchen window. She was frantically waving and pointing next door. He held up a thumb to acknowledge that he understood what she was telling him and moved towards the next house, still keeping as close to the bushes as he could.

He heard a man shouting, "Get out of the fucking car, you bitch, move, now!"

He heard a woman screaming, car doors slamming and a car engine revving loudly. A silver Rolls Royce reversed out of the drive onto the road with tyres screeching, leaving tyre marks on the road. Seconds later, the car was gone. He said that two black men had hidden in the bushes waiting in ambush for Jane's neighbours, holding them at gunpoint and telling them to get out of the car. The old man had tried to put up a fight and they'd shot his kneecaps. Then they'd dragged the wife out of the car, thrown her into the bushes and raped her.

"Oh my God, Rex, that could have been me if I'd come back five minutes earlier. They could have hijacked me and the girls, and what if they had raped me or even worse, the girls?"

"Oh Margot, I don't think they would try and hijack an old BMW when there are Mercedes and Bentleys up for grabs, stop being so melodramatic."

"Melodramatic you say? A man's been shot, just two houses away, his wife's been raped, and their car has been stolen. I'd say melodramatic was a fucking understatement under the circumstances."

The doorbell rang. I went to answer and there were two officers asking to speak to Rex.

The officer took a statement from Rex, and thanked him for his bravery, and for stemming the blood from the man's injuries while they had waited for the ambulance to arrive.

"Rex," I said, once the officer had gone, "it's not safe here in South Africa anymore, we should seriously think about going back to the UK or Australia or anywhere. I know there's always been crime here; car jackings, burglaries, trouble in the townships, but it's getting too close for comfort now, and we have to think of the girls' safety. Maybe we should have moved to Papua New Guinea when you had that amazing job offer."

"We both know that Papua wasn't for us Margot. I know you're a little shaken, but it's an isolated case. We'll just have to be extra vigilant in the future. I'm going to shower and get these bloody clothes off."

"More vigilant you say? We already carry guns and drive around with windows and doors locked. Even the government advises us not to stop at red robots at night-time, what does that tell you? There are bars at every window, a ten-foot-high electrified fence outside and still things like this happen. How's vigilance going to work, Rex, pray tell me?"

I went upstairs to check on the girls. They were playing with their Barbie dolls, not a care in the world and totally oblivious to the dangers that lurked outside.

Monday morning couldn't come quick enough for me after another night spent in the spare room tossing and turning. I went through to the main bedroom to find Rex sipping his coffee and doing work on his laptop.

"I hope you're looking for another job abroad, because I'm not staying here waiting for the inevitable."

"I have a company to run, Margot, I can't just up and go. You're obviously distressed, but things will calm down; we have a great lifestyle here Margot."

I decided not to start another row and headed for the bathroom.

Rex was still wandering around in his dressing gown when I left to take the girls to school. I walked them to their relevant classrooms but when I returned to the car, it wouldn't start.

Not again, I thought.

I tried a couple of times but it was dead. I called the house phone but it just rang out and Rex's mobile was off.

It was only a ten-minute walk to the house. I let myself in and went upstairs. I opened the bedroom door to find Rex sat on the bed, surrounded by naked women – magazines, strewn across the bed, with centrefold naked women showing their wares. He was stark bollock naked, with the 'Crown Jewels' in his hand.

"The car won't start, Rex, and I don't want to be late for work. Can I use the Merc?"

"No, Margot, you haven't earned the right to drive my Mercedes."

"Oh my God, not this again. You admitted only this weekend how unsafe my car was." This had been brewing for a long, long time.

245

"Have you quite finished?"

"No, I haven't, you control freak. You might have a great lifestyle here, but I don't, living under your rule like a prisoner. You're a nasty piece of work. Who do you think you are, sitting there, tossing yourself off like all's well with the world? We've just had the most horrific weekend and you're sitting there getting your rocks off. What the hell's happened to us, Rex? How did it get to this?"

He looked at me. "Pass my phone. I'll get hold of Thomas to come and look at your car."

"Pass your phone! Aren't you going to come and try and fix it? What sort of husband are you?"

All the time I was talking, I noticed he was still busy with the job in hand. I just couldn't stop myself and I slapped his face. He looked stunned and in a split second he'd spun me around, face down over his knee.

"Take that, you bitch. You slapped me, well here you go, is that hard enough for you?"

He slapped my buttocks so hard and I felt that sexual urge that came with the slapping.

"Nowhere near hard enough you bastard, harder, go on, harder."

After we'd finished, Rex made the call.

"Thomas will be here in forty-five minutes. By the way, what did you mean by my so-called business trips?"

"You can't seriously expect me to believe that you need to go overseas twice, sometimes three times a year for two weeks at a time. What business could you possibly be doing in 'Disney world'? Or cruising on the Carnival Cruise Line, and while we're at it, what do you do with those wads of notes and travellers cheques stashed away in your luggage?" There was a long silence.

"You've been going through my luggage?"

"Well, what choice did you leave me? You never tell me where you're going, where you'll be staying, all I get is 'ask Sandra'. Do you know how that makes me feel, how it makes *us* look? Your secretary must think, well, I don't know what she thinks. It's not her job to tell me where you're going and for how long and why. And the 'money', don't get me started on that question. Are you laundering money, do you have another life away from us, are you doing something illegal? I never know what the hell you're up to. You never talk to me, I don't even know how much you earn, how well the company is doing.

There's something majorly wrong with this relationship, Rex. With you!" I stood up and left him sitting naked on the bed.

I could hear Sophie singing in the kitchen as she washed up the breakfast things, even though there was a perfectly good brand-new dishwasher. I went down and poured a coffee and sat outside looking out over the pool while I waited for Thomas. Bessie the boxer was running around the pool trying to catch the dragonflies as they hovered over the clear water when the doorbell rang.

"Hi Thomas, how are you?"

"I'm good Ma'am, thank you."

"The car's broken down at the school, Thomas, I'll have to come with you."

We drove around the corner to the school and within minutes, Thomas had the car started. He did explain what was wrong but he may as well have been speaking Chinese.

"Thanks a lot," I told him.

"That's okay, Ma'am, you have a nice day."

I sat in the car and cried. My world was falling apart.

I drove to Sandton City and headed for Kaldis. While sipping my Americano, I recalled the vision of Rex masturbating and tried to mull over where things had gone so wrong. Our sex life had been amazing to begin with; two, three, even four times a day, every day. Our lovemaking had been something movies were made of. Meeting in secret at my house every lunchtime with a bottle of champers and ham sandwiches.

I was brought out of my daydream when the waiter approached with my panini.

"There you go, Ma'am, enjoy. Is there anything else I can get for you?"

"Yes, an Americano, thank you." *A holiday would be nice,* I thought, a long holiday with me, myself and I. I imagined myself on a beach somewhere far away from Rex's droning, demanding voice. But no, I couldn't leave the girls with him, how very cruel that would be, for the girls.

I finished my breakfast and went straight to the travel agents.

"Good morning, Madam, how can I help you today?"

"I need the next available direct flight to London. One adult, two children, one way."

"Okay, Ma'am, let's have a look. How old are the children, Ma'am?"

"Seven and ten."

"Okay, we have a BA flight tomorrow evening, non-stop, or Wednesday SAA, also non-stop."

"Which is the cheapest?"

"BA is slightly cheaper but SAA is, in my opinion, far better than BA."

"Okay, South African Airways it is then."

"I need your passport – I take it both children are travelling on your passport?"

"No, actually they have their own passports, but I don't have them with me."

"Not to worry, we can do the necessary paperwork and I'll reserve the booking for you. If you give me a quick call later, with the passport numbers etcetera, I can go ahead and book it for you."

"Okay, I will call you as soon as I get home, thank you."

"No problem at all Madam."

As soon as I arrived home, I found the girls' passports and rang the travel agency to give them the details.

"Okay Margot, everything is booked. You need to check in two hours before that time and your tickets will be ready for collection later today, or you can collect them anytime tomorrow. Would you like me to order any travellers' cheques?"

"No, thank you, I have to go to the bank anyway so I can order them myself."

I then called Kelly Girl and told them that I had to go to the UK for an indefinite period of time due to a family crisis. They were very understanding and said they would pay any outstanding money that was owed to me.

I booked a room at the airport hotel for Tuesday evening, so that at least I would get a good night's sleep before the long flight.

Then, lastly, I phoned Rex.

"Hi, Rex, how's it going?"

He sounded slightly confused, as I rarely ever rang him at work, andhe asked what was wrong.

"Nothing's wrong. Just thought that after the dreadful weekend we've had, we might go out tonight for a meal or something. We need to talk."

"Well, that sounds ominous. Leave it to me, I'll book somewhere."

"Actually, I fancy the Top of the Carlton. You know where you took me that first day, … you know, when we made the connection."

He laughed.

"Okay, Top of the Carlton it is then. See you later."

I replaced the receiver.

I drove to the bank and ordered travellers' cheques, and then tried to withdraw a rather large amount of cash from my savings account. The teller explained that such a large amount had to be ordered before 11 am and told me I could come and collect the money any time after 10h00 the next day.

With the banking out of the way, I picked the girls up from school and dropped them home to Sophie, then went to get my hair done.

By the time Rex arrived home, late as usual, I was bathed and busy applying body lotion. He quickly showered and put on his dark-blue Dior suit, a crisp light blue shirt and one of his many hundreds of ties. Suit and tie and evening dress were essential for the Carlton. He looked so handsome and I remembered the first time I'd set eyes on him, how his vivid blue eyes had looked at me, right through to my soul. I slipped into my long red dress, which showed off every curve, with its low-cut front revealing my bountiful cleavage. I checked myself in the mirror and thought, I'll show him who's 'earned the right'.

As we pulled up outside the Carlton Hotel, the concierge approached the car.

"Good evening, Sir, Ma'am, may I park the car for you?"

Rex handed him the keys. "Yes, thank you."

Rex walked around and opened my door and we made our way into the white marble-floored lobby, towards the reception area and the Roof Top restaurant. Once inside the lift, I pressed the button for the top floor.

"Do you remember that time when I'd just started working for you Rex, and you took me to visit John, and we went up in that glass elevator on the outside of the building, about forty floors up?" I asked him.

"You mean when you held on to my arm and couldn't look out?"

We smiled at one another.

"Do you love me, Rex?" I asked him.

"What a silly question, I'm here, aren't I?"

"So why don't you tell me anymore? I can't remember the last time you told me. You know, actually said the words."

He put his arms around my waist and kissed my cheek.

"I love you, Margot, really I do."

I felt my heart quicken as his moist lips touched my cheek and I smelled that oh-so-familiar aftershave. He tightened his grip around my waist and I felt that familiar throb way down in my tummy. I wasn't expecting that.

"Well, that's nice to hear. It's been a long time." I began to doubt now if I was doing the right thing.

Why don't I just go and live in the house in Cape Town? I thought to myself. *Why run away to the UK?* Of course, that wouldn't be an option as the house didn't belong to Rex totally. He'd bought it in a 'consortium' with three other guys as an investment to be used as a holiday home. The doubt in my mind now made me feel sick; was I really going to leave him and my beloved South Africa which I loved dearly? The evening was wonderful. I couldn't fault him. I began to feel myself trying to back out of what I was about to do, when Rex said; "Shall we get the bill and go home and have dessert Margot?"

"Yes, I'd love to, do you want me to drive?" I asked, knowing full well that he was way over the limit. I was also over the limit but as I was leaving anyway, it didn't really matter now, did it? I felt good driving the Mercedes, even though it would be the last time.

While I parked the Mercedes in the garage, Rex went inside and poured two glasses of wine.

"I thought we could go for a dip to cool off," he said.

Rex put the wine down onto the small table between the sun loungers and turned around, and grabbing me by the arm, he pulled me close and kissed me with such ferocity that I almost fell over. He pulled the straps of my red dress down and undid the back zipper, then yanked the dress down over my hips. It fell to the floor. I was wearing absolutely nothing underneath.

My nipples stood erect with excitement as he slowly flicked his tongue around them, then slowly kissing his way towards my shaven mound. I felt myself slightly moisten. I could feel his hot breath on my body and, as he gently flicked his tongue between my legs, my knees trembled. I let out a small cry of ecstasy and held his head, pulling him further in. He sat me down on the lounger and unzipped his bulging trousers, letting the 'beast' loose.

"Suck my cock," he said, as he took me by the hair and pulled my head towards his erection. "Suck harder, deeper, go on, Margot, suck, suck."

"Now turn around and bend over," he ordered.

As I bent over, he spanked me so hard that I shrieked.

"Again, harder, Rex, much harder," I cried.

"Do you want this cock inside you? How badly do you want it, Margot, hey, how badly?" He was panting and ready to go.

"Fuck me now, Rex, fuck me hard and make me come, come on, you bastard." My orgasm came pretty quickly and Rex carried on thrusting until he reached climax, then he picked me up in his arms and we fell into the pool. When we surfaced, we were still clinging to each other.

We were woken early next morning by a loud knock at the bedroom door. We heard Sophie calling,

"Boss, Madam, are you awake? It's past eight."

"Yes, thanks, Sophie," Rex replied. "Oh my God, I have a nine o'clock meeting." He jumped out of bed and went to the bathroom.

I went down to make coffee and was sitting out on the stoop thinking about how magical last night had been. Was I really going to leave him? I wondered if at last I had 'earned the right'.

Rex came down, suited and booted, ready for his meeting.

"Can I use the Merc today, please Rex?" I asked.

He kissed me on the cheek and said, "Not this again, Margot, we've been over this a million times."

"Oh, you mean those special words of endearment you use so often? 'That I haven't earned the right to drive your Merc'?"

He looked at me in exasperation, raised his eyebrows and said, "See you later Margot."

As soon as I heard the gates click closed, I went upstairs to find Sophie getting the girls dressed for school. "They're not going to school today, Sophie. Please, can you pack as many of the girls' things as you can into the four cases in the spare room?" Sophie just looked at me. No explanation was necessary. Sophie knew what life with the 'boss' was like.

"You mustn't say anything to the boss, okay? Tell him I gave you the day off and you don't know where I am, do you understand?"

"Oh yes, Ma'am, Sophie understands." Sophie began to cry and bent down to hug the girls.

Suddenly, I realised the enormity of what I was doing, taking the girls away, and not just from Rex. She had nursed them through their childhood illnesses, looked after them while Rex and I had been out in the big world, working for our piece of heaven on this earth, and now I was taking them away forever. My eyes filled with tears. I too bent down and the four of us sat huddled on the floor in a heap, crying.

While Sophie took the cases downstairs, I had one last thing to do. I retrieved the envelope I had kept safely for so long and opened it. Inside was a copy of the final decree nisi, dated 1995, which I had never given to Rex; a copy of the ante nuptial contract dated 11 September 1991; and a note saying:

'Hope you enjoy your cars, your money and your own company.'

I sealed the envelope and wrote on the front:

YOU HAVEN'T EARNED THE RIGHT TO HAVE A WIFE AND TWO BEAUTIFUL CHILDREN.

***